Huntsman

Huntsman

A
Novel
By

M.A. Cumiskey

Copyright © 2010 by M.A. Cumiskey.

Library of Congress Control Number: 2010916315
ISBN: Hardcover   978-1-4568-0734-4
                Softcover   978-1-4568-0733-7
                Ebook   978-1-4568-0735-1

All rights reserved. No part of this book may be reproduced or transmitted in any form or by any means, electronic or mechanical, including photocopying, recording, or by any information storage and retrieval system, without permission in writing from the copyright owner.

This is a work of fiction. Names, characters, places and incidents either are the product of the author's imagination or are used fictitiously, and any resemblance to any actual persons, living or dead, events, or locales is entirely coincidental.

This book was printed in the United States of America.

To order additional copies of this book, contact:
Xlibris Corporation
0-800-644-6988
www.Xlibrispublishing.co.uk
Orders@Xlibrispublishing.co.uk
301179

'Still, still shall last the dreadful chase,
Till time itself shall have no end;
By day, they scour earth's caverned space,
At midnight's witching hour ascend.

This is the horn, and hound, and horse,
That oft the lated peasant hears;
Appall'd, he signs the frequent cross,
When the wild din invades his ears.

The wakeful priest oft drops a tear
For human pride, for human woe,
When, at his midnight mass, he hears
The infernal cry of "Hoila, ho!"

(The Wild Huntsman; Sir Walter Scott; c.1796)

Chapter One

As a child I was often described by my mother as being timid, 'Too timid for your own good' she would say. Although exactly how much timidity would have proven to be good for me she never explained. Neither did she appear to appreciate that such a statement (often made in public) inevitably increased my timidity quotient by at least a factor of ten. Being aware of her expectations however, I struggled to change my image unfortunately I only succeeded in causing a succession of further embarrassments for myself. Indeed for some large part of my later childhood a feeling of being embarrassed is probably my most prevailing memory. I felt I was forever being 'found out' or about to be found out; I was the one making daft statements, or the one who didn't get the joke. Consequently I grew up used to being the butt end of everyone's ridicule. It seemed then that all my efforts at redemption were doomed to failure and for a considerable period this situation caused me to deliberately distance myself from my peers and to reside comfortably in the quiet security of my imagination. With hindsight in adulthood eventually I grew to understand that it was the nature of my upbringing that was the root cause of my difficulty.

A single parent with ultra conservative tastes, my Mother prized learning above social grace and save for a privileged few generally preferred her own company to that of friends or associates this, was the basis of my problem. My social environment was further aggravated by, what I came to believe was a mistaken dedication on her part to religious belief and practice—especially the practice. In my Mother's case the chosen religion was the Roman Catholic Church but it might well have been Islam or Hinduism as much as Protestantism or any of a myriad of other spiritual leanings. Not surprisingly as a result, my early life was as cloistered as it was proscribed and the value system I inherited included all the traditional limitations and distortions one might expect. It naturally contained a large slice of the, 'Don't speak until you are spoken to,' philosophy and as a result I rarely got to speak at all. It was not surprising that initially I became somewhat introverted.

When I was still a pupil in Primary Education I adopted an attitude that sought to hide my lack of all those qualities of exhibitionism I could identify in my friends. Save for English and History my academic achievement was modest; practical subjects escaped me completely and in sport justifiably I was the last member of any team to be chosen. In any running competition whether it was cross-country or sprint inevitably I came last; my long-jump was the shortest on record and my high-jump the lowest; PE staff refused to entrust a javelin to my hands and they measured my attempts at the shot putt in centimetres rather than metres. My few friends tolerated my company, I believe simply because I was the proud possessor of a very creative and very lewd sense of humour most of which had been acquired without understanding via the collection of novels I was able to read in the library. Needless to say, if my affections served any purpose at all, it was only to secretly fuel my fears of forthcoming embarrassments providing me with yet more secrets to hide.

In this context my first and possibly my worst disgrace occurred in my early years when I was an altar-server. Shortly after starting my first school and no doubt through my mother's devout observance of the Roman religion, I was encouraged to train as an altar-boy. Often this was seen by Catholic parents as the pinnacle of achievement for their tinniest offspring—another confirmation of the gender bias for which this Faith is infamous (and the converse of the Greco-Roman practice of employing vestal virgins for much the same purpose.)

The principal ritual in the Roman Catholic Church is the Mass. It is characterised by the priest who conducts the service on an altar and is assisted usually by two young boys. Whilst every action of the Mass is charged with symbolic meaning its purpose is built around the belief in a miracle called transubstantiation: the changing of bread and wine into the actual body and blood of Jesus Christ. And however similar this may appear be to the cannibalism sometimes found in the jungles of Borneo, Catholics claim it relates to Jesus' actions and instructions at the Last Supper. In its Tridentine form the ceremony of the Mass was carried out in Latin. This procedure necessitated the priest's prayers being answered in Latin by the altar-boys. The learning of the Latin responses was therefore a major part of the induction process for new altar-boys. Consequently, at aged six years I found myself attending classes two evenings each week for instruction. These classes provided occasions to rehearse the Latin and to become familiar with the detail of the activities needed. It did not matter that the words we learnt were so much Donald Duck language to the ten boys who attended the classes. Indeed I suspect that our ignorance like that of most congregations who attended Mass was as much a part of the magic as were the costumes we were obliged to wear.

Repetition was the order of the day a tried and tested learning process with which we were already familiar through the same practice employed in our regular classrooms—learning times tables was much the same as learning Latin responses. Thankfully the Ecumenical movement has done away with this chore and responses during the Mass now occur in the language native to the host country.

The preferred atmosphere during our classes was one of serious intent: formal in the extreme. The ethos generated could not have been holier had we been asked to seek the Grail: a mandatory rigour that was best otherwise associated with high security prisons. Needless to say therefore my enjoyment of these occasions had nothing at all to do with the content or form neither of the lessons nor in the anticipation of their intended application. Due to inherent shyness I was not by nature a gregarious child so to find a legitimate reason to dress up and perform was in some sense a new joy.

I had survived my first year at school only on account of the large class size. Amongst forty other children I found it relatively easy to submerge and go unnoticed. In a group of ten the same was not possible. I was therefore drawn into relationships with my classmates and forced to respond. The most stimulating time was when five of us walked home together. This was when my education proper began. Conversations were illuminating. I learnt about the sexual act; what one called girl's genitalia and what they looked like (Gordon Bundy was always drawing them) and my vocabulary was extended by the use of new swearwords. There were so many new words almost as foreign as the Latin. Once I was accepted by the group I was also given a crash course in petty theft: how to steal small things from the newsagents and the corner shop. Best of all I was introduced to the mysterious ritual of group masturbation. It was a whole new world.

At such an early age and having only my mother for company I lacked the criteria on which to evaluate the quality of my friends' influence. I only knew that what they offered was new and exciting and if it was regarded by adults as naughty then that only added to the attraction.

With hindsight I appreciate that the value systems apparent in the group reflected the diversity of their backgrounds. As a result, the possible exchange of information provided me with street-level facts that were far more compelling than anything I'd ever found in books. It seemed that whatever the query someone in the group would have answers. I was particularly intrigued by the facts I learned about sex. I discovered that really girls like to be kissed but only men liked fucking. I was informed that too much masturbation would make you go blind and that once we grow up we would be able to spurt tiny babies out of our willies. To my horror I found out that most foreigners—especially Black people were infected with something called the pox this was a disease that made your Willie go black and fall off. It seemed that the variety of my ignorance was matched only by the complexity of the answers my questions generated.

Just before my eighth birthday, being an experienced performer of nearly two years on the altar, I attended a special Benediction service. That evening there was a full compliment of ten altar-boys all dressed in black cassocks and crisp white and lace-edged cottas. We attended on Father Martin the Parish priest and our presence there was to signify our formal acceptance; the satisfactory completion of our probation. Each boy sported a freshly scrubbed face; hair slicked down with Brylcreem or spit and teeth whiter than white. Our arrival at a slow march in two practised columns had been synchronised with an exactitude as precise as any found in the British Army and the posture of hands together made a perfect pattern beneath the rows of sparkling eyes. Needless to say the beatific expressions had been rehearsed to perfection.

When the moment arrived we were called forward one at a time and given a tiny sacred heart medal which we were to pin to our school blazer lapel. I was to discover much later that these medals had a different currency amongst some older boys in school. In their eyes the wearing of the medal was similar to a sign signifying a plague carrier: an invitation to have one's backside kicked. Significantly I was only one of three who did not know we would become targets of abuse. The first time my lapel-badge was used as an excuse to give me a drubbing, I removed it and thereafter denied all knowledge of its existence. Under those conditions I would have denied the existence of God himself.

With the passage of time the enthusiasm for performing on the Altar gave way to complaints about the drudgery of early morning Mass. Getting out of bed at six o'clock in the morning suddenly seemed less of a privilege—more so still when was expected to attend four services on a Sunday. By the time I was ten boredom had set in. Our new occupation was high-profile providing teachers and parents with a whole new armoury of threats. Whether we liked it or not we had to set a good example.

'Altar-boys don't behave like that . . . . What would Father Martin say if he heard you talk like that?' and so on. Being used in this fashion tended to alienate other pupils and place us in isolation. As a result it was natural if not inevitable that our little band of altar servers sought to find things to distract them. We needed diversions and it wasn't long before a whole hierarchy of mischief-making evolved. We found that by arriving early and being the last to leave we would have time to sample the altar wine. On rare occasions, if the time lapse was sufficient, we could try on the priest's vestments. However these were only the first steps. We learned how to change the rota for altar-servers by forging Father Martin's signature; having installed mice in the tabernacle and a dead rat in the vestment drawers in the sacristy, the more adventurous amongst us went that bit further. We located the cupboard where the holy-communion wafers were stored and we decided to try and consecrate them into hosts ourselves; a sort of DIY Mass making for beginners.

'If they really become the actual body and blood of Jesus Christ,' Danny Moon said, 'then when we break one open if should bleed.'

Danny was an imaginative boy with a fine sense of Gothic humour. His proposal was a match for any Hammer House of Horror film and no matter how abhorrent the notion might have been to some amongst us, *en masse*—to a man or rather to a boy we were mesmerised. The prospect of calling down the Lord God was irresistible—certainly a lot better than Saturday morning pictures. That day we took turns to read the relevant Latin with all the solemnity we could muster, observing the detail of the ritual as accurately as possible. Danny even wore the priest's cope and his stole. That it did not work was eventually put down to the fact that we had not performed it on the high altar and that it had not been part of a full mass.

The next step was terrifyingly obvious.

In the spring the good women of the parish took it upon themselves to clean the church. The designation of the epithet 'good' was one endorsed and repeatedly referred to by Father Martin. In his innocence he probably intended it as a non-discriminatory description much in the manner it was used in the Middle Ages. However, whilst the term satisfied the ladies in question, according to my mother, it alienated many others. Clearly some took the priest to imply that if they did not volunteer to scrub and clean the church—they were not so good and this divided the congregation.

Actually the schism was only a manifestation of the jealousy already well-established between two groups of women. There were those who annually scrubbed the floors, dusted the statues and polished the pews and then there were others who arranged the flowers, polished the candlesticks and swept the floors weekly. The weekly performers—all members of the Catholic Women's League claimed that their more regular efforts were surely more important. Whereas the others—who were all members of the Mothers Union, would claim that their annual work schedule was necessary only because the church was not properly maintained throughout the year. No one could ever explain to me how two groups with such similar aims and good intentions could find themselves at such odds.

Nevertheless despite the back-biting that year the annual cleaning programme was planned to take place as usual during the spring half-term. Generally the work took one week and it was accepted that it would be a time of upheaval: a short period when all services save for the morning mass would be suspended. Significantly it was Mrs. Moon—Danny's mother who led the assault on the dirt and grime in the church.

Danny told us, 'That starts on Monday morning, and for a few days they get there early and work till late. But by Thursday they're arriving later each morning and on Friday they won't arrive until after one pm. Now I can get the keys say for Friday morning and we can have our own mass done long before the cleaners arrive.'

'Won't your Mum be suspicious if you ask her for the keys to the church?' Henry Johnson asked.

After me Henry was regarded as the weakest link in our chain and some of the others immediately took his objection to mean he was about to chicken out. Dug Watson, by far the biggest and nastiest of the group was not going to permit such transparent cowardice. He had long since appointed himself the role of enforcer and enjoyed nothing better than bullying anyone smaller then himself.

'If you don't turn up 'enry ah'll kick yer fuckin face in.'

Subtlety was not his *forte* but what he said, he said with heartfelt meaning.

Henry protested that he had every intention of being there and that if the others wanted, just to prove his good intentions, he would volunteer to say the mass himself. It was a safe bet. We all knew that Danny had set his heart of the lead role and before anyone could comment on Henry's offer he made it clear that was how he felt.

'Ah mean me mother is the one with the keys, an' I'm gonna get 'em—so I reckon it's only fair that I do the priest bit.'

No-one argued the point.

During the following week we met to discuss the plan and to finalise the detail several times in the playground. School was even more boring than usual most especially because four of us were in the scholarship class and could only look forward to the 11+ test coming up in the near future. However, that was not my only concern. Now that Danny's project was drawing closer I began to have some doubts about having a part in it. It was all well and good for the prophets in the Old Testament to call on God and maybe it was okay for priests to do it as well—but ten schoolboys calling on God was a very different matter. There was also the unthinkable possibility of being caught in the act. The vision of my mother's disgrace not to mention her retribution was almost too much.

The holiday week sped past and the sense of anticipation was ever stronger. A shaky feeling nevertheless permeated the group: a premonition of disaster. At last the big day arrived and despite my fears I waited after the seven o'clock mass to see which of the others remembered to turn up. Young Father Thomas put away his vestments and left me to tidy away the cruets and straighten the changing room. Time dragged as I waited, stretching the slow minutes on the Sacristy clock. My tasks were soon completed and I wandered the church still dressed in my cassock, still tense. At eight fifteen exactly Danny appeared. His face was just as flushed as mine but in his case I felt sure it was through excitement rather than terror. Ten minutes later Henry arrived with Jimmy.

I imagine that those secret service units who were sent into occupied territories during WW2 would have had the same moment of trepidation just before they jumped: a moment when they questioned the sanity of their actions. For me that moment became ever more elastic. My conscience had been increasingly at odds with the plan. The ground far below lacked the necessary substance and my doubts about the communal parachute increased by the second. The appearance of the others—or at least some of the others helped, providing security in the comfort of numbers. The gnawing doubts nevertheless continued to tease me just beneath the surface of my apparent confidence.

We waited until nine o'clock for the rest to turn up by which time it was apparent that we were on our own. Danny was furious.

'Fuck 'em . . . . ' he kept saying, 'Yellow bastards.'

Whilst we waited Jimmy served us generous portions of altar wine in cracked cups and we shared a packet of crisps Henry had brought along. The wine affected us all in different ways. Danny became ever more truculent and determined; Henry discovered his bravery; Jimmy was the first to get pissed and I grew more and more morose. Dug who had been the last one to appear simply fell asleep. At nine o'clock sharp Danny allocated our roles. He was to play the priest whilst Henry and I were to be the altar-boys. Jimmy was to be the look-out as he wasn't capable of anything else by then and Dug would serve as the congregation.

I helped Danny into his cope in the priests' dressing room and Henry lit the candles and laid out the cruets of water and wine on the altar. Standing before the long mirror just before he took the chalice and the wafers Danny turned to me with a twinkle in his eye.

'S' gonna be a special mass this is Paul—and when God comes down, like I know he will—then I'm gonna ask all of you to 'ave a wank. All of us along the altar rail celebrating with a 'J. Arthur'. In fact better still—we'll say this mass without our pants on eh?'

Henry caught the end of this statement as he came in from the altar—just as Danny began to loosen his belt. Henry looked nervous.

'What are you doing Danny?'

His voice was small.

'Get yer pants off 'enry—me and Paul think it would be a good laugh if we tossed-off just before communion when God arrives—so we're gonna do this mass without our pants on.'

Having been described as one of the originators of the idea there was little I could do but agree. I started to undress and Henry quickly followed suit.

A moment or two later the three of us in procession took to the altar. It was no wonder that Jimmy broke down in peals of laughter at our appearance. The white cottas we wore only came down to our hips leaving our bare bums clearly visible. Danny spun round at the sound of laughter. He shouted the length of the nave.

'Shurrup . . . yer drunken sod . . . . And get yer pants off now.'

The laughter subsided and I saw Jimmy struggling to follow our example.

Danny mounted the altar steps to locate the chalice and a moment later he stood between Henry and me to start the service.

'Introibo ad altare Dei . . . . '

He intoned the Latin in the same expressionless manner to which we had become accustomed and our responses followed in the time-honoured pattern in a similar vein.

'Ad Deum qui leafiicat juventutum meam . . . . '

The responses delivered in unison secured for us some sense of normality. As if the phrases themselves magically transformed the sacrilege into acceptable if not holy practice. My mind was befuddled through the wine I'd drunk. It was usual for altar-boys to forgo their breakfast until after morning mass consequently I'd had nothing to eat since supper the night before. The alcohol therefore made my head light, my vision blurred and my sense of reality impaired. Once or twice I staggered and Henry was much the same. I noticed that his concentration wandered occasionally and he sometimes missed the responses. Increasingly however I was impressed by Danny's performance. He used the thick missal to great effect easily able it seemed to find the right prayers for the day and the Epistles and Gospel references without effort. Indeed at least as far as I was concerned other than the fact that our act was sacrilegious and performed in a state of semi-nudity and for dubious purposes the mass progressed with all its usual assurance of propriety.

The ritual moved on to the time for Holy Communion and Danny turned to face Dug his congregation holding the ciborium before him. He strode down the steps, his bared genitals wagging between the tassels of his stole and we joined him at the altar-rail. Jimmy had apparently dozed off and Danny had to shout to get his attention.

'Jimmy!' he yelled breaking the spell completely, 'get y' self up here now . . . ' then out of the corner of his mouth he muttered to me, 'the bastard's gone to sleep.'

At last Jimmy arrived to kneel next to Dug facing Danny, Henry and me.

I suppose we were all so engrossed in the final act of irreligious defiance that no one noticed the arrival of Father Thomas. The first we knew of him was his scream. It was a piercing, heart-rending screech of protest; a wail sufficient to chill the blood of any Christian. He shrieked his objections in a gibberish of shocked protest. Words like profane, desecration and unsacred tumbled from his lips as he ran down the central isle. We all froze, each of us still clutching our respective willies.

It was not until Father Thomas grabbed Jimmy by the neck that we came back to life. His eyes blazed like a mad man and in terror we all tried to exit the place. Danny dropped the heavy silver chalice spilling holy wafers across the mosaic floor and made a run for the sacristy door. In turn Father Thomas let loose of Jimmy and leaped the altar rail in one bound. He grabbed the cope from the retreating boy's shoulders, in the process tripping him and a struggle began between Danny and the priest. Henry fell over backwards dropping the communion plate. I tried to intervene in the struggle but found the front of my shirt caught up in the priest's fist. He lifted me almost off my feet completely. Still struggling Danny was tucked up tightly under his right arm; like me Henry was grabbed from the floor by Father Thomas's other hand and a tangle of torn clothing, screams and bare bottoms completed the ensemble. Dug stood to one side throughout the struggles looking to be traumatised if not mesmerised.

Given my less than lucid state it is difficult to recall precisely when I became aware of Danny's mother. Father Thomas's screams mixed with our protests had created a tumult in which the addition of female voices was momentarily hidden. It was only when Mrs. Moon hit the priest over the head with her zinc bucket that I realised like the cavalry in any western movie; the women of the parish had arrived. Their conclusions as to what was actually happening were welcome however misplaced.

In the assault that followed the boys were all cast aside as if they were made of straw. Mrs. Moon and her three associates, all ladies of generous proportions took to beating the priest. They used their mops, their sweeping brushes and whatever other cleaning utensils they had to hand. Their screams enjoined with his in a cacophony of equal dimensions to that of a philharmonic orchestra and in a very short while he was beaten to insensibility.

It was only then that they stopped.

It was months later after the Moon family had moved from the district, in the process changing their allegiance to the Methodist persuasion; after Father Thomas had been found a posting in a distant far flung foreign part and after I had been enrolled in a private school before my mother approached the question of culpability with me. Like the other parents involved and despite the confessions of the boys she nevertheless still harboured a suspicion of the priest. What I did not appreciate at the time was that her doubts also encompassed the possibility that my own involvement may have been more than it appeared. By the time

I understood the implication of her thinking in this regard I was old enough to find the idea humorous. By then I had also grown to admire the creative side of my mother's thinking. She would never acknowledge these skills but it was an area to which I always felt in her debt: a suitable development from the daydreaming of which I had ever been accused.

Fortunately my daydreaming had its own rewards, eventually allowing for a career writing biographies albeit mostly of lesser known poets. Despite being thorough in terms of the research necessary they proved to be works without very special literary distinction. They were—and are—typical of my intellectual prudence; careful pieces that seek to fill historical gaps rather than expose long forgotten scandals; works that unashamedly take a joy in the mundane. Needless to say before she died, my Mother was full of praise for my efforts but conversely this was an accolade that caused me to question the direction of my career.

Looking back it is significant that I regard her funeral as the fulcrum about which my life turned. It was the start of a series of events that would quite literally change my way of perceiving the world and the way in which I responded to the stimulus it provided.

The occasion of the funeral both in terms of the church ceremony and the social gathering afterwards was organised by Aunt Polly, my Mother's younger sister—the dominant sister. However, the fact that the religious provision was focused on a Methodist chapel was initially something of a surprise. Privately Aunt Polly explained that Mother had fallen out with Father O'Brien, the Catholic Parish priest. Apparently he had had the temerity to change one of her flower arrangements: his Pink Chrysanthemums instead of the more tasteful Arum Lilies and Ivy. His small misdemeanour; however irritating for my Mother and her coterie of colleagues in the Woman's League, was apparently described by her as, 'the last straw' and prompted her switch of allegiance. The Catholic Women's League consisted of a small group of stalwart, well-meaning females (in their middle years or older) who took responsibility for cleaning and decorating the church interior. Selecting and arranging the flowers on the High Altar was seen as the pinnacle of achievement within this group and only the older more experienced ladies accrued this honour. Clearly Father O'Brian's preference for chrysanthemums had no place in the hierarchy of choices exercised by his well-meaning volunteers.

Despite my familiarity with the Roman Faith, I did not realise that the tenants of that faith could so easily be changed to suit a quite different belief system not even when subjected to anyone's 'last straw' Nevertheless, Aunt Polly was in charge (as she was so often) and I concurred with her wishes for the use of the Methodist Chapel followed by a short service at the crematorium. In all honesty I would have preferred a more traditional Requiem Mass at St.Ignatius's Church accompanied by some solid organ music and a burial. This was a vain hope. Given the poor state of my relationship with my Mother however, it would be unfair to express any serious degree of disappointment with Aunt Polly's decisions. Indeed, try as I might, I did not feel anything like the degree of responsibility that a more devoted son might feel. My Mother and I had become increasingly estranged over recent years and I was no more aware of what might constitute her final wishes than I was able to describe her preference for wallpaper patterns.

It was in this context that much against my better judgement I was persuaded to read something appropriate as part of the crematorium service. Aunt Polly thought it would be a 'nice' gesture and so it became part of the itinerary. Being a Classics graduate, a sometime journalist and biographer my experience with regard to choosing a suitable passage was naturally judged to be insufficient. The sole arbiter of what might be seen as appropriate was of course my Aunt Polly. Even had I been suffering a hangover I would never have chosen anything by Sir Alfred

Lord Tennyson but if I had been sufficiently mistaken to do so, I would not have chosen to read 'A Dirge.'

With hindsight perhaps it was because I felt the reading set an unfortunate tone that I was so distracted. On the other hand it may well have been my inherent fear of public performance. Since my disastrous appearance with Danny Moon and friends I have never enjoyed standing before an audience; I never give talks or lectures and have never accepted any of those roles so often pressed on one by friends such as Best Man and the like. Basically being a shy person, if pressed I always plump for a supporting role rather than one in the spot-light.

On this occasion when it was my turn to perform, my thoughts were elsewhere and I missed the polite cough which was the priest's cue. Aunt Polly—the guardian of all things in their proper places—sought to remind me albeit with a sharp elbow in the ribs—a timely reminder. Once at the lectern, my faulted start went almost unnoticed however, due to the fact that the Pastor's cough, redolent of a smoker on forty a day had turned his face puce and thoroughly rattled his frame the congregation turned their attentions and considerations to their vicar. I was therefore allowed to revise my beginning again almost unnoticed.

My dry throat and clammy hands were accompanied by an undeniable premonition of disaster. I scanned my text which up until that moment I had committed to memory and then looked out on the faces below me. By then Mr. Burse the vicar had recovered himself behind a large pocket handkerchief and the silence was overwhelming. I suppose I had not been prepared to see such a large turnout. From my vantage point the chapel appeared to be filled to the brim. Dozens of pale wrinkled faces, crowned with dark coloured hats of every conceivable size and shape watched and waited. I cleared my throat and began:

> 'Now is done thy long day's wait . . .'

The print swam momentarily and the next line became an homogenous squiggle. I stopped and adjusted my spectacles, involuntarily noting the predatory cough from Aunt Polly in the process. I began again:

'Now is done they long day's wait . . .'

This time a tickle in my throat caused me to need to swallow or to clear the airway. I tried to do both and almost choked. Composure restored I glanced over my glasses and mumbled an apology. It was becoming rather more of a long day's wait than even Tennyson could have imagined. However, the third attempt took me through the first two verses without further mishap and my confidence grew. It is odd how those of us lacking the skills of public oratory, given some modicum of success will become over-confident—irrationally over-confident. Nevertheless with two verses under my belt my rehearsals began to pay dividends and I recalled the third verse without need of my text. I felt that the congregation now hung on my every word; I was able to stare down at them; I became expansive and at some point with arms outstretched I leaned forward placing my hands on the console and exaggerated my pause. Glancing at the fifth verse, I read:

'Round thee blow, self pleached deep,
Brambles roses faint and pale,
And long purples of the dale.
Let them rave.
These, in every shower creep
Thro' the green that folds thy grave,
Let them rave.

It isn't possible to say precisely when I first felt the concern of the congregation but it was certainly during verse five. I glanced up as I recited the final line only to find that every eye under every black hat was focused on some point beyond my left shoulder. It was then and only then that I became aware of the soft sound of machinery: the steady whirring of a conveyor belt. In the distant corner of my field of vision I caught sight of the coffin as it began to move and it was only at that moment that I realised my outstretched hand rested on one of the buttons on the control panel.

In cold desperation I jabbed again at the button but my Mother's sedate progress was not to be denied. Frantic now I began to press other buttons. The lights dimmed and then brightened again and the curtains began to close and open in spasms of indecision. My actions, agitated as they were must have left an impression of an old time cinema organist. And if I could have found a button that would have sent me and the pulpit down into the basement I would have pressed it willingly.

Eventually Mr. Burse the vicar came to my rescue. He appeared alongside me like Marley's ghost and with the dexterity of a computer analyst, he flicked a switch and pressed a button and soon calm was restored. Unfortunately by then Mother had disappeared.

In response to my look of concern, he whispered in my ear,

'Sorry, the conveyor belt goes only one way . . . . should have warned you.'

Given the context, his message might well have been a religious metaphor. My embarrassment was total and I crept from the lectern red-faced and downcast.

In the final part of the ceremony Aunt Polly insisted on leading the congregation in a recitation of two decades of the Holy Rosary. Presumably this was her attempt to restore a relationship between the non-denominational character of the service and the Roman faith she shared with my Mother. How appropriate this might have been proved doubtful as only a minority of the people present were of the Catholic persuasion. More significantly the particular mysteries we were asked to contemplate during this litany were the assumption and coronation of the Blessed Virgin. These were from the third chaplet, termed the Glorious Mysteries and however complimentary to my Mother's memory I wondered if at least for the most devout practitioners, the choice might not have been seen as sacrilegious.

Sufficient to say few had brought rosary beads, a curious practice in my view to count the prayers. However, the use of beads for this purpose is not distinctively Christian. Palladius a writer of the fifth century described an Egyptian monk who employed the use of pebbles to enumerate his delivery of three hundred prayers and William of Malmesbury wrote that lady Godiva who founded a religious house in Coventry in 1040 AD left a circlet of gems, strung together on which she used to tell her prayers. Bearing in mind that these were simply methods of counting, it is interesting that the emphasis they enjoy has imbued them with their own mystical importance.

Afterwards everyone was extremely polite. Save for Aunt Polly, no one referred to my impromptu rearrangement of the service. The line of mourners shook hands with me as they left and I caught Uncle Desmond's eye as he and Aunt Polly approached the chapel door. His expression said it all. After what she would undoubtedly see as the successful part she had played Aunt Polly clearly felt better equipped to criticise mine.

'Well done Paul . . . . but if I'd known we were to have a light show, I'd have booked Go-Go dancers and some lasers.' After delivering her coup de grace she turned leaving me to my private shame. A moment or two later, still smarting from her comment I followed her dutifully to the black car.

Chapter Two

A group of selected friends and ex-colleagues collected after the service at my Mother's cottage. A respectable sherry with a finger buffet was on offer and although I had played no part in the provision of the food I had chosen the sherry. Needless to say the guest list had been decided by my aunt. The cottage was tiny and although the original intention was to site the gathering in the small back garden, the English Autumn weather made that impossible. It had rained all day. Consequently, the guests were crammed into two small reception rooms and an even smaller kitchen. I had been ordered to circulate and to make folk welcome but I found any kind of movement almost impossible. It was difficult enough just to turn around. For the most part therefore, I found myself jammed against the kitchen door trying to balance a tea-plate in one hand and a crystal glass in the other.

Secretly I was glad that there were few relatives present. I have a persistent phobia that has me believe that graveside gatherings bring out the worst in people, especially amongst those who could boast blood-ties with the deceased. In my view there is often what I call a vulture complex evident at funerals. This manifests itself by anyone with the most tenuous the most distant link to the dearly departed imagining that they have a claim to valuables—or even the 'not so valuable' of any description that they may fancy. Much like competitors in the ubiquitous TV panel game they vie for any old bits and pieces they can find. Sometimes the post-burial greedy bun-fight is characterised by a question and answer session in which the bereaved are closely cross-examined. Fortunately my Mother's last will and testament made her intentions perfectly clear. Everything, save for a few items of jewellery for Aunt Polly was left to me. This however, did not arrest the attempts by some of the carrion-eaters. Clearly I was seen as the 'soft-touch' whereas Aunt Polly was not bothered by the thinly veiled suggestions and was able to return rudeness with rudeness.

I was cornered briefly by Miss Thomas and Miss Evans who were Mother's next door neighbours. They had proved to be a caring couple who had been valued friends and of all the people there I was most glad to speak to them. They spoke of my Mother with real affection and told me how she had often boasted about her talented son. This came as something of a surprise as she had not been one to exhibit the more obvious signs of mother-love publically. Indeed although we continued to exchange letters our discourse had been mainly factual. I wrote concerning the things I did, places I visited and work projects. She would write about the garden, village life and express opinions about my work. I therefore knew much about her philosophy but little of her feelings.

I am led to believe that my Father disappeared from the scene apparently at about the same time my Mother's pregnancy was first announced. At the time they were both lecturing in the English Department at one of the red brick universities. Their 'fling' had occurred around the time he was applying for teaching Posts abroad and I once heard my Mother cynically observe that his success had proved her undoing. He left her to fend for herself as best she might and as far as I was aware she never heard from him again. Her career was thereby truncated according to the ethic of that time and his influence on any proceedings affecting our future was consigned to the file Mother would call: 'Items not wanted on voyage'. It was ever her practice to invent such categories, designing them to suit a myriad of situations. Perhaps the 'Things to Remember' files were the most used but the catalogue of convenient depositories seemed to cover every eventuality bringing order to my childish thinking—or so my Mother would argue. The files also comprised an extensive list of sub-headings under: times of day; days of the year and lessons. There were also 'Unacceptable behaviour' files and 'Good Manners' files. Having witnessed some small transgression, I have vivid memory of my Mother saying, 'Paul—I wish you would consign that to the unacceptable behaviour file; sub-heading: at the breakfast table.'

It is only now as an adult that I examine such memories that I begin to appreciate how my repetition of these pat euphemisms must have appeared to my teachers. Clearly they must have added further testimony to what must already have been my unbearable precocity. The attentions lavished upon me by my only parent were not without the demands of certain responsibilities. For example my education was taken most seriously. I was enrolled at a local school but they were able to provide little more than the basic tuition and my presence there was more to do with satisfying social strictures rather than any serious expectation of education as my Mother knew it. For a while after the Moon family had left the district, she tutored me at home. Such was the intensity of her system, by the age of eleven years I was beginning to read the Classics, becoming familiar with Latin Greek and French and spending one hour each day practising the piano. The very same piano that I could now see was festooned with glasses of sherry and plates of half eaten cheese biscuits.

When the crowd began to thin a little—about the same time that the duck pate and the smoked salmon were running out—a spritely white haired gent approached me. He introduced himself as James Collins and told me he had been a colleague working with my Mother many years ago. He also claimed that he had known me when I was just an infant. Curiously he then congratulated me on the publication of my last book. And even though his language was flowery, praise from my public was so limited (almost non-existent) that his comments were most welcome.

'I thoroughly enjoyed it,' he said 'Cumbria and the Border country were the stomping grounds of my youth providing a seminal experience beyond material wealth. I always believed that the legends and myths of the region had been badly neglected and your little volume stirred pleasant memories.'

'My thanks but unfortunately I appear to have done little to increase the popularity of the subject or the area. You're one of only a very select band who purchased the book. The critics thought it was pedantic and the public ignored it almost completely.'

He laughed.

'I'm sure you didn't imagine it would be a best seller or that it would make you a millionaire. Are you working on anything currently?'

I told him a little about my project with regard to Sir Walter Scott.

I've been researching him for the last twelve months—in fact I was in Edinburgh when news of my Mother's death reached me.'

Ah—Sir Walter—that is interesting. I have a proprietorial interest in Scott. An ancestor of mine is mentioned in one of his lesser known verses. You may recollect it—in the introduction to 'The Bridal of Triermain—there was a line:

> For Lucy loves—like Collins, ill-starred name!
> Whose lay's requital, was that tardy fame,
> Who bound no flower round his living head
> Should hang it o 'er his monument when dead . . . and so on.

The Mister Collins referred to was William Collins—my relative—a much misunderstood poet and scholar who died in the middle of the eighteenth century.'

I was intrigued and entertained by his recollections. A coincidence of some scale I concluded, almost enough to have be believe in synchronicity. I certainly knew about William Collins not surprisingly his name had cropped up several times during my research. I was also familiar with Scott's poem, sufficient to know it had been misquoted. The line actually read:

'Who bound no *laurel* round his living head.'

Signifying that, just as his relative had stated, he was largely unrecognised during his life-time. However, having promised my aunt to be on my best behaviour and also because I had already begun to like Mr. James Collins, I resisted the temptation to correct him. After all it was not every day that one met with such a distinctive link with the eighteenth century. Later I glad that I had held my tongue. James Collins turned out to be an exceptionally well read and informed observer of the very period I was studying. This made him a valuable contact. We hit it off so well that we arranged to meet for a drink the following week when we were both back in London.

If only some of the other people at the party had been half as interesting maybe I would not have given so much ammunition to Aunt Polly. Always on the lookout for reasons to criticise me later in the afternoon she had plenty of evidence to call on. I was thereafter forever condemned as the irresponsible and thoughtless son. I still choose to believe despite what happened that the cause of my misbehaviour was not entirely of my own making.

As was expected a number of the guests left early and these included my new friend James. Nevertheless our conversation had given me a lift and I had begun to feel that the reception was not entirely the waste of time I feared it might be. In this new frame of mind I helped myself to two more glasses of sherry. It should be said that my Aunt witnessed my indulgence and caught my eye from across the room with her warning stare. I smiled my assurance at her between the black hats that separated us and semaphored that this would be my last drink.

As luck would have it I hardly had time to sip the drink before I was accosted by a Mr. And Mrs, Flinthorne. It transpired that they were leading lights in the local literary circle and as amateur writers and dramatists they were keen to make my acquaintance. I had met the type before and was never able to persuade them that I would not be able to help them find a publisher. My well-worn prejudice, honed to a cutting edge by countless embarrassments at the grindstone of their ignorance was again amply confirmed. There is something about pushy amateurs that makes my skin prickle and those well intentioned and enthusiastic acolytes of the Arts—often retired folk with nothing to do—come top of my list. I can tolerate their affected displays of knowledge and I appreciate that they do not go out of their way to be offensive. Indeed, they are characterised by the way they hang on one's every word and see significance in the most trivial detail of one's comments. Rather it is their expectation of instant gratification that offends: their vain and stupid hope that they will witness some act of genuine creation.

Emma Flinthorne Typified the breed.

'I do enjoy meeting Artists; they're so much more sensitive to the issues that really matter.'

Her husband smiled his agreement and added:

'We write a bit you know. Not that what we do could be termed Art—like yours—but we do try. Don't we dear?'

Not knowing how to respond politely I gave a return smile and nodded. Unfortunately this was taken as encouragement and Norman (the husband) immediately launched into a description of his wife's latest play.

'It is a bit sort of Becket-y . . . No my dear, sparing your blushes the influence of the great man was there for anyone to see.'

He gave a knowing nod in my direction and added:

'I'm sure you would have seen it. Anyone with a trained eye could tell . . . '

His voice droned on acquiring an insistent tone. Its effect on me resembled that produced by piped music in lifts or supermarkets: I recognised groups of words and even some whole phrases but so pedestrian was the content, I found it impossible to devote the whole of my focus to what was being said. I need not have been concerned. Neither Norman nor Emma needed my direct participation. They were happy just to have me there as a passive recipient: someone to bounce their words off.

Until that afternoon Uncle Desmond had never been one of my favourite relatives. He'd always been seen as Aunt Polly's whipping boy; a long-suffering appendage or an extension of her will, sent to take messages or to make the tea. His early retirement had provided his wife with a constant attendant, someone who would devote his time exclusively to her requirements. However, it was Uncle Desmond who saved me from the Flinthornes. Just about the time Emma had been persuaded to recite one of her poems to me Desmond burst into the performance.

'Sorry—sorry Emma, I have to stop you there. I have to steal this young man away, something urgent has cropped up needs his immediate attention.'

I grasped the straw gratefully and followed him leaving my excuses trailing behind.

A few minutes later and we were seated opposite one another on single beds in the spare room. I was pleased with the rescue but I was delighted to find that the urgent business that had occasioned it was contained in a full bottle of fifteen year old single malt whisky.

Desmond poured very generous measures in each glass.

'Just couldn't leave you to Fred and Barney.' He grinned and answered my questioning frown saying, 'The Flintstones—as I call them—a terrible pair. They over-dosed on culture in their early old age and now they are addicts—a real pain in the arse. They qualify for the 'Boring' Olympic Gold Medal.'

I laughed feeling all the day's tension suddenly lift.

'That's better; you've had a face like a bad foot all day. Can't have you behaving like this was a funeral can we.'

He held out one of the glasses.

'I thought you might want to toast your Mother's spirit with something a bit more substantial than that poisonous sherry being foisted on the mindless ones down stairs.'

The golden fluid burnt its way through my system with instant results. By the time we had absorbed two such dinks tongues were loosened and the foundation of a new friendship was in the process of being established. Desmond refilled the tumblers.

'I hope you don't mind my saying so but I don't think you knew your old Mum all that well Paul. To be honest, even though Polly is her sister she didn't know her either.'

I accepted a cigarette from him which he lit for me. It did not seem to matter that I had stopped smoking some five years ago, having a smoke with him hidden away from critical eyes was somehow appropriate.

'How d 'you mean I didn't know her?'

He gave me a sly look.

'Well for example—did you know she was writing again?'

I nearly choked on my drink. It was almost twenty years since she had written anything—not since her last thin volume of verse. Once upon a time she had been quite prolific. I think the total was something like twelve novels, two bits of research and five books of poetry.

'No I didn't know—any idea what it was about.'

His grin this time was lop-sided and he made a pretence of drawing deeply on his cigarette—a theatrical gesture in the best Hollywood tradition.

'Ah—now that would be telling. It might surprise you to know that her subject wasn't too far from the kind of things you like to write about.'

He sipped his Scotch again.

'She was always interested in matters of what she liked to call—the soul—and seen through folk-lore.

'Are you trying to tell me she got hooked on that old time religion? That doesn't sound at all like my Mother. Catholicism was enough for her.'

'Far from it—she was far too keen an observer to swallow any clap-trap. No—what I meant was that she had taken an interest in legends and myths and had begun to uncover all sorts of beliefs and practices some of which had been adopted by Christianity and Islam.'

He gave a belly laugh and then paused for moment before continuing.

'That is the sort of thing you're interested in—isn't it?'

'Not really it isn't.'

I'd answered slowly trying to be as precise as I could but hearing myself I began to question myself. Sure I was interested in myths and legends especially as they were recalled in poetry. I'd researched all manner of cults and obtuse groups through their written word. I was intrigued by the structure of language and its development in the poetry contemporary to the period under the microscope. I tried to tell Desmond what I meant but long before he grasped my meaning we slipped into silly verse brought on by the whisky. In a more sober moment my uncle offered his best advice.

'It all sounds a bit dry to me. I think you might have had more commercial success if you'd concentrated on stories that were more accessible. People want a good read—tell a story folk can identify with—then you'll sell books.'

There was a ring of truth in what he said echoed precisely by the comments made regularly by my agent. Before I could argue with him however, Desmond changed the subject.

'Did I see you talking to that Collins fellow?'

'Yes you did, we had quite a chat. He was apparently one of Mother's teaching colleagues. Nice guy and interestingly enough we talk the same language regarding an interest in Sir Walter Scott.'

Desmond shook his head.

'Don't like the man—I never trusted him. I always advised your Mum to steer clear of him. He's a slime-ball only out for his own ends.'

The depth of his feeling and the way he expressed it made me laugh. His confession earlier that he'd known my Mother better than any of her relatives had made me suspicious—it was more than a platonic interest. Clearly he was jealous of James.

'That's a bit strong Des—are you sure that you're being entirely objective?'

He snorted down his nose and his face reddened.

'There you go again—of course I'm not being objective. I'm being entirely subjective and there's nothing wrong with that. I never did like the feller, always reckoned he was up to no good. You take my advice and keep well clear of him.'

He was adamant and, not wanting to create a difference of opinion after his kindness in rescuing me from the boring Flintstones and the generosity of malt whisky, I allowed the warning to remain unchallenged.

Instead I began to tell him some of the spicier tales from North of the Border. They caught his imagination just as I thought they might.

In all we spent two hours together in the small room and once the subject of James Collins had been exhausted our conversation was less than serious. Conversely the manner in which we attacked the bottle of Scotch was very serious indeed, so much so that a second bottle had appeared by the time the knock on the door sounded. By then we had both removed our jackets and ties and Desmond was in the process of trying to demonstrate a proof of one of the less comprehensible scientific conundrums associated with flight.

'But man can fly.' He said.

He was balanced precariously on the end of one of the thin beds as he spoke, a half empty glass in one hand and a feather in the other. God knows where the feather came from but he but he waved it as he was in the act of conducting the London Philharmonic orchestra.

'And to prove the point I will now . . . . '

With hindsight it was probably a good thing that Aunt Polly did not wait to be invited into the bedroom, as it was the knock and her sudden appearance seemed be simultaneous. From my position next to the sash window which I had just opened on Uncle Desmond's instruction, I could see she was more than a little upset.

Her voice was like a breadknife cutting a crusty loaf.

'You fools—you pair of stupid idiots—just look at the pair of you.'

Always obedient to her requirements we looked. Desmond looked at me and I looked at him. She was quite right—we were fools. Desmond posed with his feather was apparently ready to dive from the end of the bed and out of the window and, at least in his imagination, soar like an eagle over the roof-tops. Due to a broken sash-cord I stood there holding the window open waiting for him to make his leap into the history books—or perhaps more accurately into the undertaker's arms. It had not occurred to me up until that moment that if Desmond had made his leap I would have been the only witness left and my story would have undoubtedly left me behind bars for the considerable future.

'And where did that bottle come from?'

Her question rang out and I saw Desmond blush again. A moment later to my consternation I heard his reply.

'Paul brought it. He just asked me to join him for a quick snifter . . . and . . . well one thing led to another. No harm done though eh old girl? Been a bit silly—but it's all over now—back on the straight and narrow eh?'

His wife was unimpressed. By now she was inside the room with the door closed firmly behind her. I remember thinking that the only avenue of escape left was the window. Unfortunately by then the sobering effect of her presence had ruined the magic and flying was definitely off the agenda.

She ordered Desmond off the bed and then she turned her attentions to me. Given the circumstances I suppose her speech was predictable. However, to the casual eavesdropper it might have seemed that we were being castigated for transgressions against the national interest. If we had organised the storming of Parliament or the sale of Britain's atomic submarine fleet we could not have been more roundly criticised. I imagined her sending us to Guantanamo Bay.

In the end we were informed that as we were in no fit state to mix with the other guests, we should stay in the room until everyone else had gone. Her decision was guaranteed by the fact that she locked the door when she left.

Chapter Three

London has always been one of my favourite places, a fact I associate with its size as much as to my temperament. I like its urban sprawl and the excitement of its cosmopolitan ethos. I am prepared to suffer its crowds, to tolerate the traffic and to suffer its dirt and its dangers in the belief that all of it adds to the creative thinking process. When in London I feel part of what is happening. Rather than having one's provincial nose pressed against the window of national events, Londoners feel to be participants.

The excitement is due to the evident variety of sights, sounds and activities; to the pulse quickening opportunity and the potential of hidden danger. It is not so much that anything might happen (although well it might) rather that it is literally about to happen round the next corner, in the next house or as soon as I look away. I always found it to be a place where one can so easily overdose on anticipation: a refuge for the hopeful and a ready stimulus for anyone's imagination. How much of this reaction is self-induced it is difficult to say. I have never quite managed to overcome that first feeling of awe the shock when, as a boy of fourteen years I stepped out of the tube station at Piccadilly to witness for the first time the centre of the civilized universe—or so I imagined. At that time my experience of any kind of universe, civilized or otherwise had been severely proscribed by my upbringing in the far north of England. My conclusions therefore may have been just a little over the top. Nevertheless even if my later maturity brought greater awareness that ultimately begot cynicism, the excitement remained and I am as ever I was a moth to London's flame.

For some years I became a resident. I found a basement flat and through careful management of my frugal earnings I was able to secure a foothold and my independence by the purchase of an extremely long lease. Since then there have been many occasions when it may have been advisable to sell the flat but I kept it. I held onto it even when my work took me abroad; when property prices soared and selling would have cleared all my debts. I kept it despite the painful associations with Deborah and I kept it even though for a long time I didn't use it. The ties were indefinable I simply wanted to maintain the link.

I left the tube at Oxford Circus and walked down Regent Street. The air was cold under a grey sky. Pedestrians were muffled against the wind causing them to appear as armless mounds of heavy cloth: heaped up and formless bipeds from some sci-fi movie. I kept my gloved hands deep in my overcoat pockets and my chin well hidden beneath a woollen scarf. Winter was no friend of mine. Perhaps an émigré from the colder climes of County Durham should have been able to boast a greater tolerance but I had found as I grew older the cold was ever more difficult to tolerate.

Just before Piccadilly Circus I crossed over to enter Swallow Street. The wine bar was down a steep flight of steps in a basement. As I turned the corner the outstretched hand of a homeless man caught my eye. He was crouched on a quilt of newsprint topped by a piece of old carpet. His worldly goods were contained in a plastic carrier bag and secured under one arm. Not an old man, perhaps in his late thirties, he was clean shaven and beneath his woollen hat, there had been some attempt it seemed to comb his long lifeless hair. The apparent bulk of his body was consistent with the many layers of coats and pullovers he wore. It was only the thinness of his face, the drawn skin over sharp bones that confirmed the fact of his actual physical state.

I struggled to remove my glove and then again in search for my trouser-pocket beneath my overcoat. Whilst he waited his eyes were fixed on mine. They were not cowed or in any way shame-faced. They were bright inquisitive eyes full of questions. It was not the stereotypical face of a down-and-out. At last my fingers closed around the coins in my pocket.

'Been out long?'

My question was as much to relieve the tension as anything else.

'Long enough!'

His answer was in a Scottish country accent.

At a rough guess the coins in my hand must have amounted to four pounds and some change. I dropped them into his palm and he acknowledged the gift with a short nod but continued to hold my gaze.

'Well—good-luck. Hope it works out for you.'

I was pulling my glove back on and beginning to walk off as I made my last comment. He still stared at me, the coins still showing in his open hand.

'And Fuck you too!' he said.

His was a dismissive gratitude that let the cold under my scarf.

A moment or two later and I was descending the steep stairs down into the wine bar. I went through the archway and into a large room. A long bar was situated along the right hand side wall and opposite another room could be accessed by way of two more arches. In all there were about twenty tables but only one or two were occupied so the place was still quiet, a sharp contrast to the noise of Regent Street above. I guessed that the lunch-time trade would not begin for another hour or so, consequently it was a good time to order food. As I reached the foot of the stairs I saw James. He stood up from behind a corner table clutching a half empty pint glass. He gave me a huge smile. Hung my coat on a nearby stand and approached the bar with James at my elbow.

'My shout,' he said, 'what'll you have?'

'Bitter—a pint in a straight glass please.'

The barman a young Irishman raised his eyebrow at the row of labels.

'Bass please and could we order something to eat?'

The smells from the kitchen were already making my juices run so after an extended discussion I chose sausage and mash in onion gravy whilst James opted for the shepherd's pie. The selection of food on these occasions I perceived in a similar way to the significance attributed by some to body language. There was therefore some security in knowing that we both ordered 'real' food leaving the hamburgers and breaded chicken to those without respect for their digestive systems or dietary wellbeing.

James was obviously pleased to see me.

'I'm glad you made it. I wondered if you might forget what with all the fuss of the funeral.'

I shook my head.

'No I've been looking forward to seeing you again. I think I might have recognised a kindred spirit.'

The beer was cold, unnecessarily so and I found myself staring at the glass critically as the first draught traced its icy passage. James took note of my reaction and asked if the beer was off.

'Difficult to tell—they keep it so cold one can hardly taste the stuff. Maybe they think its Lager.'

My friend laughed into his glass.

'It's easy to see you hail from the North. Would you like a short to warm you up?'

I refused the offer but had to admit to my objection to the now fashionable cellar technique of keeping all the beers very cold. I said I believed that there was a preconception about cold beer, one that could be blamed on the Germano-American influence.

A little while later the food arrived.

'I hope you're going to tell me about your new book.' James commented between mouthfuls, 'I had another look at your last publication this morning and it only confirmed my previous observations.'

It is a common sign of human frailty that if a stranger pays complimentary attention to some aspect of one's work, suddenly the sky is blue, the birds are singing and one's most private thoughts are immediately an open book. I confess that I am just as likely to be swayed by compliments as the silliest schoolgirl. This occasion was no different. In no time at all I was describing my latest venture.

For me Sir Walter Scott was a paradox. Despite all his poetry; his vivid imagination and it must be admitted, his romanticism he had been trained as a lawyer, a profession not usually given to flights of fancy. Lawyers, especially in his time, had hardly been known to provide the seed-corn of literary endeavour and still less to encourage the Arts generally.

Sir Walter was called to the Bar in 1792 at the tender age of 21 years. He practised for five years before publishing his first volume anonymously. His first book was a translation of 'Burger's Der Wilde Jager' (The Wild Huntsman). During that same year he married a Frenchwoman Margaret Charlotte Charpentier, daughter of Jean Charpentier from Lyons. Within the next fourteen years Scott became a partner in James Ballantyne's printing business and four years later (1809) became partner in Ballantyne's Books.

I recited this litany of achievement without hesitation. The poet had been a favourite of mine since I was a boy and I felt that I knew him well. Dealing with the product of pen however, was not quite so easy. I had learned by was of a regular mauling by critics that he was an acquired taste. To the modern reader he appeared sentimental, his aspirations naive and his language antiquated. It was and is my contention that there is a rare quality to be found in his writing especially in the construction of his verse. I proposed that it was the form of his poetry that maintained my interest. For James's benefit I stressed the historical background rather than involve myself too deeply in a lengthy description concerning structure.

James listened attentively but when I paused for breath and a gulp of Bass, he leaned forward and asked if the book was intended simply as a biography.

'Certainly not—I must confess I have almost as much curiosity about the man as I do about his work.'

Giving this response left me flushed with embarrassment. I knew that I always described my work as writing biographies even though I felt it delved rather deeper than itemising a simple chronology of events. I imagined that my feeling of awkwardness must have communicated itself because James became solicitous.

'I grant you there may be hidden clues to his writing in his personal history but surely the content of his narrative, if not the quality of his verse, transcends what was in fact a rather pedestrian life.'

I was to find on closer association with James Collins that he possessed a unique conversational style. His appearance and the tone of his delivery often belied the content of what he said. For example at one end of the scale, nodding as he disagreed was one of his more discernable habits. It was not that he was an unsympathetic listener or that he lacked charity as a story-teller. Simply that in any debate he had an ability to weave a cloth that appeared to be an agreeable dialectic apparently for the benefit of his companion but when worn, was found to prickle and irritate. In the beginning I therefore found him elusive in conversation and often found myself unable to say precisely what his opinion might be. Needless to say I still found his company intriguing.

Our conversation that day lasted until well after the normal trade for that period had expired. We were the last customers to leave and only then when we were pressed to do so. In terms of matters discussed, our spectrum was catholic if not exhaustive. Our talk about what we termed was writing for work contrasted with that which we did simply for pleasure. We argued about narrative style and blank verse; we debated the importance of myth and legend and finally via a difference of opinion about the Green Man we explored notions of the Noble Savage.

I had long-since harboured the belief that the closer mankind could operate to nature then the better and probably the longer our life-span, not to mention the reduced wear on the planet. A modest enough thesis—I thought and entirely in keeping with the sensible and liberal tradition of the middle classes. On closer examination however, it proved a vague and somewhat amorphous intention, not bounded by an identified time-scale or by any limit to the intensity of involvement. James put that down to a generation of Hippy/ New Age Traveller thinking.

'I suppose my main objection,' he said draining his glass, 'is the lack of intellectual rigour in that kind of woolly thinking.'

He claimed that mine was an amorphous intention not bounded by a time-scale or by any limit to the intensity of possible involvement.

'As I said before I suppose my main objection, is the lack of intellectual rigour in that kind of woolly thinking.'

He had an irritating habit of summing up an argument and drawing conclusions long before I had finished describing my viewpoint.

'Good intentions by themselves only serve to muddy the waters', he continued, 'and as long as no-one asks for explicit clarification—then you're safe. But look for a commitment; seek out necessary change; examine the minutiae and what are we left with?'

'I'm sure you are about to tell me.'

'Indeed I am,' he replied ignoring my sarcastic tone, 'I believe there is nothing worse than being 'well-intentioned'. To say someone meant well is to admit he did not organise his thinking effectively. In my view that is operating at less than even an instinctive level. At least in the rest of the animal kingdom, the denizens know what they want and they generally know how to go about getting it.

'D'you not think to claim they 'know' is too strong a word?'

Now it was my turn to play the pedant.

He laughed and shook his head, 'If our discussion is to turn into an argument then I'll stop now.'

His comment made me feel embarrassed and I made a great pretence of denying my irritation. I do not think he believed me but he allowed himself to be persuaded to continue.

'I'm sorry if I appear bombastic Paul. I was only trying to make the point that perhaps we have much to learn from our animal neighbours. Their 'knowing' is at a base level, it's instinctive, felt with the whole of their being. They are really close to nature. They don't need to form a 'Green Party' or to proclaim they are 'Friends of the Earth'. By comparison we've forgotten how to respond honestly to our environment. We've lost our understanding of the essentials. The only thing we commit to is our own comfort. If we are so superior to our less fortunate neighbours surely we should be able to employ all their abilities plus those of a higher intellect.

Secretly I found myself agreeing with his argument and that perhaps my annoyance had only been an appreciation of my own lack of foresight. On the other hand I also realised my change of heart might be yet another instance of my suggestibility. Faced with strong opinions I often found myself changing sides. It was a character fault that my Mother had often referred to but one about which she had often taken advantage.

It was clear from their behaviour that the people at the wine bar were waiting on us to leave. Rather than pursue a discussion about what might constitute a way forward we paid the bill and made our way out onto Swallow Street. James suggested we might find more sympathetic surroundings at his club which was only a short walk away.

'I presume you don't have any important appointment this afternoon?' James asked.

I told him my day was free and that I would spend the night at my flat in Elgin Crescent. He seemed pleased. As we left the wine bar I noticed that the homeless man was still crouched on his newspaper bed, this time as I passed he spat on the pavement but refused to look me in the eye.

James was a member of the Garrick club, a long established gentleman's meeting place of considerable reputation. Amongst its facilities it could boast as good a restaurant as any in London. Its premises were festooned with paintings and memorabilia representing a history of association with artists and writers; dramatists and their patrons over several centuries and the furnishings would not have looked amiss in any of the grand mansions in the locality. I had been invited there only once before but such was the impression made on that visit, it was still a vivid memory.

We mounted the dusty grey steps to the reception area where the doorman greeted James with a warm welcome. After we had deposited our coats we climbed the winding staircase to the bar on the first floor. There were several other occupants in the large room but we easily found seats in a corner near one of the long windows and settled to resume our conversation. This time we were fortified with large glasses of single malt.

During our short journey neither of us had spoken. However, once we were settled James began to reconstruct his argument. I concluded privately that his silence had provided him with time to rehearse his view-point. He spoke with elegance drawing on a wide range of source material, not all of which I was familiar with. I found he could quote as comfortably from Thomas Aquinas as he could from Nietzsche; as easily from Homer as from Dante or Tolstoy. The breadth of his reading was impressive. Nevertheless as he developed his theme I felt increasingly uncomfortable.

In the beginning his proposals were so obtuse that I could not be certain where they might lead. In one breath he appeared to castigate religious practice and in the next he protested his evidence of an after-life. He talked of earthly powers; the strength of nature and of the planet as a living being but it was only when he began to talk of primitive folklore that I started to understand him. He was a Pagan, proclaiming Paganism imbued with at least some of the clutter of the modern world.

I could not resist.

'If as I suspect you are preaching Paganism, I wonder if we might agree what the modern Pagan actually stands for?'

He started to reply in his usual oblique fashion and I found myself having to interrupt.

'James, just for once can't you give a straight answer to a straight question?'

He stopped at once making neither protest nor complaint just studying me from beneath his thick eyebrows. When he did speak this time his words were slowly and carefully enunciated leaving me with the impression that they had been just as carefully chosen.

'Seeing that it's precision you require the fact is that Pagan is a village in the Myingyan district of Burma on the Irrawaddy River. The Pagan Burmese were in fact originally Buddhist but changed to a modified Hinayanism. Their kingdom existed between 1050 and 1300 and in terms of their religious beliefs they had two main sects: the Sinhalese order which was orthodox and the order of the forest dwellers which was more appealing to the general population . . . . so the answer to your question is no I am not a Pagan. I do have some sympathy for some of their beliefs but I have never been a Buddhist. If you need a convenient label for me, the closest would be a Druid.'

He paused again and looked around the room. The barman caught his eye and immediately began pouring a repeat of our previous order. James lit a cigarette and inhaled deeply.

'So Paul,' he said at last, 'does that answer your question?'

Of course it did not, it only raised others.

'If I had any idea what a Druid might be . . . I mean, I know there is a connection with Stonehenge and that it relates to Celtic practices . . . but today—what does a Druid do today?'

My question brought James's smile back.

'What does a Catholic do today? Or for that matter a Jew, let alone a Druid? I suppose it is fair to say a Druid does much the same as a non-Druid—for much of the time.'

'Okay,' I said accepting what I saw as a reproof, 'Let me rephrase that: tell me about Druids . . . there how's that?'

Suddenly his smile had gone cold.

'The short answer to that is 'no'.'

His reply was clearly the end of that discussion, that particular route for conversation was closed—as if he had taken offence. It was propitious that at that moment our drinks arrived by way of the silently gliding waiter: another pair of large glasses containing generous measures of Single Malt Whisky. It proved to be the start of many such deliveries by our waiter.

I remember thinking that part of my problem was that the beer laid heavily in my system robbing me of my usual inhibitions. By comparison the Scotch allowed my sense of decorum to evaporate I can only recall mere snatches of the rest of the evening. I know that at some stage we ordered steak sandwiches and I had a disagreement with the waiter about which mustard was most appropriate. I also have a memory of making rather loud comments concerning a prominent politician, a member of the Cabinet who just happened to be sitting at a nearby table. None of this I take pride in. I suppose it is fortunate that when we feel shame concerning our behaviour, more often than not it occurs far away from our more usual habitat and on this occasion in my case I was glad to find myself alone.

The next morning found me making apologies to my bathroom enamel in the early hours and hoping and praying that James and his fellow members could forgive the bad manners of my rudeness. It would be a long time before I would dare to show my face in that particular bar again.

Chapter Four

Despite the fact that my presence in that particular place at that precise moment was accidental, I could not help but feel that I was a voyeur. I kept telling myself that I should move or at least that I shouldn't look but I was rooted to the spot. My instincts insisted that as a well-brought-up Christian man I should respect the privacy of others and either leave immediately or make my presence known.

In the event I stayed to watch.

Afterwards, trying to be objective, I agreed with myself that it had been the sight of so much bare skin that had made the scene compulsive. It had been some time since I had shared the company of a woman and never in quite so energetic or original fashion as that before me. I suppose I could argue that it was feeling of shock that immobilised me and there was no doubt that I was shocked. However if I am honest it was the sensation of almost being a participant that fixed my attention.

The action took place only feet away from where I stood and my view through a sash window was so detailed that I swear I could see the young woman's tiny nipple-hairs. Consequently by the time my conscience was activated I was already committed.

With hindsight, I suppose my qualms of conscience that were concentrated later were also a surprise to me. The knowledge that I was just as able to be attracted and intrigued by pornography (or at least the individual variety of 'gold medal' rutting demonstrated before me) as any reader of those glossy top shelf magazines, came as something of a surprise. By comparison my own sexual adventures could only be described as modest in proportion and traditional in content. The culture of such behaviour as I had witnessed therefore, was known to me only by repute.

Normally I am a lights-out-first practitioner whose adult working knowledge of female anatomy and the act of love-making was derived from very limited, very jaundiced Catholic sources. My other research included illustrated medical journals, novels of ill-repute and Continental films. My personal endeavours in this regard had virtually terminated some time ago, nevertheless to see the act performed—in the flesh, as it were—proved to be still of significant academic interest. What it satisfied in terms of my curiosity however, was small compared to the glandular stimulation it also engendered. I could not look away.

In this context as in much else, my childhood had been conservative. At that age when my Mother deemed it appropriate I had been given copies of Grey's Anatomy, Sons and Lovers and the Karma Sutra and told to read them in that order. In most respects my Mother was a conscientious parent but thereafter, in her own eyes, having provided for my education Vis a Vis procreation the subject was never mentioned again. Left to my own devices and armed only with those references already described plus my first growth of facial hair (hair that testified to my exaggerated claims regarding my age) I made a study of 'X' rated movies. In the process I became the best informed, if the least experienced teen-ager in my final year at Grammar school.

As a youth I enjoyed the usual speculation about the opposite sex and must confess to having taken part in a certain amount of gross conjecture: much of this focused on size and proportion, inclination and frequency. None of this however prepared me for my own first encounter.

For this I am eternally indebted to one Lizzy McDougal, a Sixth Form girl who took it upon herself to provide me with a crash course. Even in my wildest dreams I never imagined that Lizzy did this because she found me irresistible but it was never established at the time if she acted out of the goodness of her heart; for a bet or for favours in cash or kind from some of my wealthier friends. My companions it seemed were more concerned with the persistence of my apparent virginity than I was myself. It mattered not at the time that for a short period, just before she left home for a career in the Catering Corps of one of Her Majesty's armed forces, I certainly appeared to become Lizzy's pet project, if not her *raison d'être*.

Her early tutorials took place in the back row of the local cinema. I recall frantic petting and sloppy kisses to the accompanying sound of crushed crisp packets and the sound of heavy artillery in whatever was the latest war movie. I hasten to add that the crisps and the blood and thunder were all Lizzy's choice. Her training course culminated with an in-depth personal interview on her Mother's best settee in the front parlour whilst her parents were away for the week-end. It seems that the prized qualification I achieved was Lizzy's testimony to my friends that, "At last the lad has some idea about what it's for.' No one was very surprised when some years later we heard on the grapevine that Lizzy had acquired NCO status. She had pedagogical skills of a high order, matched only by her style of user-friendly management. She was a born leader of men.

I shudder now to imagine what mistakes I might have made without this extra curricular guidance. In my more honest moments I shudder to imagine the mistakes I made despite the extra curricular guidance. Although I never informed her of the fact, it was my one and only girlfriend Deborah, who became the ultimate beneficiary of the lessons I'd learnt. Evidence of this was the fact that my affair with Deborah lasted ten years, most of which was spent in co-habitation in my little flat. And whilst I eked a living as a cub reporter she typed one hundred words a minute for an advertising executive. In fairness our relationship was at best a pale imitation of connubial bliss, the nature of which was derived in our innocence from images prompted by Hollywood and a value system foisted on the public by middle-class women's magazines. That ambience once generated for me by Simone Signoret and Brigit Bardot never permeated our basement flat and our love making could only be described as sanitary rather than exotic.

With hindsight it was clearly an affair doomed to failure and I suspect it only lasted as long as it did because neither of us (me especially) could achieve sufficiently attractive alternatives. Having made that claim however, I was never certain if her unexpected departure one Saturday morning after breakfast, was prompted by my continued resistance to the nuptial ceremony she was wont to plan, or through my sexual inadequacy. Eighteen months passed before I discovered that Deborah had been seduced away by her advertising executive's sports car and his West End lifestyle. In the event I couldn't blame her at all. Indeed I might have been tempted myself if I'd had the offer.

Up until the night in question therefore, when I caught sight of my near neighbour's activities, I had had little or nothing with which to compare my own coupling technique. The performance of the male partner under scrutiny changed my thinking completely. I concluded that if the level of expertise I witnessed through the rear window of 69 The Mount (as appropriate an address as I could have ever conjured from my imagination) was in any way typical, then Deborah's departure had nothing to do with promises of marriage or sport's cars. Clearly either Lizzy's reputation had been founded on misinformation, or she had faked my final test results in order to be rid of a hopeless case.

I stood there that night in the shadows of the first cold of a Yorkshire winter to spy on a virtuoso sexual performance and despite my amazement; the element of black comedy did not escape me. I found myself wondering just how I had arrived there and why I continued to watch.

I was partially hidden by the outside lavatory of a two bedroom cottage situated near the top of a steep hill isolated high on one of the less popular North Yorkshire Moors. By any measurement the word ludicrous seems insufficient to describe the situation. The cottage was one of seven that stood in a crooked terrace alongside a seldom used road. It was as if the fates had conspired to direct my footsteps; that in some strange way I had been drawn to this wilderness. It was to prove a place of curious ambiguities.

James Collins had much to answer for.

In the same way that I had retained my flat in Nottinghill as a kind of bolt-hole, James had maintained his cottage. For him as for me it was somewhere to which he could escape from the pressures of his everyday life. Unlike my own hideaway his could not be reached via the Circle Line Tube. Indeed there was not so much as a bus service stop within four miles and the quoted taxi-cab fare from Pickering would have bankrupted the Sultan of Brunei. James had told me it was situated on the edge of the known world and he had not exaggerated.

Apparently James had offered his cottage to me in a spirit of kindness at the end of a long day spent drinking together in London. I had little memory of the conversation let alone of my accepting his suggestion. Significantly by the time the offer had been made, we had fortified ourselves with another kind of spirit to such an extent that my perceptions had been badly impaired. In fairness even though my recollections remained faulted next morning, I found James's note giving me directions and telling me he was sure I would enjoy the place. He said he would leave the keys within twenty-four hours and he was as good as his word. However, it was not until I received the padded brown envelope the next day that I began to take the notion seriously. The maps excited me and the instructions regarding switching on the electricity, where I might buy provisions and who the neighbours were made it sound like an adventure. Consequently I began to think it might make a pleasant change and an opportunity to spend some real time finishing the book—a concentrated burst of creative energy was just what I needed.

The key to his front door (also enclosed) became a metaphor for a new and vigorous resolution on my part. His letter also recalled my decision to seek a distant place where I might complete my book. He also claimed to share my love of primitive locations and said his Yorkshire retreat would be ideal in this respect, more importantly he said I could use his cottage for as long as I might need it. His generosity impressed me, as generosity in others always does. But the reference to primitive places left me wondering if the alcohol had caused a change of personality. I decided that I had probably just been a little less truthful than usual, trying to be agreeable. Bearing in mind the insecurity I felt when faced with any large space not surrounded by urban development, I just could not imagine myself making such claim. Added to that I must confess I have a less than complimentary regard for country-dwellers; a fear of farm animals and an almost complete ignorance of all things rural. Nevertheless in my still unstable state due to a hangover, the prospect inspired me and I made my preparations and left before mid-day.

Although I do own a car, usually I like to travel by public transport. In London that means the choice of the Tube, a taxi or the bus. For mainland journeys of any great distance I am one of an apparently declining public who still prefer the ministrations of travel by rail. However, due to the inaccessibility of my destination, I felt obliged to use the car. I was to find that this was an error of judgement; the first in a long line of similar errors.

To begin with the road map that I kept in the glove compartment proved to be out of date. Several pages were stuck together apparently through the liberal application of sticky 'goo' that may have been decomposing sweets (I used to keep a few sweets for long journeys). The possibility of any reference being made to a whole chunk of North London was therefore obviated. I was therefore left with an A to Z that was more aptly and an A to D and a P to X. I gave up smoking about six years ago—about the same time as I stopped storing sweets in the car. The 'goo' remained a mystery.

To make matters worse I soon found that since I had last used the map and in fact since I had last driven through North London someone in their infinite wisdom had seen fit to create a quagmire of one-way systems. Beyond that a whole new collection of roads, no entry signs and detour directions conspired to confuse me. I began to feel like a tourist. It was more by good luck than good judgement that I eventually found the route north.

Like many of my generation despite my alienation from the Church I still keep my St. Christopher medal fixed to my car keys. Like some other saints I always regarded him as user-friendly; always easily approachable. His demotion to obscurity by the Church establishment was in my eyes a totally unnecessary and unworthy act. He was ever welcome to stand knee-deep in water with baby Jesus on his shoulders in my car for as long as I had one. There are few alternatives guaranteeing safe conduct in my book. I suppose I could have petitioned St. Jude the Patron of Lost Causes or St. Anthony the Patron of things lost. But I preferred to keep St. Anthony for those occasions when I couldn't remember where I left my glasses or keys or the like and St. Jude, I hold in reserve for really important petitions. He is the 'big cheese' in this context. This line of thinking alongside the examination of my conscience regarding the appropriateness or otherwise of a lapsed Catholic maintaining contact with holy icons kept me occupied until I reached the Motorway. On reflection it was a curious subject remembering that my rejection of religious belief was synonymous with the development of my friendship with Lizzy all those years ago.

The second and far more basic irritation associated with this trip was when I experienced what passed for road-side fare. This came about when I stopped for a much needed coffee at one of the so-called service stations. I had travelled only about ninety miles before sawdust collected in my throat and the demand for coffee grew to an undeniable obsession. I have and always have had a low tolerance for driving. My eyes were sore, my head ached and I felt stiff and uncomfortable. Some kind of rest stop was essential. The car park was not full so I was able to park close to the facilities. My satisfaction was short lived when I discovered that the cafe/restaurant on my side of the motorway was closed. If I wanted to have a drink or some food other than pre-packed plastic sandwiches I had to cross by the bridge. I put my annoyance on hold and persuaded myself that a short walk would probably do me good. At least the bridge was a closed environment, it was brightly lit and after the cramped car it would make a nice change.

The deserted landings and stairways were mounded with litter. It may have been my imagination but I swear I could smell the acrid stench of male urine. Determined to be charitable I blamed it on a stray dog. Although where such a creature might have come from—some several miles from the nearest human habitation, I could not guess. My imagination accelerated to supply an answer. A rogue animal I decided, stranded by its owner; left to fend for itself in this plastic oasis; a tramp canine exiled and homeless. Who could blame it? The matter was settled for me when I was halfway across the bridge. I had to detour to avoid a pile of empty beer-cans and to tip-toe past suspicious puddles that flooded one side of the passageway. The stink was overpowering. When

I eventually located the serve-yourself-Teflon-coated food hall it was crowded to capacity. The car park on that side of the motorway was full.

In marketing terms, bright lights imply that nothing is hidden from the customer and there is nothing about which to be wary. The sanitised-instant-E factor-food bubbled unashamedly under Perspex hoods trying to tempt traveller's palates. The fact that the chicken something-or-other looked remarkably similar to the simulated beef stew stopped me in my tracks and caused the queue behind me to grumble loudly. Instead I chose a sausage roll and served myself to a cup of tea or coffee and just like the notice promised—I got tea or coffee. One could not actually tell which was which. From my plastic seat at a plastic table I was able to survey the facility in its entirety. It was decorated in a non-offensive basic colour scheme, harmonising perfectly with the background Musak, the stainless steel kitchen and the pink faces of the attendants. As far as the public were concerned the hygiene was impeccable and bugs and germs were unknown. The sausage roll was a cardboard cylinder in which a coagulation of preservatives had lodged, without the watery ketchup there was no taste.

What price the modern mirage?

On account of the poor provision at these roadside food parlours, the last leg of my journey was tackled in one long continuous burst. My gastric juices felt inadequate in the face of another plastic food oasis. I did make a brief stop in Pickering but that was only to seek directions. It had been bad enough trying to navigate the London streets but once I was adrift in the countryside I lost all confidence in my map reading ability. Not surprisingly when I finally located the cottage it was already dark. I parked the car, unloaded my luggage and looked over the place. Once I had the electricity on and the place flooded with light I sought the toilet.

The bolt to the back-door had seemingly been fixed with the aid of a steam-hammer—or so it seemed and by the time I had it open I felt ready to burst. Beyond the ring of light from the open kitchen door the Yorkshire countryside was pitch black and impenetrable but I had no difficulty in finding my way. There was a waist-high privet hedge to the left and the traditional brick lavatory to the right. Access to the Water Closet was just round the corner through an old and battered door. Clearly designed more for decoration than to ensure privacy it fitted so badly it resembled those so-called bat-wing doors one sees in Westerns: the saloon entrance. The cubicle was lit by a 40 watt bulb that constantly flickered: a Morse signal perhaps alerting the district to the arrival of a stranger. I had only been seated for a minute when another light filled the gaps in the door. This was a much brighter illumination and although I could not make out its point of origin it left me feeling exposed. English mentality concerning bodily functions is curiously delicate and never more obviously so that amongst city dwellers. It seems that from early childhood the earliest notions of shame are associated with a bare arse and we become shy and embarrassed once our trousers have dropped. It is almost as though the voiding of bowels is self-indulgence peculiar to the individual alone. Not so out in the country where given an emergency, every hedgerow offers a facility for relief. However, my appreciation of this state of affairs did nothing to restore my security and when distant voices accompanied the light I almost panicked.

A woman's voice protested but without conviction and a man's voice insisted with great conviction.

The man laughed and I began to hear snatches of what was being said.

'Come on Kate . . . . the table . . . . been two days or more and . . . . '

I found myself listening. Eavesdropping is the writer's curse.

It was difficult to attribute ages to the voices but I guessed that the woman was somewhat younger than the man.

'You dirty . . . . ' the woman said.

I quickly made myself respectable and peered through a gap in the ill-fitting door. If I kept beyond the light I knew I would remain hidden in the shadow. Just over the thin hedge a few feet away next door's kitchen was brightly lit and I could see directly into the room: a ringside seat.

The couple I'd heard were struggling in what appeared to be a passionate embrace it was a love tussle in which the woman's resistance was obviously only role play. Now he searched energetically beneath her blouse top and although she pushed him away with one hand the other was meanwhile loosening the waistband of her skirt. The noises they both made were loud and enthusiastic.

I blushed. My first inclination was to rush away. The intimate nature of the activity precluded a audience and my feeling of reserve borne of maternal warnings about good taste left me in a quandary of confusion. Before I could decide, the skirt slipped away and although her legs were hidden behind the kitchen table the tight silk of her knickers held my attention. I changed my position back into deeper shadow.

The blouse was suddenly cast aside and thrown into the far corner; his clothes were pulled away in frenzy and he pushed her back onto the table-top. I had never imagined that mouths could be used with such creative endeavour, not still less with such effect. The first minutes were filled with slappings and suckings and bitings and lickings and when the bodies heaved against one another, eventually joining in moist satisfaction, I found I had been holding my breath.

It had been a devastating performance. Her cries were those of a she wolf, his were those of an unnamed wild animal. One could have been forgiven for thinking it had been rape, but that was not the case. In the end they stopped. She lay twisted with one buttock pressed hard against the cold window and her arms bent back behind her head. He draped across her, still joined between her legs: eyes staring body spent. My own breath echoed theirs in gasps. I was just about to sneak away when to my amazement they started all over again.

This time she was the aggressor. She first slipped away from him, tempting his body only her touch. She left the table and turned to examine her partner much like a surgeon in an operating theatre then for a moment or two she worked on him with her hands, insistently, gently. Suddenly she bent forward and took him in her mouth. His words were lost beneath the pounding in my head. Without warning he sat up, straight backed facing away from me. She remained bent to him: a calf at its mother. He reached over beyond my field of vision and produced a length of coarse string. He used this to tie her hands behind her back after which he began to slap her back-side. The sound of his assault, his big hands on her soft skin made a sound like a shot from a pistol or cracking glass. Soon he was swinging his arm in a big arc, apparently using more force with each successive blow. The woman stood her ground but as the rate of the blows increased, I could see her thighs begin to quiver then she stood up. Tears streamed down her face. Gently now and without a word he turned her around, bent her over the table and entered her from behind.

The shock of their encore left me weak. I could not tolerate much more and in a moment of confused desperation, I stepped out and hurried past to the kitchen door. It was only a matter of a few steps but as I stepped out into the full light from their window, I could not help but glance across once more. The man's eyes were shut tight as he worked on his quarry, the woman however faced up at me from the table and for just the briefest of moments she caught my eye.

My state was such that I could not be sure but when I got back to the security of the kitchen, I found myself left with the distinct impression that she had winked at me

Chapter Five

I slept badly. A lumpy night disturbed by dreams in a strange bed: erotic nightmares left on the fringe of memory next morning. An exhausting night spent in a half-awake state: heavy sweats and a frustrating ignorance of the story-line causing them. I was conscious of strange unfamiliar noises. They were far from the friendly fire from Ladbroke Grove. No Police sirens, no Portobello Road traffic sounds and no voices—often shouting voices of homeward bound drunks. There was just the wind, the creaking trees and the creeping debris of leaves and twigs.

When consciousness finally established itself I found myself staring at a silent ceiling landscape of cracked and textured plaster. A weak light filtered through the old cotton curtains that I had drawn hastily last night before I undressed. Bearing in mind my earlier experience who could know who might be watching from the nearby dark. Casual curiosity made Peeping-Toms of the most unlikely folk.

The thought freshened the memory of my vigil in the shadows: the shock of what I had witnessed; the compulsion of my viewing and the conviction that the girl had winked at me. No small wonder my dreams had been erotic. What kind of creature had that kind of confidence—I asked myself. For the first time I began to consider how I might act if and when faced with the young woman of last night. It would be difficult to say the least to find myself standing next to her in a queue. As is my want on occasions such as this, I took the concerns along with the visual record of what I had seen and closed them up in a specially designed 'mind' box made for the purpose.

I glanced at my watch and saw it was already ten o'clock—so much for my good intentions. The designer-self-discipline planned to bring rigour to my schedule had fallen at the first fence. There had been an intention to make an early start each day, to take some much needed exercise and to eat only wholesome fat-free foods. I had convinced myself that this would increase my rate of word production and enable me to complete the book through two weeks of intensive effort. With all that in mind I tried to focus on my last notes, unfortunately Scott's poems were from a past that pre-dated the persistent visions of sexual perversion that inhabited my mind. I could think of nothing else.

What kind of people practised such behaviour—and in the kitchen?

The girl—her hands tied, her torso pressed flat against the rough table-top; the man—his eyes tight shut banging into her buttocks and wearing a silent grin as he grabbed at her thighs.

It was only when I re-examined the memory that I realised for the first time that the man was older—considerably older than the girl. She was probably in her early twenties and he was about thirty years older. Older even than me!

I surprised myself with the depth of my revulsion.

I swung my legs out of the bed. There were two single beds in the room placed side by side and I had taken the one nearest the door. There was no bathroom on that floor so I went down to the kitchen to shave. Due to the cottage's orientation the kitchen received the fullness of the morning light. It was a treat to shave and wash in the brightness of a livid winter sun. The electric water heater provided the first artificial warmth of the day and I steeped my hands gratefully restoring circulation. On my return through the living room I lit the fire, it had been set with logs and coal before I arrived and it quickly burnt up. I unpacked my case and a clean shirt, a thick sweater and heavy cords soon made me feel better. With my new resolution I laid out my mini office on the living room table, the pens, pencils the notebooks and the thin stack of typing already written. I positioned the chair, adjusting its height with a cushion and finally set up my old portable typewriter. Now I was ready. Now I could breakfast.

The kettle was boiling when there was a knock at the front door. For a second I was unsure. My occupation was surely too new for visitors—and what if it was one of the people from next door—what if it was the girl.

The visions forced their way onto my sight screen but I opened the door anyway.

An old weather-beaten face greeted me with a broad smile.

'Mornin—Jim Brotherton. You'll be wantin some dry firewood I expect?'

Behind him stood a tractor and trailer, the latter loaded with neatly stacked logs. Clearly a local farmer from his mode of dress but the only acknowledgement of the freezing cold was his cap. Typically his face was blotched with a red speckled bloom and when we shook hands his skin was as coarse as animal hide.

'Thank-you—yes that would be a good idea'

'Y' can't be usin th 'electric fer heatin—cost you an arm an' a leg. Anyway best you 'ave a log fire—keep the place snug.'

I nodded and asked him to estimate how many logs I might need. He studied me for a moment and when he stroked his chin I noticed one of his middle fingers was missing.

'Depends 'ow long you might be stayin . . . ow big yer grate is an 'ave you got a tarpaulin?

'Sorry?'

I was finding it difficult to follow his logic still less make sense of his accent. He grinned again and shook his head—like I was intellectually challenged.

'T' covers over the logs. Y'll need a sheet to keep the snow off. If they get damp they'll never burn up. Less you're gonna stack 'em indoors?'

The technicalities of country living were unfolding slowly.

On an impulse I invited him to have a coffee and I was surprised when he accepted. I calculated that all his questions about the size of my hearth could be answered by him looking for him. When I returned from the kitchen Jim Brotherton was crouched before the fire poking at the burning logs and muttering about it being a slow starter. He accepted the mug of coffee, loading four teaspoons of sugar even before he tasted it. He sat back on his heels and turned to me.

'Pity t' throws yer money away usin the electric. S' a good hearth here—take up t' five logs at a go—an' if y' clean out the oven y' could cook yer dinner in there—save y' self a fortune.'

I nodded in agreement, bowing to his superior knowledge.

He accepted a couple of digestive biscuits without comment and sat back in the nearby armchair clasping his mug of tea as though to warm his hands.

'What I'll do is leave you a half load of logs this time. If you need more then you'll have to walk up to the farm.'

This time as he spoke he scanned the room, his eyes finally resting on the typewriter.

'So—yer a bit of a scribbler then?'

'Yes—I write books—and articles and things.'

It was then I remembered that I had not introduced myself. I reached forward offering my hand.

'Sorry—how rude of me. My name is Paul Denley.'

He looked amused but took the hand and crushed it in a steely grip.

'Never shook 'ands with a scribbler before, mind—t' be honest we don't get much call fer shaking 'ands round 'ere—less its a deal—selling a beast or the like.'

I could not be certain but I had the distinct impression he was having a laugh at my expense. Nevertheless we drank our coffees and then went outside to settle the matter of siting the logs. We found a space just round the side of the cottage. A site that was flagged and alongside it a folded tarpaulin. Clearly this was the wood store. He backed up the trailer and tipped the load in a neat pile, with his assistance I spread the canvas and secured it against the wind. He seemed to be content with the result.

'There—snug as a bug.'

'And what do I owe you for that?'

'Call it a tenner eh?'

I paid him and he spat on his hand and we shook in it. He grinned.

'Now that's when we do sheck 'ands.'

He drove off promptly, turning to wave back at me before he disappeared over the brow of the hill. I was left standing outside the cottage facing the Spartan landscape alone. It was not much more inviting than it had been the previous night.

Although I had planned to organise my day around a strict writing schedule, intending to start as I meant to go on, that first day was spent in a kind of disorientated reverie. Perhaps it was simply the strangeness of the location or maybe the knowledge that I was in a distant place, and a place with hardly anything that could be termed a population. On the other hand maybe it was the severity of the change: leaving the hub, the centre of the country's capital city where I had lots of friends and knew my way through highways and byways, in favour of a shadow-land consisting of peculiar accents; of open houseless hills; of fresh air and of memories of a wayward girl and a kitchen table. Taken as a whole it was not so surprising that I was experiencing some degree of shock.

Settling to my allotted task was difficult and after several attempts I decided instead to pay a visit to the shop—the only shop within easy reach. In his letter James had told me the shop was open only from ten in the morning until mid-day and that it was located at the end of the terrace.

I slipped on a heavy jacket and went out.

It was only a walk of about a hundred yards or so but it was uphill, a steep climb up a cobbled half street. In the distance to the west the hills rose up patched with the last purple heather and half hidden by a thin mist, as if a conjurer's silk handkerchief was disguising the peaks. As I passed by I noticed that each of the cottages had been carefully maintained. The paintwork was clean and bright and the curtains in the sash windows were crisp and fresh. The only sign of weathering was on the sandstone fascias where there was some evidence of pitting and flaking: a patina applied by the prevailing westerly winds and entirely consistent with the patchwork evident in the rest of this landscape. Nevertheless these were house built to last; built to resist the harshness of the climate and as natural to their setting as any of the stony outcrops that pushed through the coarse grass beyond. Surprisingly however, other that the trails of smoke that issued from squat chimneys there was no sign of life and, until I reached the shop I saw no other living soul.

The bell on the shop door was loud: an incongruous sound too large it seemed for the small interior. I crossed the threshold and down a step into an Aladdin's cave. It was packed. Every fraction of wall-space was shelved or hooked and every shelf was filled to capacity; every hook full of suspended items. Packets of breakfast cereal squashed against jars of sweets; bottles of lemonade, orangeade, and Dandelion and Burdock gathered dust in a corner, another section hosted a stack of shoe boxes.

Most significantly there was that smell that shops used to have in my childhood, a mixture between fresh yeast, newspapers, sliced ham and chutney mixed with tobacco and soap and leather goods. A welcoming smell redolent of infancy that immediately coloured my judgement of my new surroundings.

The counter-top ran the full length of the room but other than for a yard or so in the middle of it, the whole surface was stacked with every conceivable item of every possible purchase one might imagine. Cards of buttons, hooks and eyes, lighter flints, needles and pins hung precariously on a wire display stand. A glass topped case boasted a selection of screw-drivers, chisels, mallets, and hammers; rows of toiletry articles were stacked in a pyramid whilst pans of every dimension hung from the ceiling cosseted by a variety of kitchen utensils tied in bunches. I stood savouring the moment until a face emerged from behind the talcum powder tower. It was a very small face surmounting a very large body. A mountain of a woman appeared, more in scale with the outside landscape than with the domestic intimacy of the shop interior. The orange flowers on her dress made a discordant contrast to her environment and for a second I could not believe that she would ever be able to fit between the chest freezer and the counter top.

'Yes young man an' what might you be wantin?'

As she spoke she slipped into the space in question. A feat of magic as if her bulk reformed itself amoeba like, changing the spread of its proportions to accommodate the limitation of the vacancy.

'Good morning. I wonder do you have any milk.'

In the momentary pause before she replied, and despite myself, I found my eyes searching her immensity. There is inevitably a compulsion to stare at unusual physical characteristics and the more unusual the greater the compulsion. It is a habit that civilized society frowns on—a rudeness regarded as unnecessary and often embarrassing for all concerned. As it was in this case I was caught off guard and allowed my control to slip.

Her face blossomed into a huge grin and her colour heightened slightly.

'Bless you—these 'ave dried up years ago.'

As she spoke she made an almost imperceptible adjustment to her bust a kind of shuffle with her wrists as though to relieve the weight of the mighty overhang. This time it was me who blushed—furiously and deeply.

'However, there's some cartons in t' fridge . . . . and they're almost as good as the real thing.'

Then she laughed and her enjoyment made me laugh along with her. She stretched behind her and produced a pint carton of full cream milk. At the contortion the thickness of her reaching arm quivered but she was still smiling when she placed the carton in front of me on the counter.

'You 'ave enough fat—'ave you?'

I stared in silence. It was as if she had read my mind.

She shook her head appreciatively and explained.

'For frying of course—I know you young fellers—soon as yer on yer own everything gets fried.'

'Actually I'd prefer olive oil—if you have any.'

'Aye we 'ave that too—fer me I prefer a dollop of beef dripping—a better flavour some say, but if you prefer oil then oil it is.'

She stretched again this time with the other equally large arm and a large can of olive oil appeared next to the milk. I decided that it must cause considerable effort each time she negotiated in the tiny space. Consequently I purchased a number of smaller items especially those close at hand, as much to make her struggles worthwhile as to satisfy my limited needs. Significantly each of my requests was satisfied without effort and despite my sympathy for her situation; she found what I wanted within easy reach. Clearly the radius of her stretching arm had been calculated to allow her access to most essential items. On each occasion she moved instinctively almost without looking. Despite my sympathy for her difficulties, I found myself wondering if I could think of something beyond her reach.

'R you gonna be 'ere fer long then?'

Her question was asked as she licked the dull end of a pencil stub prior to totting up my bill on the corner of some wrapping paper.

'I can't be sure really, Mr. Collins loaned me his cottage—number 69—so that I could finish a book I've been writing. It might take a few days—on the other hand it could take me weeks.'

At the mention of James's name she smiled.

'James is a nice man—generous to a fault, 'and well respected round 'ere. D'you works with him?'

Her questions were put casually but there was no mistaking the probe of her enquiries. I guessed that she represented the public face of this remote constituency and that the need to know about strangers was entirely consistent with the natural curiosity found in any small community.

'Not really—he was a colleague of my mother's and I met him quite by accident at her funeral a few days ago.'

I did not appreciate the effect my declaration might have. With hindsight I should have known that those inhabiting small villages have a distinctive reaction to talk of death. And whilst they may treat it in the abstract—as another fact of life sometimes even to the point of irreverence, in the particular especially when referring to those known to them, it becomes a serious business necessitating condolences and a show of sympathy.

'My poor lamb,' she whispered, her voice adopting a funereal tone, 'so yer lost yer mother. Well now know this—if there's anything you might need—anything at all you come knocking on Bessie's door. 'An even if we're closed I'll open fer you—'and if you need to talk about it, come and see my Gerald. He lost his mother last year . . . '

Long before I could decide how I should respond to her offer she turned and shouted at the back of the shop.

'Gerald—Gerry my love.'

A sound issued from the bowels of the house in answer, an indistinct sound. She replied immediately.

'Gerry come 'ere my love—come 'ere can you?'

Footsteps sounded on creaking floorboards and a moment later a head poked around the distant retail pyramid.

'Y-y-you wanted m-me Bessie.'

The face asked, fixing me with a baleful stare at the same time.

'Gerry I want you t 'meet a friend of James's. A nice young man, he's down 'ere to write a book.' She turned back to me, 'This is my husband Gerald.'

The man stepped into view and without a change of expression reached out a hand for me to shake. He looked to be only about five feet tall and wore a plaid shirt with the sleeves rolled up to expose thin scrawny forearms. As he reached forward I could not help but notice his spine was twisted into a hunchback.

'Paul—Paul Denley—pleased to meet you Gerald.'

We shook hands in Bessie's shadow. Gerald said nothing more but his wife broke the silence.

'Paul's just lost his mother Gerry—buried her a few days ago.'

Now they both stared at me, sad-eyed and mournful. I blushed at their attention, struggling to try and remember anything that might inform me of the behaviour expected of me. The culture gap was more like bottomless pit at this point.

There are times when understandings cannot be taken for granted when despite the commonality of shared language communication is inhibited by differing traditions. My grief was a private affair. A belief cultured in the hot-house of city society; the response of the sophisticate. I had experienced a detached bereavement, a controlled feeling of regret—one step removed from remorse—anything else was in bad taste.

Suddenly Bessie placed her hand over mine as it rested on the counter top. I could swear she was close to tears.

'Never mind my lamb. Yer among friends 'ere and if you needs t' talk you cum an' ave a word with Gerry—eh Gerry?'

She turned back to her diminutive companion who nodded his agreement enthusiastically.

'J-jus 'cum round a-a-anytime.'

As he replied Gerald's head twitched to one side and his hand fluttered—a disjointed animation and a reflection of his stutter I thought. I found myself thanking them both for their kindness and the words proved a balm for my feelings of awkwardness and embarrassment. Such naked sympathy caused me serious problems and I was much relieved when at last I could retrieve my hand, pay my bill and leave.

Bessie made one last comment, delivered as she put my change into my hand. She looked into my eyes and promised that she would ask the whole village to pray for my mother's soul. A promise that in retrospect I found rather more disconcerting than anything else that had taken place.

I was glad to get back to the cottage. I made myself busy carefully storing the provisions and tidying an already tidy kitchen so that I did not have to dwell on Bessie and Gerald. I made myself a cup of strong coffee and a sandwich and sat down before my typewriter determined to make a start. Unfortunately the encounter in the shop permeated my thinking, arresting any possibility of concentrating on Walter Scott.

The fact of the couple's appearance made the incident all the more unusual. The contrast of their distinctive individual characteristics only exaggerated the abnormality of their presence and their relationship. That they were of a different context was patently obvious but allied to the intensity of their concern it proved so unorthodox as to make a burlesque of the situation. I sat over my coffee staring out of the living room window for most of the following hour. The view was uninterrupted and the quiet of the distant hill hypnotic. The winter light made the limited colours all the more magnetic. Patches of green and umber were mottled with purple flecks punctuating the pinkish grey of the far slopes; the sky was sheer, a continuous shield of pale blue providing a cold backdrop to the far horizon. There the eye-line was burnished with a golden glow casting ever longer shadows in the late afternoon. I rambled in my imagination and a curious feeling of acceptance predominated complimenting the silence. Suddenly there was a loud knocking at the front door. A savage disturbance to my reverie.

On the doorstep to my further embarrassment I found the young woman of yesterday evening. She stood there dressed in sweatshirt and jeans, her hair tied back in a pony-tail and sporting a friendly smile.

'Hi,' she said, 'I'm Katherine—Kate—from next door.'

She stuck out a small hand and her eyes twinkled as I took it in mine.

'Hello—Paul, Paul Denley—it's nice to meet you.'

Her smile turned quickly into a grin.

'Sorry if we shocked you last night. We didn't expect an audience. Duggie's an animal when the mood is on him and the kitchen is as good a place as anywhere else—he says.'

I released her hand reluctantly, not quite knowing what to say next. Thankfully I wasn't given an opportunity to design a response.

'We wondered if you might care to join us for a meal tonight—an olive branch if you like. Just to prove we aren't quite as ridiculous as we must have seemed.'

'I'd be delighted. I was just trying to decide if I should open the sardines or settle for beans on toast. So—yes thank you, I'd love to join you . . . . and . . . . not that it matters but I didn't think you looked at all ridiculous.'

She laughed out loud, high pitched laugh wrinkling her nose and making her eyes sparkle. She was very attractive.

'Great, the fatted calf is on a final warning—about eight.'

I agreed and with a last grin in my direction she turned and opened the door next to mine.

I spent the rest of the afternoon reading extracts from Scott's letters and later from The Lady of the Lake. It seemed appropriate and at that juncture any thought of writing was completely out of the question.

Chapter Six

Scott finally completed his poem The Lady of the Lake in 1810. It was a work of significant import that was to inspire a generation of artists from a variety of disciplines and for some considerable time. It appears that much of his scenic imagery was derived from Loch Katerine in the Western Isles of Perthshire, by all accounts a location of great charm and mystic beauty. I discovered that the derivation of the name Katerine in the Celtic pronunciation becomes Ketturin and in his notes for The Fair Maid of Perth, Scott signified his belief that the lake was named after the Catterine or wild robbers who haunted its shores.

This caused me to wonder if the name Katherine had originated from a similar genus. Given the synchronicity that my new friend from next door shared this name, the coincidence did not escape me. The wild Kate of my recent acquaintance could certainly have been related to bandits or robber bands. Clearly she was self-willed and determined, confident of her sexuality and no doubt on closer inspection would prove to be a shrew of equal dimensions to that lady of the same name who married Petrucchio. The notion implied in my use of the phrase, 'closer inspection' entertained me. After my vision of the previous evening the only closer evaluation one might achieve would be by actual physical contact—a stimulating idea. The expression, 'dirty old man' immediately sprang to mind: one of my mother's favourites. She had never been able or willing to accept that older men might feel a serious attraction to younger women or that it could be anything but a demonstration of the basest form of lust. In her view any relationship that concentrated on carnal activity to the exclusion of true love was illicit.

I read the extract all over again:

> *'On his bold visage middle age*
> *Had slightly press'd its signet sage,*
> *Yet had not quenched the open truth*
> *And fiery vehemence of youth;*

The knight of the poem, James Fitz-James was middle-aged as was Kate's kitchen lover and as I was myself.

Another coincidence?

There was however, an irreconcilable contrast between the romantic chivalry of the knight and the recurrent memory that stirred of the man at work over the kitchen table. I held both in freeze-frame, examining the detail carefully. Set somehow between them I found myself adopting the role of mediator, negotiating the value of each of the participants. My inclination for things intellectual made me feel admiration for the former; however, my rediscovered instinct for the fleshly pleasures suddenly made me jealous of the latter.

Kate winked and won me over again.

My preference finally admitted, I dwelt on the possibilities. Clearly despite her apparently wanton behaviour, Kate's attitude was infused with charm—even innocence. She was certainly not the Lady Ellen Douglas of Scott's poem—not literally but perhaps a new version in a modern idiom. I shuddered at my sacrilege.

One of the legends that reputedly informed Scott's endeavours claimed that King James the Fifth of Scotland would on occasion disguise himself and travel about the country to test the justice of his administration. I preferred to believe that if the Scottish monarch had travelled incognito his motive would have been more likely to reflect his inclination to pursue women. His practice had afforded him numerous opportunities for romantic adventure and his affair with Lady Ellen certainly fell into that category. My own visit to this remote spot did not reasonably equate to the travels of a king, nevertheless, in the new spirit of adventure that I had begun to feel, I left myself open to persuasion that I might have opportunities previously unimagined.

*

It was dark by six o'clock and I changed my shirt in the bedroom in the dim of a 60 watt bulb. It was becoming increasingly obvious that the comfort James enjoyed regarding his financial status was absent here in the economy he practised. There wasn't a bulb in the cottage bigger than the one in the bedroom. The fridge was empty when I arrived and I had had to buy logs for the fire. Given his generosity when we drank at the Garrick Club I was forced to conclude his was an odd mix.

I could not decide if I should wear a tie or to have an open neck. It was hardly a formal affair but I did not want to leave a wrong impression. The messages implicit in local customs here had already left me confused. The farmer's comment about not shaking hands had been contrasted by everyone else from shopkeepers to Kate. I did not want to get off on the wrong foot—or at least any more wrong a foot than I had already. In the end I rejected the tie. Instead I wore a jacket and put the tie in my pocket. A compromise designed to satisfy the broadest spectrum of possibility and a conclusion I knew full well illustrated my insecurity.

In the kitchen I inspected my alcohol reserves—as yet untouched. I enjoyed a drink, especially a good wine or a malt whisky but I kept it under control. I had brought with me two bottles of malt, a very dry sherry and six bottles of decent wine. I selected a nice bottle of Bordeaux and told myself that it should set the tone. The face in my shaving mirror was non committal.

I stepped from my own front door sideways and knocked on the door adjacent. It opened immediately almost as someone had been waiting for me to call. Kate smiled and waved me across the threshold.

'Very punctual indeed, I'm impressed. Please come in Paul.'

The room was a mirror image of the lounge in next door. The only difference was the hatch that had been cut into the far wall, presumably to access food from the kitchen. As I stepped in she shouted over her shoulder.

'Douglas—Douglas he's here.'

She accepted the bottle and thanked me for my thoughtfulness.

'Perfect—Douglas has prepared a Stroganoff and the Bordeaux will compliment it nicely. Please have a seat.'

She led me across the little room to a fireside made welcome by more of Jim Brotherton's logs. I took the seat offered on the small settee which was angled to half-face the matching armchair. It was not until I had settled myself that the thought struck me that this was probably their place. Couples and two seater settees go together. However, I wasn't given time to ruminate, Kate sat down opposite.

'Duggie will be through in a moment—he's fastidious when it comes to cooking. He used to work in a big hotel down south—now he cooks for the pair of us thank God. I hate working in the kitchen.'

At the mention of the kitchen my imagination flared once more and whilst I did not yet know my hostess well enough to employ sarcasm at Douglas's 'fastidiousness' in the kitchen, I allowed the images to entertain me secretly for a few seconds.

'Now—what can I get you to drink? Are you a whisky drinker perhaps?'

'I suspect that my friend James may have briefed you on that score. Yes a whisky would be fine, thank you'

She laughed but denied any prompting by James. She went over to a chest where a drinks tray had been prepared and uncorked a bottle. With her back to me I had an opportunity to examine the room more openly. It was decorated in a traditional country style: flowered wallpaper reflected in the Chintz covers; horse brasses alongside the fireplace and a mixture of old if not antique furniture. It was a comfortable room with only a stereo-player paying respect to any trace of modern facilities. Significantly there was no sign of a television set.

'Do you take water with this?'

'If I knew you better I would now begin a short but instructive half hour lecture on the lengthy process of whisky making; the importance of the water source; the aging preferably in old sherry casks and even the intricacies of the blending. The intention would be to illustrate the fact that despite evidence to the contrary in Scotland, I believe a true whisky drinker never dilutes the golden liquid. Now you may not believe this but I've even been known to get pompous about it . . . . '

By now she was laughing.

'Never, I wouldn't have believed it,' she said sarcastically, 'not pompous really!'

A moment later just as she was handing me the drink Duggie came through the door from the kitchen. He caught the tail-end of our conversation.

'Ah—a real whisky drinker—that makes you doubly welcome. Hello I'm Duggie—as you've probably gathered the chief cook and bottle-washer, skivvy without portfolio for her ladyship here.'

We shook hands and he sat beside me on the settee. On closer inspection he was a well-kept man of about forty-six with a flat stomach and muscular arms. His grip was firm and he seemed genuinely pleased to have me as his guest.

'If Madame will allow, I'll join our next door neighbour and have a shot of whiskey.'

Kate continued to play steward and delivered another glass which Duggie promptly raised in my direction.

'Cheers and welcome.'

The darkish smoky liquid was delicious.

'That's a grand brew.'

'It's from Islay—fifteen year old and just the thing for a cold autumn evening.'

Kate wrinkled her nose.

'I hope you two aren't going to be whiskey bores all evening. I imagined that with a real writer next door we might be able to raise the cultural tone of our little community.'

Duggie shook his head in mock despair.

'I'm afraid Kate is a terrible snob. When she heard that you actually wrote books that were published she went faint. Poor thing, living here with me she has to rely on my limited sense of appreciation of the finer things in life. My educational achievements were very modest and my tastes—she tells me—are pedestrian. I like thrillers and hot sexy stories.'

Kate was quick to respond.

'So you see it's Duggie who is the snob.'

At which we all laughed.

It is always difficult to tell with new acquaintances how much of their performance might be an affectation for their new audience, or if what one witnesses is an accurate reflection of their normal behaviour.

They appeared to understand one another well and I was—so far—very impressed with the obvious closeness of their relationship. I concluded that if he regularly did the cooking the balance of their mutual respect was genuine.

A little while later we sat at the kitchen table and Duggie served his Stroganoff. It was exceptional. The rice was cooked to perfection with just a hint of cloves and the meat a pure delight. My wine was supplemented by two more bottles of comparable quality and by the time the treacle-tart appeared hot from the oven, all our tongues had been suitably loosened. The subjects of our various conversations ranged across a double spectrum. The first—consisting of all that information sought by people meeting for the first time was about jobs, background, and interests; the other—more interestingly was about beliefs and philosophies. We discussed politics and religion; we talked about society's shortcomings, about education and the Welfare State and we even agreed about most of it.

Throughout the meal, despite my being on my best behaviour, I could not help but be conscious that we were sitting at and eating from the very same wooden surface that less than twenty-four hours before had facilitated a quite different function. Now however, the bed of their endeavours was clothed in a crisp white tablecloth and the hot human flesh of the previous evening was replaced by steaming beef. Neither of my hosts seemed to be embarrassed or affected in any way by the juxtaposition of these two events. I would have been mortified if a stranger had witnessed my act of intimacy but there was no evidence that my feelings of ambiguity were shared by either Kate or Duggie. The meal that night was from a quite different menu, pandering to a quite different appetite but I found myself wondering which I might have preferred—given the option.

When we finished we retired to sit around the fire in the sitting room and Duggie served us brandy with strong black coffee. Once settled he stretched out in the armchair and asked,

'So tell us a bit about the writing. I'm intrigued by the notion that anyone can make a living and keep themselves entertained just by telling stories.'

'There is a bit more to it than that,' I replied, rising to what was clearly a deliberate provocation. 'I spend a lot of time doing research and anyway most of my stuff is factual. Rather like biography.'

'And this latest one is about Sir Walter Scott?' Kate asked.

'Yes—in particular I'm having a look at some of the border legends on which he based much of his verse. Stories of ladies and knights; of love and cruelty of intrigue and murder; stories I like to think that have some physique—some guts and blood.'

Duggie affected a deep horror-movie type laugh that ended in the traditional curdled gurgle. 'And magic,' he said, 'there has to be some magic and tales of griffins, goblins and fairies.'

I laughed but Kate added that she would settle for something a bit less frightening.

'I enjoy that grisly bit between hard boned fact and the flexible muscle of fantasy, the kind that leaves one wondering if the verse was more of an incantation—a spell to ward off evil perhaps.'

I shook my head.

'Sorry to disappoint you but Scott's work is mainly narrative. It was the quality of the story-telling that made it so popular: lots of esoteric and flowery descriptions but nothing that could be remotely seen as an incantation.'

Duggie grinned then added, 'It's a fact you know that many of the most serious, most famous spells are simply descriptions of the intention. Have you read anything about the period around the Hell-Fire club?'

Satanists had never interested me and I said so. Duggie was surprised.

'I'd have thought there would be a wealth of reference about primitive belief systems. And even if Crowley and his mates were self-indulgent layabouts—his written work was extensive. Anyway the notion that narrative became intrinsic to magic practice is as old a belief as you'd find.'

I made no response and this encouraged him to pursue his point.

'Take for example the North American native Indian—they used Wampum as currency—little pure white shells made into beads. Even some of the early settlers used the stuff and for some it became their most valuable possession. They would weave it into belts and these were often used as ceremonial gifts. However, the Wampum was known to have magical and medicinal properties and its value was on that account. From the 18th century these belts contained mnemonic or pictograph devices, symbolic of the occasion—in effect a narrative.'

It was an interesting argument and the idea began to fascinate me.

'So perhaps I've been writing magic spells all these years—and here was I thinking they were just stories.'

The looks on both their faces left me to understand that they did not share my sense of humour. It was apparent that they took this subject very seriously. For the first time that evening I began to feel some small sense of reservation.

Kate was the first to take me to task and the next hour or so was devoted to an instruction in what they called the natural arts. To begin with they talked of healing and the use of herbs and wild-flowers and then about primeval beliefs associated with the earth, eventually they raised the subject of the Green Man. Much of what they said rang bells in my memory; half remembered folk tales, the kind I associated with Grimm's Fairy Tales. Eventually I categorised their message under the general heading of conservationist theory and despite the sympathy I felt for the underlying principle, their particular emphasis was hardly one I could take too seriously.

I was however, conscious of my role as their guest and therefore struggled to keep my sarcasm under control and limit my criticisms. When they began to describe how they thought their beliefs might be interpreted in the modern world, I detected a subtle change in the level of their enthusiasm. They both grew more enervated—excited even. Duggie emptied his glass three times to my once and Kate paced him. At some point I found myself referring to the emergence of Christianity.

'In a secular sense at least, psychologically Christianity satisfied many of the needs of the common people: to believe in heavenly reward; to propagate forgiveness and love and to accept one supreme God rather than many had to mean progress.'

Duggie laughed derisively.

'Christianity was a political solution,' he argued, 'not surprising really that the Jews—as a conquered people—would seek to claim rewards in an afterlife. It made the horror of their day to day existence more acceptable—and same goes for loving one's enemies If the Romans had loved them all then their problems would have been over. The Christian ethic was really just an aberration. Jesus was a compromise between the incipient selfishness that is the capitalism of the Roman Gods and the emergence of Jewish socialism. Despite the fact that he was described as a revolutionary Jesus could well have been the Palestinian equivalent of the leader of the local Liberal Party, only good for attracting middle-of-the-road voters. Christianity appeared by default. It was and is a make-do-and—mend belief; the sort of process we might expect a politician to invent. All their festivals were pinched from previous religions under different names and they even used most of the same symbols.'

'And the belief in one God?' I asked.

'Their monotheism was another compromise—Zeus had long since been accepted as the king of the gods—the father—God the Father. The so-called Holy Family could be found in ancient Egypt and the retinue of saints were the bevy of minor gods—war, love etcetera. Heaven was still to be located in the skies and Hell or Hades still beneath the earth—most significantly access to the ultimate reward was still through conformity.'

The drink thickened his voice but there was no doubting the fire of his sincerity. He emptied his glass once more before continuing.

'What was really needed was a return to more basic beliefs, those proven to be effective in life on earth . . . . ones that predated the Romans and the Greeks. Unfortunately by then society was obsessed with a singular view of progress and to go back was unthinkable.

He sipped his new drink and Kate took up where he had left off.

'Society is prejudiced against any belief in old religion. That's all part of the brainwashing despite the fact that in terms of living life to the full the old beliefs make more sense. In Britain we have experienced a culture shock since having to comprehend the new religions of ethnic minority groups. Multicultural tolerance is alien to the approved national pattern of thinking—a sad state of affairs.'

I watched her as she spoke unable to account for her agitation. During the course of our conversation she had moved about the room on the periphery, as though disengaged—unable to settle. Occasionally she stopped to offer her contribution and only then did she move into our physical sphere. Clearly she listened to what was said but spent her time piling logs on the fire; straightening a picture on the wall and looking out of the window. Having shifted seats several times during this uncomfortable performance, she finally joined me on the small settee. Her face was flushed, a fact I had originally associated with the drink or her proximity to the fire. Her excitement I attributed to the depth of her feelings concerning the discussion. However on closer scrutiny and if her body language was anything to go by, she appeared to have been struggling against becoming involved in the conversation at all.

'So what's wrong with pleasure seeking?' Duggie asked suddenly.

I had not been aware that this had been anyone's preference or even that it had been in contention. I was not given time to record a response as he continued almost without a pause.

'Nothing—nothing at all I say. We all have our own problems to suffer, so why not look for some extra enjoyment—it makes up for other things . . . . not so Kate?'

By now he was staring at Kate with serious concentration as if they shared something more than the obvious. She stared back arrogantly, unaffected by his comments.'

Conscious of a possible rift in their private relationship I attempted to quiet the turbulence by playing the innocent.

'I've nothing against pleasure, but you two seem to have found an ideal situation here. A haven far from any madding crowd and one you can both share.'

Duggie turned to me by now he had more difficulty in focusing.

'But pleasures have to be paid for. I would have thought a writer would appreciate that.'

I could not resist and bit back immediately without thinking about possible consequences.

'That's a peculiarly Catholic idea for someone claiming to scorn the Christian ideal. I thought Alistair Crowley taught . . . what was it? 'Let whatever thou wilt be the rule' or some such.'

Duggie got to his feet. He swayed and had to lean against the chimney breast to balance as he looked down on me. The glass in his other hand dribbled scotch onto the rug and for a second I thought he intended to throw the drink over me but he just stared. He stared for several seconds until Kate broke the silence.

'Douglas!'

Her voice was crisp and it changed the mood in a flash. He looked over to her and finally grinned.

'Sorry—sorry old thing. Sorry Paul—must be something I drank.' He laughed. 'Think I'd better retire—had too much of the amber liquid—sorry folks—really sorry.'

At the door to the stairs he stopped and started to say something else but changed his mind and all we got was an unfinished jumble. He laughed again and closed to door behind him. We heard him stumble in the bedroom and then he flopped heavily on the bed—then silence.

Kate grinned ruefully and shook her head.

'I'm afraid we so seldom have guests for dinner that Duggie . . . . as you saw—sometimes he forgets to curb his drinking and gets carried away—he doesn't mean any insult to you.'

She made her statement not as an apology, more a simple observation of fact.

'If I wasn't trying to be on my best behaviour tonight I might be in the same state myself.'

Now it was her turn to smile and conventions were apparently satisfied.

I finished my drink and stood up signalling it was time for me to go home but she wouldn't hear of it.

'There's no need to go as yet. Have another drink and tell me some more about your writing. We got sidetracked by all that talk about primitive religions and the like—and I am really interested.'

A little reluctantly I accepted another glass of the Islay scotch but instead of talking about my book, I instigated a conversation about Kate and Duggie's relationship. In answer to my question about how long they had known one another, she said she had known him for most of her life. Naturally I took this to be a poetic estimate rather than the literal truth.

'We've lived here at the cottage for the last four years, ever since he took early retirement.' She told me, 'Duggie was one of the first wave of computer analysts—he made lots of money but lost interest. We were left this place from a parental bequest and it seemed like the answer to all our requirements. We found the little community here to be quite exceptional.'

'And did you used to work?'

'I trained as a Primary School teacher but never actually practised.'

Now my curiosity was aroused. I found it difficult to understand how one so young—one with professional qualifications could find any kind of fulfilment in such a remote and primitive location. She had described the community in glowing terms but those that I had met with were hardly the sort to provide any kind of intellectual stimulation for a teacher and a computer expert.

A silence developed and when I looked up again she was grinning at me.

'Go on,' she said, 'I know what you're wondering about.'

'Well,' I said, half embarrassed, 'what do you find to keep you occupied out here? I mean what do you do all day?'

'We like to walk, we share an interest in bird watching, we grow a lot of our own food and we engage in whatever communal activities that might be current. We both have hobbies—you saw us practising one last night!'

I choked on my drink and she laughed.

'You see—you are from London and would probably claim to be worldly wise, knowledgeable about life but when I refer to what you saw last night, it's you who are embarrassed. So which of us is the prude?'

'I have to admit,' I answered when the whisky had cleared my throat, 'you are surprisingly direct. On the other hand, I can't ever recall anyone calling it a hobby before.'

'So what would you call it then?'

'It's—I suppose I still think of it as love making. Is that naive?'

'And I suppose you never do it just—just for fun; casually, occasionally—on the spur of the moment or with a stranger or someone you hardly know?'

I shrugged at the suggestion, not wanting to admit to anything in case it made me look weak. She studied me with what could only be described as a maternal smile. After a moment she leaned over and put her hand on mine.

'For example—how would you like to have sex with me?'

Chapter Seven

The rain came on with the intensity of a tropical storm and like its counterpart it proved an assault on the ears. It was what I called aural GHB. Unlike the tropics however, the Yorkshire downpour had a durability as tenacious as the character of the people; as immutable as the rock of their mountains. The storm's ethos felt as though it challenged the perspective of my inner landscape and became an assault on my soul. No small wonder that some primitive societies worshipped the sun.

It goes without saying that wet weather depressed me—the wetter the weather, the greater the depression.

To satisfy a job interview—incidentally one in which I did not succeed—my travels had once taken me to the West Indies, to the island of Trinidad. The annual monsoon on those islands lasted several months and although it was characterised rather more by the daily rise in humidity than by the storms, the strength of the rain was impressive. Its ferocity was frightening. In just a few minutes storm drains would flood, traffic would stop and the streets would clear of people. The temperature would rise and the air would become electrifying leaving a feeling of isolation of being surrounded and enclosed. Islanders believed—naively perhaps—that one must never allow the top of one's head to get wet. They claimed this would cause all manner of death threatening colds and flu. Consequently at the first sign of a downpour the local population would flee to the nearest shelter and would remain there until it stopped. Fortunately those rains never lasted too long, seldom more than an hour—not so the Yorkshire tempest.

By first light the driving thundersqall had given way to a silent, fog-drip-mist. It settled and clutched the hill-top community with a cold dread hand. The air itself seemed to thicken and visibility was clouded. Without the promise of a respite it produced an atmospherically induced austerity of spirit the like of which I had never experienced before. From the bedroom window I could hardly see the garden fence.

I felt I should know something about mists, they had long since figured in stories and legends around the border counties. Indeed the mythology would have one believe them to be variously, the result of magical conjuring; the unhappy souls of warrior kings or—in Welsh folklore—the breath of the dragon. The incidence of silent barges disappearing into clouds of grey damp fog are countless; the appearance of stone-faced armies surprising their foe from a curtain of dense mist are equally numerous and the last glimpse of a lover's horse or the flash of her blond hair are too frequent to itemise. Such fine sentiments however, played no part in the disturbance that occurred that Monday morning.

I had intended to sleep late but the clatter of the rain and vibration caused by the thunder woke me at five am. The street had become a cobbled stream, an echo of the speeding sky. Spikes of rain swept horizontally across blackened roofs making me glad to be safe and dry indoors. Eventually I went back to bed and drifted off to sleep despite the environment. I was awoken again at eight, this time not by the noise but by the silence—an almost complete absence of sound.

The second waking was at first confusing and it was only after listening carefully for more than a minute that I realised the cause. The storm attack had passed but in its place there were no bird-songs; no sign of life and no sign of nature. I peeked past the bedroom curtains and found that in pursuit of the storm a dark cloud had squatted over the land filtering the morning. The added moisture content made breathing difficult and allied to the quiet stillness; it made me feel as though I had been plunged into the depths of a deep lake.

I went down to the kitchen and hurriedly lit the fire. The kettle boiled quickly and after tuning the radio into the morning programme I cooked myself a fried breakfast. I was glad of the sounds I made and for a moment I was tempted to walk to the shop to buy a newspaper. One look at the sullen outside from my front door convinced me it was a day to spend by the fire doing what I do best. A day to be spent writing. For the first time since I had arrived the prospect of work held its usual appeal. I pulled the curtains, mounded logs on the fire and settled to my notes.

My copy of 'The Lay of the Last Minstrel' had been published by Adam and Charles Black of Edinburgh in 1875 but the Editor's note described how Scott had completed the poem in 1830 and had made corrections to the text in the autumn of 1831. Unfortunately the original manuscript had been lost I was therefore denied the advantage of comparing the author's various readings. As in the case of other works such as 'The Lady of the Lake'; 'The Lord of the Isles' and 'Marmion' reference to the original manuscripts had proved invaluable. Nevertheless an introduction written by Scott served to fill some of the gaps and to set the contemporary scene to good effect. Further to this same end his 'Essay on Limitations of the Ancient Ballad' proved most instructive. Over the years I had found that it was always necessary before setting out to write, for me to absorb the historical context by reading whatever was available. It was inevitably a task that demanded serious concentration. In assuming the mantle of a previous age an attitude of mind consistently focused on the reference material was essential. I was half way through this last document when I found my mind drifting, my self-control slipping. I began to recall Kate and the events of the previous evening.

The human psyche or sub-conscious mind is a peculiar mechanism. If in a healthy state it shields and protects the host consciousness at every turn. Often seminal experience in childhood however influential is consigned to the deepest memory pit. Equally those actions that might cause alarm to the conscience are sometimes similarly disguised waiting to be rediscovered by some later capricious circumstance.

It was just as if the events of the previous evening had happened to someone else. Inevitably however, once the curtain lifted the mind-pictures surged back completely displacing my concentration on the work in hand. Suddenly I could think of nothing else. I had no idea what triggered the memory at the time but later on reflection I imagine it was probably the peculiar atmospheric conditions.

I had been surprised if not shocked by Kate's blatant offer. At the same time I could not be certain if she was simply trying to shock me or whether it was a part of some complex game she had devised to play at my expense. There was no doubt that she was amused at my embarrassment more so still at my confusion. However, she appeared to understand my hesitation an instinct clearly founded on experience.

'Is it such a hard decision to take?' she asked me coquettishly.

I could remember the feel of her hand warm and dry on mine and the smell of her perfume. I told myself later that my qualms had been as much to do with Duggie's proximity as they were to do with cuckolding him. On the one hand he had welcomed me into his home and treated me with respect; on the other, he was in bed just above our heads. I did not fancy the scene should he discover his wife's infidelity—in the act—as it were. Kate had no such reservations.

Eventually we did it on the rug in front of the fire. And whilst I would like to remember the occasion as being a romantic interlude: the dim lighting, the flickering reflections of the fire and the danger and excitement, in truth it was not. It was more like a scene from a pornographic movie than from a chapter of Byron's verse. Kate behaved like an animal both in the nature of her appetite and in the manner she chose for its satisfaction. I was devoured and was expected to devour; the brutalising was as much in the giving as it was in the taking and the permutations of her imagination were as diverse as the various ways she sought to be penetrated. To begin with I found her aggression quite foreign to my taste and it was only when she switched roles to become the passive recipient that I began to appreciate the game plan. I was very much the pupil under her instruction but being a quick learner I soon adopted a more demanding role myself.

I have a memory of hastily discarding clothing; of the contrast between sharp nails and eager soft skin; of gasps and cries (hers and mine); of the pounding pressure of blood and of tortuous effort and the loss of control. Finally there was the feeling of consummate satisfaction—being spent—completely spent.

In the early hours of the morning we had sat beside the dying fire and shared a cup of cocoa in almost complete silence.

My reflections again generated all the alarm I had felt the previous night. The prospect of a scene, perhaps even a violent scene with Duggie made me break out in a sweat. Not having the temperament for it, I was ill-cast in the role of Don Juan and I found myself questioning Kate's motives as well as my own weaknesses. There was no doubt in my mind that she had been the instigator—but who would believe that. More to the point—would I ever be so crass as to claim it that line of reasoning was a cul-de-sac. Trying to measure the likelihood of Duggie discovering what had happened was another problem—I was certainly not going to tell him but would Kate?

I was aware that my experience with women had been very limited. I knew many as colleagues and one or two as friends but hardly any as lovers. Much of my education in this regard had first been with Lizzy then via the popular media. However, the role of females on television or in films included a consistent theme of them seeking vengeance for some terrible wrong done to them or in some cases their perception of offence. It was always possible that Kate had this in mind as payment to Duggie for some imagined wrong; that I had been the instrument and if that were the case then she would need to let him know in order to sink her vengeful hook to sufficient depth for her satisfaction. My mind raced trying to examine all the possibilities—could I expect Duggie to come knocking on my door seeking his own pound of flesh?

My knowledge of their relationship was at best superficial and as it stood I could not hope to resolve the conundrum. In the end I decided I would just wait and see. The next time we met I would take my cue from their attitude and in the mean time I would have to endure the uncertainty.

My period of reflection left me disenchanted with my task. My mind had wandered far from Scott's poems making further work impossible. I am well aware that some artists and writers thrive on emotional tensions. Indeed some have claimed that their romantic deceptions and affairs of the flesh were the very meat of their existence; the stimulus they needed for the development of their work. There are others who, seeking to expose political, financial or religious intolerance also live on the knife-edge between the assassin's bullet and the doubtful approval of their readers. Not so in my own case, I operate in a very different sphere. My agenda consists entirely of a need for objective analysis. I find any or all of my personal involvements a distraction and have no wish to shock or surprise my audience. My prime motive is the edification of the reader through the clarification of historical nuance. Without relying on self-indulgence I seek to serve the public through sound academic research—I told myself.

It was an argument of grand proportions and even as I formulated it I began to appreciate the inherent disingenuousness. I was exactly the same person who had so recently taken a married woman—in the same house where I had been made so welcome by her husband—and most disgracefully—whilst he slept upstairs. This was hardly an act of self-control.

All creative endeavours require a high degree of self-control and supreme confidence. To write, to paint or to sculpt necessitates working alone with the singular uncertainty of any kind of recognition. Paradoxically any loss of the confidence that catalyses the process is accompanied immediately by a cessation of work. And as work is the salve for the creative mind then a circle of failure is completed when it stops.

I went into the kitchen and poured myself a large scotch, uncertain at that time of day whether this was a treat or a punishment. It went down well so I poured another. I decided that I needed to go out for a walk.

The weather conditions had settled for a mid-grey and the temperature had dropped several degrees. I pulled on another sweater, my boots, a cap and a scarf and finally a full length overcoat—about as much protection as it was possible to wear. A stroll out in the cold of the day would do me good—I thought.

The first thing that struck me when I closed the front door was that the air was damp. It seeped into the gap at my collar as it did also into any residual warm corners of my mind. It was an unwelcoming atmosphere and it embraced me possessively. The street was deserted and the curtains of the cottages must have been securely drawn as I could see no sign of light or life. The silence persisted and when I slammed the door it was as a sacrilegious act in church. Interestingly however, the noise did not vibrate; cushioned by the fog its resonance was abbreviated. I set myself to walk down the hill and could not help but notice that the colours that had been such a vibrant part of the landscape had been bled away. I found myself suddenly in a black and white movie set, not too dissimilar to those I'd seen so often in horror films of the 1950's.

The thought made me laugh but the sound was short, a very private noise made in the seclusion of a cloistered environment. Nevertheless, still determined, I stepped out. Sinking my hands deep into my overcoat pockets and shortening my neck as much as anatomy would allow I stamped out the hill and soon arrived at its base. It was only about a half mile walk but the change was remarkable. The air was suddenly crisp and clear; a return to normality. One or two shoppers chatted on a corner and a passing youth on a bicycle nodded good day. My mood lifted. The Limbo that was the Mount disappeared.

On the main street the Post Office provided a focus and whoever had designed the layout had paid at least lip service to the notion of a supermarket. The shelves were neatly stacked along two aisles and wire baskets were available at the entrance. The woman being served when I entered turned to look at me as did the shopkeeper.

The man at the till smiled.

'Good morning.' he said.

I smiled back and included the woman shopper in the breadth of my reply.

'Hello—it's such a relief to be down here and out of the fog—a different world.'

'Aye, 'tis that.' The woman said then glancing furtively at the postmaster she added, 'in more ways that just the climate.'

For a moment he frowned at her then he turned back to me.

'You're holidaying I suppose—just up for a short break eh?'

Aware of the woman's continued scrutiny I nodded not willing to give much more detail.

'Yes I've borrowed a cottage for a couple of weeks. I just thought I'd pop down here for a newspaper and a few bits and pieces.'

'It's the wrong time of year to visit the Mount!'

This time when she spoke she adopted a sly grin and I wasn't certain if she actually meant what she said because of the weather or for some other reason.

'Great view from up there when it's clear though,' I replied, 'and the quiet is wonderful.'

'Quite right too,' the shopkeeper assured me, 'does everyone good to get away from the big towns for a while—and the Mount is an ideal hideaway.'

He continued to smile adding further assurances for my benefit but I noticed that his attitude to his customer had cooled. It was as though he disapproved of her comments. This was confirmed a moment later when he interrupted her next comment saying that I should be allowed to get on with my shopping and that I probably didn't want to listen to more gossip.

I laughed and picked up one of the wire baskets reassuring them that I didn't mind a bit of local chit-chat. His customer however, took the hint and turned her attention once more to her list of groceries. By the time I had chose the few items I required the lady with the sly grin had left the shop. When I reached the till the shopkeeper made his disapproval clear.

'I shouldn't pay to much attention to Mrs. Harlington. She loves to gossip and pays far too much attention to old wives' tales—doesn't have enough to occupy her mind.'

I smiled grateful for his explanation.

'I suppose in a village like this there must be lots of old tales handed down.'

I could not resist testing for new material.

'To be sure,' he said, ringing up my purchases as he spoke, 'we go back to the Doomsday book—and a lot of water, not to mention blood, has flowed under the bridge since then—if you see what I mean.'

'Blood?' I asked.

He grinned, knowing I had taken the bait.

'Aye blood and especially because of the Mount.'

I waited as he filled a plastic carrier-bag with my shopping, knowing there would be more to come. Sure enough, once I paid the bill he continued. As I guessed the delay was only the strategy of a skilful story-teller.

'The story goes,' he muttered in a low voice as though imparting a state secret, 'that in the Middle Ages a group of gypsies stopped here. They came up from the south so they say looking for a spot to settle. The squire then was Sir Gareth St. John Smith a widower and he would have none of it. He let it be known he knew something about the gypsies and claimed they were murderers. God knows what he meant by that. Anyway after a while he apparently took a fancy to one of the girls from their camp and she went to live with him at the big house—it's still there just off the back road a place now called Miles House. There was a fearful row between him and the girl's father and the gypsies were kicked out lock stock and barrel. Just a few weeks later the girl went as well but within a few days of her departure the squire took to his bed and died. Some said he'd been cursed other claimed it was poison.'

The Middle Ages were a long time ago,' I offered.

'Aye maybe but in the next generation history repeated itself. The Grandson of St. John Smith had a run in with another lot of gypsies and he died in mysterious circumstances as well . . . and then in the Eighteenth Century another Smith ended up in court accused of killing a gypsy. Y 'see they're fated—and the village is tainted by association—or so they say.'

'That's fine but what about the Mount?'

My question was an attempt to get him back to the start of his story as so far the connection was only tenuous.

'Of course—the Mount—once I get started on some tale I never know when or where it'll end anyway sorry about that. What happened was that in 1787 Mortimer Smith made a land grant to the descendents of the family—the one whose son had been killed—He only gave them the Mount, to keep for themselves in perpetuity. It was a kind of reparation—however the families up there now are the direct descendants of the original community of gypsies.'

It was quite a story. Nevertheless I was sceptical of this kind of oral history. In my experience the tradition, often found in isolated communities where stories are handed down by word of mouth, is fraught with inaccuracies. Often quite culpable distortions are introduced for whatever vested interests that may preside. This was a tale that was unlikely to say the least, probably an apocryphal tale. I was therefore a little disappointed. I had hoped for something with more tangible roots where facts could be checked against records.

'Surely no-one would want to claim that the various generations of gypsies were in any real sense related . . . would they?'

In the absence of factual evidence to the claim, my question only sought to test the validity of the belief amongst the locals and it was meant in a kindly way. Unfortunately the story-teller seemed to take offence at my doubts.

'I can't see why not—it's like questioning the relationship between the various generations of the Smith family. Just because they were travelling folk doesn't mean they wouldn't have a traceable family history.'

He paused leaving the logic of his statement to argue its own cause.

'Anyway—the proof of the pudding is that the families who live on the Mount will tell you—if you bother to ask. Let me tell you they can trace their history back as far as I can my own and probably further than you can. If you don't mind my saying so, I'm a little surprised to find the likes of your good self staying up there. Usually the only visitors asked to stay are relatives. You aren't related are you?'

I laughed at his bluntness. People living in small communities are not best known for their tact or discretion, especially when strangers are involved. His curiosity was typical and it had taken rather longer than usual for it to manifest itself.

I explained about James's cottage and his association with my mother and about my writing. All that seemed to satisfy him. I couldn't help but add that I had been made to feel most welcome up at the Mount and that the locals there had been accommodating and friendly. Contrary to the impression made by the postmaster and although my words prompted guilty images of Kate I nevertheless felt justified in testifying to the friendly ethos amongst my new neighbours. My rendition was further evidence of the fallibility of the description of local history I had just been subjected to. Fortunately the Postmaster appeared to accept my reservations with good grace and we parted amicably.

Before making the steep climb back up to the Mount I decided to explore the village a little more. A weak sun now warmed the morning air and the previous crispness had softened into a fine autumn day. To the west the entrance to the little hamlet was clearly marked by a sign proclaiming the name Rosedale. Beyond the sign, the open fields persuaded me to turn back east. After following a slow bend in the road I spied the church. It sat in all its Gothic splendour across a small green juxtaposed nicely to the Black Bull, the local pub. The front gardens of the houses I passed were well kept, tidied away for the onset of the cold that comes early in that part of the country. Lawns were trim and garden gates painted in pastel colours. Past the church and at the end of the row of dwellings stood an impressive entrance it sported two well worn but imposing sandstone columns. The gates had long since been removed only the rusted gudgeons remained testimony to the grandeur of their wrought-iron counterparts. The house beyond could not be seen because of a mountainous cedar and a clump of laurel trees that bent to obscure the view. A carved stone plaque employing Roman lettering was mounted on one of the columns and I could just read the legend: Miles House. I concluded this must be the home of the Smith family. There was a coat of arms above the plaque but it had all but worn away. I was in fact trying to decipher the shield when a voice interrupted me.

'I'm afraid there is very little left, it has nearly disappeared—the weather you know.'

I turned to find a man on a bicycle; he had stopped at the edge of the grass verge.

'Yes—it is such a pity' I replied.

Initially I thought I was speaking to a gardener. Except for the quality of his deeply melodious voice and cultured accent he might have been any kind of labouring countryman. He wore a heavy sweater with the sleeves pushed back to reveal deeply tanned forearms; old cord pants and a shapeless battered old hat. His hair was white and I guessed he must be in his late sixties although his obvious fitness belied the fact. As I spoke he dismounted and moved to where I stood.

'Let's see if I can describe it to you.' he said.

As he spoke he stepped up to the base of the column and ran a hand over the surface of the carving.

''Fraid I can't recall all the proper heraldic terms but I think I can give you the gist of it. Atop the shield is the cross of St John—soldier knights—Malta and all that. Then in the first quadrant a mailed fist; then a rose—I think it was a rose—probably relating to Yorkshire. Beneath was a fish—the Christian sign and next to that a crown'.

He stepped down.

'There—not bad for an old man.' He smiled and turned to me, studying my face for the first time. He held out his hand, 'Richard . . . . Richard Smith, forgive my bad manners.'

I took his hand realising at the same time that this must be the owner of the house.

'Paul Denley—I'm delighted to meet you Sir Richard.'

He smiled coyly at my recognition.

'Now you're clearly not from these parts so how did you know?'

'Let's just say that my occupation makes me eternally curious—I'm a writer.'

'And are you staying locally Mr. Denley?'

I hesitated and then rejected my caution.

'Yes—I borrowed a cottage from an old associate of my mother—up on the Mount—lovely views—quiet—nice people.'

'The last bit was thrown in as a tempter to test his reaction but the smile stayed firmly in place.

'Just the place for a writer—I would have thought.' he added, 'and no doubt you've been hearing all the gossip about my ancestors and their dubious reputation.'

I laughed at his candour and for the first time began to like him.

'I have a healthy scepticism for history handed down by word of mouth—especially when the oration is from an interested party. Often all one hears is as you say gossip. But as you've asked—yes I have heard some stories.'

'Perhaps when I know you a little better I'll make the case for the plaintiff.'

'I'd be intrigued to hear it.'

By now he had strolled back to pick up his bicycle which he had dropped on the grass verge. He stood it up and began to push it towards the entrance. He stopped between the columns and turned back.

'Would a writer accept a dinner invitation sometime? I enjoy new people but have rarely had the chance recently . . . . if you are too busy with your scribbles I'll understand.'

I could hardly hide the pleasure at such an invitation and told him so. I said that as I could make my own timetable, I was free anytime that was convenient to him.

He smiled and nodded.

'What about Friday evening then—say eight for eight-thirty?'

'I'll look forward to it.'

He started to wheel the bike again but stopped to add, 'Nothing formal mind you—just come as you are and—I forgot to ask, have you a wife in tow, or a girl-friend? If you have do bring them along—all the more the merrier.'

He vanished round the bend in the path disappearing behind a giant rhododendron bush calling back as he went. 'See you Friday then . . . '

When I got back to the cottage some time later, the mist had cleared leaving a bright fragile sky. A note had been pushed through my letterbox. It was from Kate and although it was brief, I felt myself flush with excitement as I read it. It said, 'Paul you must have been up with the lark this morning. Knock when you get back. Luv and cuddles. Kate.'

I quickly put away my shopping and made myself a cup of strong tea. My manuscript lay untouched, still neatly stacked as I had left it. The sight generated a surge of feelings of guilt but as soon as I began to study the note the guilt was suppressed by resurgent memories.

The memory of her warm body, her moods and her passion were all still fresh. It had been a long time since I'd felt such compulsion. I realised that since that morning I had tried to avoid any thought of her.

With the prospect of a likely negative reaction from Duggie it had been easier to ignore the possible outcome but the note brought it all back. I drained my cup, stood it in the sink and made my way to the door. I was just reaching for the handle when the knock came.

Duggie was at the doorstep with a frown on his face.

Chapter Eight

Apparently, the condition of Homo sapiens in this the twenty-first century is one of supreme tolerance. If he keeps abreast of the latest news and pays even a minimum of attention to his environment he will be made aware of most of the excesses practised by society at large. And some argue that with such information at his fingertips his tolerance for the unusual is considerably enhanced. Consequently for some years and as a result of such reasoning I have considered myself well beyond being shocked. Sadly this increased tolerance apparently does not always extend to include the media. The popular Press appears to revel in the tragedy of war casualties and terrorist atrocities; they often make cynical and hypocritical observations of victims' families, encouraging a melodramatic and entirely inappropriate ethos around the event; they print provocative pornography often in the form of nude or semi-nude women, at the same time paying lip-service to the supposed standards of the Christian ethic by castigating the often minor sexual transgressions of public figures. Theirs is a shadow world of amorality sheathed in the guise of public interest and all this in order to sell newspapers or to persuade viewers to watch a particular channel.

However, whilst in print the agenda purports a concern expressed as moral outrage, in the medium of the moving image the sub-text promotes a puerile sentimentalism of a kind most often seen in American films:

the starving child; the down and out sleeping in doorways; deserted animals and the like and so on. One might say for example that sex on television is coated in a veneer of Art prompting 'good-taste' rape and apparently justifiable violence, (often excessive violence). And as long as the context is a soup of serious relationships amongst the middle classes then anything is deemed acceptable—but who am I to criticise.

Given the degree of my cynicism and despite the limitations of my actual experience, I was nevertheless surprised when Duggie was able to deliver such a profound shock to my value system.

When I first opened my front door to him I feared the worst. He was there to confront me; he was about to charge me with seducing his wife; he was prepared to shout and scream and perhaps in a worst case scenario—to become violent. Physical violence has never been my forte and since my first schooldays I had resolved to talk my way out of any such problem and if talk failed then to run and run as fast as I could. These thoughts and the possible consequences challenged my conscience and brought a flush to my face.

'Hi Paul—could I have a quick word?'

His voice was quiet and well modulated and I shook myself mentally. Taken by surprise I stood for a long moment without answering.

'Do you mind if I come in?'

I shook myself.

'Of course—sorry Duggie I'm still half asleep—do come in.'

I stood to one side and he stepped into the room.

'Please have a seat—would you like a coffee or something?'

He sat in the armchair.

'I know it's rather early but—do you think I might have something stronger—a scotch perhaps?'

I poured his drink in silence still not knowing what to expect.

'There,' I said handing him the glass, 'decadent to the last eh.'

He sipped the drink and seemed to relax.

'Ah that's better—I had to drop by—just wanted to say one or two things on our own as it were—without Kate being around.'

He sipped the drink again and I could feel my flush returning. He didn't seem to notice and continued.

'I enjoyed last night and I'm sorry I flaked out when I did . . . . can't take the booze like I used to . . . . I know that Kate also had a good time.'

The *double entendre* did not escape me but I added nothing and waited for him.

'Please Paul believe me when I say I—I don't want you feeling guilty. I know how it is with Kate—in fact that's part of what I came to say . . . . I mean I don't mind. What Kate does and who she does it with is entirely her business. We have a very special relationship—one without the strings of a more usual bourgeoisie society. I suppose what I'm saying is that I don't want you avoiding us out of some misplaced embarrassment.'

His last sentence was rushed as though he wanted to get it said without being interrupted. Apparently their marriage was just as Kate had indicated—if not in as many words. I was relieved, surprised but relieved. I muttered something about being grateful for his concern and apologised for having taken advantage of his hospitality. It was one of those occasions when the number of words used increased in direct proportion to the decrease in meaningful content. Eventually my bumbling was brought to an end when I asked him how long he and Kate had been married.

He drained his glass and without asking him I refilled it automatically. He took another drink before he replied. When he spoke this time he avoided looking directly at me and instead studied his glass.

'Actually, not that it's important but we aren't married.'

I waited not knowing what to expect.

'You see Paul . . . oh hell you may as well hear it from me as from one of the local gossips. It just so happens that me and Kate were children together . . . . you see we had the same Mother.'

My imagination went into overdrive trying to accommodate the implications of what he had just said but before I could comment he continued.

'We were brought up together—half brother and sister—in the same house. My Dad was dead and Mum married again. Kate used to depend on me for everything . . . . we were as close as it was possible to be . . . she would follow me around like a lap dog and at sixteen years of age she was already a real beauty . . . . it just happened we became lovers and we've been together ever since—off and on.'

He paused and this time my silence was entirely due to the constriction in my throat.

'We discovered years ago that I can't sire children so there's no likelihood of genetic problems . . . and . . . if she takes a fancy to someone else—well who am I to complain—she is her own person.'

I felt that I had to say something so I asked about the cottage.

'And you chose to live up here to be away from people . . . . I mean did you have a hard time?'

It was a silly question but he took it at face value.

'No—not really, Kate went to college and I followed behind doing all kinds of jobs. Given that my interest is in IT it has always been easy for me to find employment. We inherited the cottage from our step-father. Like my mum he belonged to a long line of travelling folk—real Romany stock. Once we got to know everyone up here we found there isn't anywhere else we'd rather be.'

He paused to empty his glass again.

'The nice thing about the Mount is that all the residents here have one kind of oddity or another themselves . . . so they tend not to be judgemental. We feel at home here.'

He was clearly relieved at having unburdened himself and for the first time he looked up and smiled.

'Oh yes I almost forgot—the other thing I was to ask . . . was to invite you for a lunchtime bowl of soup. I know Kate has a favour she wants to ask of you.'

I almost declined the offer knowing that before I could begin to understand, still less sympathise with their situation I would need thinking time alone. However, I also appreciated that a refusal coming so hard on the heels of his confession might be misconstrued. Instead I agreed but claimed that I needed some time to put some papers in order first.

'So—if you don't mind I'll join you in about fifteen minutes.'

He said that it would be fine and he left.

Left to my own devices I poured myself another drink and sat at the window to try and sort out my feelings.

Incest was one of the few remaining taboos in a civilized society. There was a general consensus and there was no debate about it. It was still regarded as incest even with different fathers and the known consequences had been qualified by research over many years. The results of such research had only exaggerated the abhorrence felt by society in the face of such conditions. Besides all that it was considered a crime. The question was—if there was no possibility of children from the relationship should it make a difference. I questioned myself and tried to balance my immediate revulsion against my own recent behaviour. Were the genetic dangers the sole reasons for the taboo? And if so, once removed should the objections be diminished? One could reasonable argue that, at least in theory, moral standards were set by quantifying the danger to physical and mental health. After all social preference and behaviour were governed by needs of survival—not so? The fact that safe practice produced social morays that in turn acquire their own value is incidental. Apart from religious belief—and much of that is governed originally by knowledge acquired—moral and ethical values have their foundation in society seeking to continue—to survive. Without the consideration of health and welfare, being known to one's half sister in the biblical sense is surely no worse that marrying one's cousin—was it?

My dilemma was far from over however, even with this dubious level of accommodation. The fact that Kate and Duggie were also willing to indulge in what used to be called free love—was something else. It was also part of the equation that I felt less secure in offering criticism about. My own culpability hardly equipped me to pronounce judgement. My conscience ached for an easy solution, something that would satisfy the disparate conditions and the vagaries of my considerations. There were none available. In the end, despite myself, I went and knocked on Kate's door.

The broth she had made was a steaming orchestration of seasonal vegetables and at least for a little while it took my mind off more serious thoughts. The leeks and carrots were enhanced with selected herbs from Kate's kitchen garden and thickened by a late crop of potatoes. It was a meatless concoction but for all that it was nevertheless satisfying: just the kind of mid-day meal to allay the effects of the weather. However, whereas the lunch worked its magic to good effect its powers were limited. The atmosphere round the table was strained and I found myself choosing my words very carefully. And when I was not speaking instead of listening I found myself studying the pair of them. It was just as if I expected to see some tangible outward sign of the corruption evident in their relationship.

Due to my preoccupation I misheard things several times and once or twice missed the comment aimed at me altogether. By the time coffee was served my distance was becoming obvious. Kate finally broke the spell.

'Does it make such a terrible difference Paul?' she asked.

I must have looked confused. She continued.

'I know Duggie has enlightened you about us . . . . But does it really change anything?'

For once in my life I struggled to find an answer and after a moment or two she said, 'We enjoyed a good fuck didn't we?'

This time the tone was more aggressive and the use of the expletive made the emphasis she clearly intended. It was a shock tactic. I have never been happy with the frequent use of the more common swearwords and have found difficulty employing their use with anything like conviction. On her tongue the word was especially productive, it wakened me but my reply still lacked conviction.

'Of course we did—but you must appreciate—well—hearing how you are—it came as a shock.'

Duggie gave a low chuckle.

'I'm afraid Paul has had a very sheltered upbringing Kate. You'll need to educate him.'

She ignored the jibe and continued to direct an uncomfortable stare at me.

'So it makes no difference?' she asked finally.

I mumbled my agreement.

'Good!' she said, 'I was beginning to think you might have moral limitations after all. Had that been the case it would have been difficult to invite you to the party.'

Before I could formulate a response there was a knock at the front door. Kate turned to Duggie.

'Get that will you love.' She said quietly.

He left the kitchen and went to the door. When he had left Kate pulled her chair closer to mine in a conciliatory gesture. She reached out and took my limp hand in hers.

'I'm sorry,' she whispered, 'I should have known it would be hard for you to accommodate—but just trust me eh?'

Close to her all my reservations faded. She was far from a traditional or classic beauty but there was a light in her green eyes that made the impish smile all the more attractive. As usual she wore her old jeans with an old shirt tied in a knot around the flat of her stomach and the variously exposed patches of bare skin seemed to glow. She smelt of excitement and the touch of her hand was cool. On an impulse I leaned forward and kissed her quickly on the mouth. She smiled, bit my lip and playfully pecked me on the nose.

'Now that tells me more than any number of words ever could.' She said.

Suddenly and without warning I wanted her. I wanted her there and then and she knew it. She stroked the back of her hand along my cheek and gave me a secret smile just as the others entered.

'Paul,' Duggie announced, 'let me introduce you to Malcolm . . . . a good friend and one of our special neighbours.'

I stood and turned to take the outstretched hand. Malcolm grinned and gripped my hand firmly. He was a tall man, well over six feet and thin almost to the point of emaciation. His clothes hung on a skeletal frame and long bony arms protruded from beneath rolled-up sleeves. The skin on his face was pulled tight and whereas his front teeth jutted forward from beneath pale lips, his eyes were sunk in deep recesses almost hidden under a heavy frontal bone. The only excess in his physical appearance was his voluminous black hair. His eyebrows were thickly matted and the pony-tail that hung down his was more than two feet long back. His head looked tiny due to the hair being pulled back so tight against his skull.

'Ah the writer—I'm told.'

As he spoke he held onto my hand and stared into my eyes.

'I'm afraid so—but since being here, the good food and other distractions have arrested any progress in that direction.'

Everyone laughed politely.

'And I am equally sure we are all delighted to hear you say that.'

I noticed that when he spoke he had a slight lisp and that my two neighbours seemed to hang on his every word.

'Would you like coffee?' Kate asked.

'Black with two sugars please.'

Even when replying to Kate, Malcolm kept his eyes on me and probably due to the strangeness of his appearance I became aware of the animal magnetism he seemed to exude. He placed a chair alongside mine and motioned in a patronising manner for me to sit.

'I make carpets and rugs—spend the winter with my looms and the summer round the markets. I choose to believe that which is beneath our feet has a special significance.'

I attempted to smile encouragingly not knowing quite how I was expected to respond. In the event Duggie saved my embarrassment.

'Malcolm's rugs are very special. He designs them as a minimum resistance to the earth . . . '

Malcolm's long glance in Duggie's direction was undoubtedly some kind of warning. A dark fiery look that stopped Duggie mid-sentence

'Duggie is one of my most enthusiastic supporters but sometimes he is apt to misinterpret my activities.' The thin man was clearly upset, 'The fact is that I believe in the life of the planet in a physical sense and in Mother Earth in a spiritual sense. Therefore the contact we make with the ground has significant importance . . . ' He paused and I returned his gaze, 'The ground coverings I make are intended to act as mediators—the materials used and the designs impregnated into their substance will help channel the earth's energy . . . ' Suddenly he stopped, glanced about him and grinned, 'But I'm sure you don't want to listen to all this mumbo jumbo. When I get fired up I tend to preach . . . I do apologise. I came over especially to meet you and all I seem to have done is talk about me.'

In one sense his apology may well have been by way of seeking approval. Clearly it would have been bad mannered of me to agree with his last statement when etiquette demanded that I should protest interest. The conformist in me made me succumb.

'Not at all,' I said with as much sincerity as I could muster, 'your thesis is one with which I can find considerable sympathy. I know little about the ability to mediate with energy, but the notion of Mother Earth in terms of spirituality is one that predates the Roman invasion. I find it interesting that the idea is gaining credibility again.'

He was obviously pleased with my comments and settled to a long and often boring description of the detail of his belief. Kate and Duggie listened attentively allowing their guest to enlarge his ideas without interruption. I suspected that it may have been even more of a trial for them as they must have heard his sermon many times before. Their patience was admirable.

It was well into the afternoon before he finally left but I was suitably relieved when, after the front door closed my new friends both broke down in fits of giggles. My suspicions were confirmed and I felt justified in joining in the merriment. The mood of our original conversation however, had been irretrievably broken and there was no way that our examination of Duggie and Kate's relationship could be reasonably scrutinised. As a result I made my excuses claiming that I was so far behind with the writing and rose to leave. There was a brief moment of embarrassment at the door when Kate asked when it might be convenient for her to visit me again. Duggie was standing directly behind her as she asked and in his presence my awkwardness returned.

'Well . . . . as I'm just next door—you can pop in anytime—anytime you like—you know that.'

Duggie surprisingly took the initiative and answered in her place.

'Then you'd best expect her tonight Paul—when she's in season she's insatiable.'

He laughed at his own crudity and although I smiled along with him, I was conscious that Kate maintained a serious expression.

'Why don't you both join me for an evening meal? I offered.

This was my attempt to dismiss his suggestion as a joke and return the conversation to more normal matters. It was a complete failure. Kate frowned as though I had rejected her and Duggie claimed he had a previous arrangement to visit friends that evening. I attempted to build a bridge by then saying that Kate and I would have to dine alone. I weighted the invitation implying it was what she might have wanted to hear but as she closed the door the situation was still unresolved.

Back in the cottage moments later I was still feeling confused. The discussion after lunch had not satisfied my qualms of conscience and yet there was already a feeling that my association with Kate had been institutionalised. It had acquired a degree of acceptance by them but nonetheless left me still somewhat shocked. Under the circumstances the expectation of our continuing to bed together was alien and for a while I found myself exercising my latent Catholic conscience—fortunately this did not last long. I knew that my inclination to moralise was an intellectual cul-de-sac, one that tended to close my mind to the context in which I now found myself. It also smacked of dishonesty if not hypocrisy. The prospect of another session with Kate naturally excited me. She was the most unusual of women but I was still wary of the situation. It would be too easy to form a deeper relationship with all the quagmire of responsibilities that might imply. And if that were allowed to happen the ripples from such a disturbance may well upset the equilibrium of the whole pond. The effect on the rest of their small community would be difficult to calculate.

I relit the fire and sat to study my last notes.

I must have fallen asleep over my books. I awoke in the late evening with a stiff neck, my head flat to the table. The fire was again reduced to red ash and outside it was already dark. I had been dreaming that I was on a long walk and the thin spidery figure of Malcolm trekked ahead of me across the moor. I knew it was him by the angularity of his silhouette—and his peculiar limp. It was only then that I remembered. I must have noticed when he was in the company next door but not registered the fact that he had a club foot. For a moment I thought it must have been part of the dream—but no—I could recall seeing it. He wore a heavy leather boot with a thick sole on his right foot and it had been the cause of his peculiar gait. It was a strange thing to forget but even stranger to remember it through a dream.

There was a sudden tapping at the back door—a noise that made me start. Finding myself in such a nervous state I quickly turned on the light before I went to answer it. Kate was standing there, a heavy overcoat slung over her shoulders protecting her from the evening damp. She smiled.

'Hope you're cooking up something nice and spicy.' She said with a twinkle in her eye.

Clearly all her previous reservations had been forgotten.

Chapter Nine

'Gerry will explain all that to you my love.' Bessie said.

She wrapped the bacon she had just sliced in sheets of greaseproof paper and laid it carefully in the carrier-bag.

'Now is there anything else? Got enough eggs 'ave you?'

I smiled and nodded. Her maternal concern I took to mean that I had left a suitable impression. Ever since my arrival at the shop that morning she had gone to great pains to ensure that I was fully supplied with foodstuffs.

'To keep body and soul together,' she'd said each time I'd said enough.

I'd realised that no matter what age I might be in her eyes as I was motherless I was a candidate for being looked after—hopefully not for adoption.

She cast an eye over the stock on her shelves, leaned back and rescued a delicately balanced tin of button mushrooms from behind her right shoulder.

'Now—these go nicely in those foreign sauces—at least that's what I'm led to believe. A large spoonful of tomato puree; a pinch of basil and oregano; some gently fried onion and a few slices of sweet yellow pepper to taste, cook it in a thick vegetable stock and you'll impress those pork steaks no end—not to mention young Kate.

Despite the reference to Kate being my dinner guest, a fact that in my innocence I had imagined to be privileged information, there was no way I could ignore such a detailed recipe.

'Okay—I'll take the mushrooms as well.'

She was pleased but as she placed the tin alongside the rest of my purchases she shouted over her shoulder, directing her considerable voice at the inner doorway.

'Gerry my love—where 'ave you got to . . . . Paul is standing 'ere waiting fer you?'

She turned back shaking her head.

'Don't know what gets into him . . . he's probably reading a book on the lavvy. He gets in there sometimes and you can't get him out.'

However, her second shout had the desired effect and Gerald duly appeared. He squeezed up next to her and she put a big arm around him like a mother hen with one of her chicks under her wing.

'Now you naughty man—me and Paul were discussing the equinox and I said you would explain it all to him—'cos of the solstice an' all.'

Gerald grinned, obviously delighted to be called on for an expert opinion. He motioned his head inviting me to join him back in their private accommodation and Bessie nodded her agreement. Since arriving in the little community Bessie and Gerald had shown me every kindness. During the last few weeks since my arrival I had been a frequent visitor to the shop. This was not surprising for two reasons: it held an almost inexhaustible supply of the widest variety of goods imaginable and it was the clearing house for local news and information generally. To some large extent the shop was the fulcrum about which the community moved and Bessie's virtuosity in handling information was unparalleled. Her knowledge about my next dinner date with Kate was a typical demonstration. My nature was such that I enjoyed pressing Bessie for information about the residents of the Mount. Secretly therefore I was pleased that the shop-owner had apparently decided to treat me as her confidante.

Gerald led the way through the small door and along a narrow corridor. This narrowest of spaces was also used for storage, mounds of magazines, packages of dried goods and boxes of tinned goods were stacked at intervals reducing the access to an absolute minimum. A bare bulb was the only light source until Gerald opened the door into the kitchen. This large room was clearly their main living space. A stone fireplace of grand proportions dominated the space and two aged armchairs—his and hers—were positioned on either side. The grate surprisingly held nothing more than the meanest fire hardly justifying the scale of its surround. The room was nevertheless cheerfully warm. At the far end of the room was a solid fuel stove for cooking purposes and that was the main source of heating. A long pine table occupied the centre of the room and this was littered with all manner of personal and commercial bits and pieces. There was just enough space left for two place settings.

'Have a seat Paul.' Gerald muttered.

Without a backward glance he then began to rummage amongst a pile of books mounded in a nearby corner. The working end of the room next to the stove boasted a large fridge/freezer and a motley collection of pans and pots which were stacked haphazardly across several work surfaces next to a Belfast sink. Several times Gerald stopped to study odd pages of books he uncovered. At some stage he even pulled one of the dining chairs across and sat to read a complete passage. In all it was about thirty minutes before he was satisfied with his search and at that point he collected four or five volumes in his arms and turned back to me.

'There's so much—so much still—Bess told me you were asking about the solstice.'

I nodded.

'D' you know anything at all about the Equinox?'

I shook my head. My only recollection of the term brought memories of Geography lessons and a teacher whose pedagogy consisted of continuous dictation muttered into the collar of an old tweed jacket. Now it was Gerald's turn to shake his head, then he read from an old edition of the Britannica.

'The term Equinox is used to describe the two points where the projection of the sun's apparent annual path crosses the celestial equator . . . . Now does that make sense—any more sense?'

I was back in school—nodding inanely. He went on now with a more satisfied smile.

'There are two occasions when this happens, one in Spring—the venal equinox and one in Autumn: the autumn equinox . . . . yes?'

My head agreed.

'One happens about March 21st and the other about September 23rd. I say this because the solstice celebrations are also associated with the path of the sun—and this also happens on two occasions: when the star reaches its greatest declination in the north and in the south about June 21st and December 21st. So as you have probably deduced the solstice celebrations are planned to occur mid-way between the equinoxes.'

Of course I had deduced nothing of the sort as much of what Gerald had said had passed through one ear and seamlessly out of the other—just as my Geography teacher had said on so many occasions. I nevertheless presented an apparently attentive pose. He seemed pleased to be able to give me chapter and verse and according to him, the scientifically agreed detail. I remained less than impressed. However, it was when he began to talk about the quasi-religious overtones that he regained my full attention. The practice he described—at least in Britain apparently could be traced back to the Druids. This was a Celtic celebration first recorded in 908AD (although presumably predating that occasion) and one, it was claimed, confirmed across the land by the Beltane fires It is interesting to note that in Cornwall these fires were known as the beacons of Saint Margaret providing a curious mixture of roots as one referred to the ancient God Baal and the other to a Christian saint.

I knew for a fact from previous research that the Scot's Gaelic 'Bealltaine' had also been a Celtic people's celebration held on May Day. How this might have been displaced to a date in June—still less in December was a mystery. Gerald seemed so pleased with himself that I chose not to mention that one characteristic of these legends is often the way in which they are amalgamated over the years by disparate groups with an unrelated variety of different belief systems. At least in Gerald's mind it was established that the occasion was one with historical credibility and that the reverence due to the sun god should be celebrated twice each year in the presence of a bonfire.

At least now I knew the nature of the party I had been invited to attend.

Trapped as I was in the kitchen of Bessie's house, it took me two hours before I could extricate myself without giving offence. During that time Gerald became increasingly keen to support his proclamations with anecdotal evidence from the myriad of Belltaines he had attended and he would certainly have kept me there indefinitely had I not excused myself. In the end I used my dinner date with Kate as my passport to the outside. It was only later over a pre-prandial Scotch that it dawned on me that I was still no wiser concerning the content of the so-called party.

The situation with Kate had taken a very convenient turn and whilst she had not exactly moved in with me she nevertheless occupied my bed each night. Despite my never mentioning it, Duggie's compliance was still incomprehensible to me. He was far more generous than I could ever hope to be and in a curious way I began to feel sympathy for his situation. Initially Kate's appetites were difficult to satisfy but what I may have lacked in terms of youth and energy I made up for with enthusiasm. I told myself that, as with any process of exercise, if the performance was sufficiently practised it would improve. There had been some progress also in the development of my book. At the half-way stage my writing project had an end in sight for the first time. The contrast of sedentary days spent in intellectual pursuit, set against nights of continuous action seemed to suit my temperament.

By now my association with Kate had become common knowledge and thankfully it had been accepted by the locals—albeit conditionally. Their approval and their consequent cooperation were clearly dependent on the successful continuation of the affair. Bessie and Gerald had been especially helpful; it seemed that nothing was too much trouble. They provided what amounted to an in-service training course consisting of supplying a directory of the names and details of the backgrounds of each resident; a potted history of the community and a review of the cultural beliefs and practices. Much of what they told me complimented the information that the Postmaster had provided only differing in detail and emphasis. By contrast however, in Bessie's rendition the members of the Smith family were forever the villains: seducers, thieves and murderers. According to her, the gift of the land known as the Mount was only fair repayment for all that her predecessors had suffered and it was actually a gift with ties. The fact was the land was leased. She insisted that her ancestors were not the gypsies of local legend but simply immigrants from Eastern Europe; that they had travelled to this country seeking a new home and being prepared to turn their hand to anything. The detail she was to provide was surprising given the time lapse but more surprising still was the fact of her continued vehemence towards the St. John Smith family.

In consideration of her strength of feeling and in order not to create a rift, I chose not to tell her of my frequent meetings with Richard St. John

Smith. By now he had become more than just a passing acquaintance; we had met over dinner on several occasions, usually on Friday evenings and had found much to talk about. We both loved literature, especially that of the 18th and 19th centuries and he proved to be generous in being prepared to loan me books from his extensive private library. His version of the Mount's history had much in common with that described by Bessie except for the attribution of blame. He would say only that the St. John Smiths were an honourable family, warriors who fought for their sovereign King over successive generations since long before the Crusades of his name-sake. There were some aspects of the history about which both parties were cautious. For example I found it increasingly significant that neither Richard nor Bessie were prepared to be forthcoming about the reason Bessie's ancestors had left the south of England. I could see that the south would have been more climatically sympathetic and that the advanced state of the settlements would have made day to day life that much easier than in Yorkshire. I concluded privately that perhaps there had been some kind of incident—some associated trauma that prompted the migration. On one occasion I even asked Richard outright. His response was typical.

'That's one area that I cannot discuss with you Paul. When the families accepted possession of the Mount it was only in part payment for the death of the young men. There had been so many recriminations over the years—so many claims of injustice that once they perceived their advantage, they insisted that no-one ever again made reference to their previous occupations.' Richard's agreement was in line with what the rest of his antecedents had done. The only clue lay in the reference to their 'previous occupations'. Whatever they had done to earn their keep had to be sufficiently serious to warrant a wholesale move to another part of the country. Alternatively their 'occupations' may have been a euphemism for some illegal activity. The only other available source of information rested with the community itself. I have always regarded research as some kind of detective work and as I was determined to find out as much as I could, I set to, to investigate by engaging my contacts and neighbours on every possible occasion.

It was therefore as a consequence of this decision that some tome later I found myself pressing Bessie for more information about her friends. There was little use in asking Kate, she seemed only interested in our relationship and regarded anything outside of that as irrelevant.

That evening when Kate arrived to join me for dinner, I was surprised to find she had brought Duggie along.

'I knew you wouldn't mind,' she said turning her most persuasive smile on me. 'He's a bit down in the dumps—and I said as you were such a generous cook that you'd probably prepared enough for six anyway.'

Duggie looked rather uncomfortable standing there behind her so I could do no more than at least pretend to make him welcome. I grinned as disarmingly as I could and endorsed Kate's concern.

'We can't have you sitting on your own in there Duggie, drinking yourself to sleep—certainly not whilst we're enjoying a veritable banquet of Italian food in here—and Kate was absolutely right, I've made far too much, more that two people could ever finish. So you'll be doing me a favour by joining in.'

My performance must have been reasonably convincing as Duggie quickly settled to his more usual self. However the fact was that I had been planning this meal for several days. I'd promised Kate that I would exhibit my culinary skills on her behalf by preparing something special. We had grown used to relying on 'instant something-or-other' from the freezer and I was conscious of the first meal I'd shared with them and wanted to repay the compliment. Given this thought it wasn't unreasonable that Duggie should join us and I felt a little guilty at my selfish reaction on first seeing him.

I had cooked the Penne pasta in a cabbage stock garnished with parsley and oregano; the pork steaks were heavily peppered and served with the 'alla Romana' sauce as described by Bessie; the ice-cream that was designed to follow was flavoured with pecan nuts on a bed of loganberries and topped with fresh double cream. A touch of Amoretto before the cream still made it special, despite my inability to find any of the requisite biscuits in either of the local shops. Three bottles of Chianti provided the final touch and by the time the table was cleared we all felt seriously stuffed. I served coffee and opened the bottle of Hine Champagne brandy and the mood was very relaxed.

Duggie—always quick on the swallow—had probably drunk twice as much wine as Kate and me; he was nevertheless still wide awake albeit between short fireside naps and continued to contribute to the conversation with his usual provocations. Our discussions ranged across all manner of subjects and although I tried to encourage them to talk about the so-called party their comments were brief and unrewarding. The chosen date for the occasion was only five days hence but each time I raised the matter Kate just laughed and Duggie became strangely mysterious, telling me that I'd just have to wait and see.

Just after midnight my mind naturally focused on bed-time. I was wondering how best I might encourage Duggie to make his way home. By then he was snoring gently in the armchair opposite. Kate was sprawled across the settee with her head in my lap. As if she read my mind she suggested that perhaps Duggie might be better off staying the night.

'He's all in and I've been a bit concerned about him—he's not been so well lately.'

'Surely he'd be better off in his own bed?'

'Maybe—but I feel partly responsible.'

'I can't see why.'

At this she sat up and faced me.

'It may sound silly but . . . well . . . since you and me got together . . . he doesn't make a complaint but he still has normal needs . . . and of course he hasn't been 'with' me since you arrived.'

She was as ever straight to the point and her comment satisfied the question I hadn't dare ask. I still had difficulty in accommodating the fact that Kate might have sex with someone other than me. I knew she would believe it unreasonable under the circumstances and I knew that in fact I was the cuckoo in the nest—so to speak—but the prejudice remained.

'I can't see what that might have to do with him being 'off colour'—or for that matter why it should prohibit him from going next door to his own bed.'

She smiled and took my hand.

'Can I ask you something—something personal?'

'Of course you can.'

'That night—the night you arrived—the first night when you saw us through the kitchen window—What did you think?'

The question took me by surprise.

'I don't remember—I think I was shocked—really shocked. Well it isn't everyday that you look into someone else's kitchen and see—see the kitchen table being misused like that.'

'And—other than being 'really shocked' was there anything else?'

I sat quietly feeling my face begin to flush but not knowing what else to add.

'Did you find it stimulating . . . was it erotic for you? You didn't know me then, I was just some strange woman getting it in the kitchen. Did watching him take me get you excited?'

'I suppose—well yes I suppose it did. Hell—seeing a young woman—a young attractive woman do the things you did—it would excite the Angel Gabriel.'

She laughed and looked relieved.

'Good, at least that's a first step in honesty.'

Now we both laughed. I was still uncertain where this conversation was leading but as long as it ended with her in my bed I didn't care too much. She studied my face.

'Having admitted that Paul—how would you feel if Duggie were to have me again?'

'I still have problems with that.'

She gave a wicked grin.

'I thought you might say that. However—how would it be if you could watch again?'

I shook my head and grimaced but she continued.

'If you could watch like you did before . . . . And than afterwards have me yourself?'

'Ménage a Trois' the phrase sprang immediately to mind—a leftover from the Sixties wife-swapping genre. The popular magazines had been full of it. The swinging set, setting a prescription to combat boredom for the middle and the lower classes—spreading as far as the suburbs and causing marriage breakdowns too numerous to count—if the Tabloid Press were to be believed. I hesitated.

'Do you find it difficult to share?'

She was pressing her point and I didn't like it.

'I find it difficult to answer loaded questions.'

That appeared to strike gold. The grin disappeared. She studied me again and for a moment I thought she would stamp out of the cottage but before I could say anything else she began to undress. She loosened her blouse, untied her skirt and in the blink of an eye she stood there in nothing but her briefs. A few seconds later she was nude.

Normally naked young women appear possessed by an aura of vulnerability: defencelessness relative to the softness of their flesh;

the question in their eyes and the hesitancy in their manner. This is especially true when they find themselves naked in front of men who are still fully clothed. At least that is what my limited experience had me to believe. Whatever the truth might have been Kate was the exception. She exhibited no shyness, no timidity; there was no attempt to hide nipples or shield her crutch; she moved about naked with exactly the same confidence and assurance as she had when she was fully clothed. If there was any insecurity present it was mine. She smiled again, this time at my obvious embarrassment. So much for man the motivator; man the aggressor; the potential rapist became homo probus: man the virtuous. Until that moment I had imagined that my recent experience had equipped me to deal with any kind of sexual confrontation; that at last the gap in my education had been filled. I was mistaken. Filled with confusion my responses became leaden and my confidence seeped away.

'Kate . . . '

I pronounced her name as a plea as if to question her actions politely. I could hear the complete gormlessness of my tone and hated myself for it. Not for the first time in my life I felt my lack of savoir faire was exposed. And all the while she stood there hands on hips smiling down at me in the firelight. The smile could have meant anything. Eventually she spoke—a more serious voice.

'Come on Paul. It isn't polite to keep a girl waiting.'

I found myself instinctively looking at Duggie. His eyes were still closed.

'Pretend he isn't here. He wouldn't join in unless he was invited.'

I still hesitated. Suddenly she knelt before me, leaning forward to rest her forearms on my knees. Thrown forward her breasts hung between us—ripe temptations.

'Do me now Paul—or I'll never see you again.'

*

It was four in the morning when Duggie finally went home. By then he was just as exhausted as I was. For some major part of the night I had been able to shut the objections of my Catholic conscience away in a secret corner of my mind; to close the door on the thinking normally governed by an ingrained morality. The urgent response of flesh had won over the needs of the intellect and spirituality. Barriers had been broken down.

I lay upstairs across a rumbled bed, the culmination of a trail of clothing left and of cushions and furniture displaced throughout the house. My mind was left in a similar state of disarray. Kate lay beside me; she was still wide awake and as far as I could judge still on heat. Contrary to my depletion it seemed as if she had thrived on the action; gained energy from the involvement and apparently she could have continued indefinitely. For me however, the night had been a revelation as exhausting emotionally as it had been physically.

I drifted off into a deep sleep charged with dreams of bonfires.

Chapter Ten

It was well past mid-day when I finally awoke. I found myself neatly wrapped in a tidy duvet, my head on a pillow and the sheets tucked tightly around me. Save for the far reaches of my imagination which was still in overdrive, the chaos that had characterised the room the night before was gone and order had been restored. There was no sign of Kate only the trace residue of her perfume.

I dressed quickly and downstairs found the pots and pans had been washed and put away and the furniture restored to its former places. There was no trace of the previous night's activities. In anticipation of the dinner I had cleared away my typewriter and all my notes, these had now been reinstated in exactly their original order. It was just as if nothing had happened. There was no earthquake damage, no cataclysm; no sign of my corruption of conscience, in fact nothing at all to signify the communal descent into anarchic pleasure. The natural world as much as that of the spirit seemed to have ignored my conduct, I thought—so much for divine disapproval.

I lit the fire, washed and shaved and made strong coffee—served with two teaspoons of guilt. My first thoughts sought to lay the blame for my behaviour at Duggie's door. He was after all the prime mover . . . was he? On the other hand, had it not been Kate who had inspired the situation: the female temptress—a role steeped in religious tradition.

'Garbage—it is utter bilge!' I told the typewriter.

Was I such a simpleton? Was I so malleable as to find myself without the balls even to take responsibility for my own choices? Surely if it had been my choice then the blame was mine also. And—what of sin, the voice of my private devil asked?

'Define it' he whispered.

More to the psychological point what of guilt? I had always believed that guilt was a condition promoted by the church by way of the priests, a stratagem employed to enable the easy manipulation of their congregation. Dress-up deviance—especially of the sexual kind in a hair shirt of restrictive morality; applaud conformity and self-denial; encourage the depression of failure and one is left inevitably with life-long mind-scars. All this is a recipe for the religious zealot. Plagued therefore with self-doubt, self recrimination and the implication of universal disapproval how much more difficult it becomes to make objective decisions based on actual need.

Intolerance, prejudice, impatience and censorship are all sign of reaction; the views of tin-pot dictators, monarchs and popes. Ask no questions they say but accept blind faith. Not, I hasten to add, the faith of Jesus or Mohammed or Allah but rather the politically expedient faith of their anointed representatives. Suddenly I was angry—as angry with myself as I was with the systems of belief I had grown up with. This was my road to Damascus. No Saul could have been any more furious to find he had been so wrong. I suddenly realised that the scepticism that had informed my attitude since puberty had been my way of accommodating the nonsense that was organised religion.

On an impulse I slipped on a coat, took the car keys and went for a drive. I needed the cold of the outside, the space, the moor: a distraction from the conflicting voices that competed for attention. The sky looked heavy with snow but I did not feel like walking and although the temperature was almost at freezing, the car started immediately. As usual the street was deserted and there was no-one to witness me turning the car and making for the hill. The car bumped on the rough road as I turned but I did not pause to see what had caused it. Just beyond the corner where the hill dipped my acceleration almost caused an accident. Two misty figures suddenly appeared in front of me, their backs were turned and it was more by good luck that I didn't run them down.

It was my own entire fault. My mind was full of pictures and strong militant sentences: a haze of grandiloquent gestures confirming a new resolve. I braked hard and the car skidded to a halt only feet from the two retreating figures. They stopped and turned to face me. They were an odd looking couple. One was a dour looking character in a long black coat and the other a tiny person wearing a fur hat. I left the driving seat and began m apologies.

'I'm dreadfully sorry. It was entirely my fault. Are you okay? I didn't hit anyone did I?'

The little one stepped back; the car bumper was only one of his small strides away. He turned to his friend.

'That was a near thing eh?'

'Too close for comfort' His friend agreed—then he added, 'Two closed for comforting—it might have been.'

The taller one had a high-pitched effeminate voice made all the more apparent when he laughed at his own obscure joke. The little one joined in and soon they were both laughing irrationally with tears streaming down their faces. I was not sure if the reaction might not have been a sign of shock so I stood and waited. Eventually the small man stopped to wipe his eyes and appeared to notice me for the first time. He nudged his companion and nodded to direct attention to me.

'Sammy—the driver . . . . the driver needs help.'

I began to assure them that I was fine but the tall one came over to me nevertheless. It was not until we were close that I realised that it was in fact a female. She wiped her face and smiled at me.

'Sorry about that Mister. We likes a good laugh . . . . 'an' you nearly killed us.'

This caused them both to laugh again, the female in a screeching giggle. She spoke in a clipped accent common amongst travellers—a not unlikable sound with words running into one another and a trace of an Irish brogue. The small man stepped forward and held out his hand.

'Celia 'an Jim Smith—she answers to Sammy but you can call me Jim.' He laughed again then added, 'We's from the Mount—sorry if we gives you a shock.'

We shook hands but when I turned to Celia she was inspecting the car.

'R 'you goin down t' hill? 'Cos we could do with a lift?'

It would have been difficult to deny my direction given the circumstances of our meeting. I therefore opened the rear near-side door and promised to drop them wherever they might want to go. They said that their destination was the Post Office shop in the village high street and they seemed pleased with my offer. Nevertheless there was a none too subtle change to their mood once we set off. They settled into the back seat smiling and waving at me to proceed as If I were their chauffeur. I decided to take it in good part even to the extent of offering them a suitably servile salute.

They talked incessantly throughout the journey, often at the same time. It became clear that they were close neighbours and in fact they lived next door to one another at numbers eleven and nineteen. This placed them next to Bessie's shop on one side and next to Malcolm the thin man at number five on the other. I had long since given up trying to make sense of the cottage's numbering system; it seemed to deliberately defy logic. Not surprisingly then that the conversation between my passengers proved a fitting compliment to such a precocity. I was unable to understand most of what was said but what I did comprehend were word games mostly based on rhyming slang and *double entendres* derived from body parts. And although the jokes were childish they were sufficient to render the participants helpless in fits of laughter.

I was delighted that neither of my passengers had been injured, more so still when they made no serious criticisms of my driving skills. I did however; find it curious that they deliberately ignored the polite conventions that regularise such meetings as ours. Indeed once seated in the car they took little notice of me except to have me feel that I was suddenly their employee. They were deaf to most of my questions and ignored any comment I made. Eventually I dropped them outside of the Post Office and they left without saying cheerio or expressing any thanks. I was glad to see the back of them.

Without intending to a few moments later I found myself driving between the stone gate-posts that marked the entrance to Richard's house. I reasoned with myself that what I most needed then was a spell of time in normal company. A pretext for such a visit was unnecessary as Richard had been most insistent that I should make use of his library whenever I might feel the need.

The grand portico of the entrance sat atop two flights of stone steps and the rhododendrons planted either side made a screen of deep green, hiding the ornate decoration of the windows. It was a lovely house, monumental in size outside yet domestic in scale inside. So much so that it was the kind of house anyone might feel comfortable in occupying. Richard answered the door himself and seemed pleased to see me. His complexion was flushed and I noticed he was wearing his gardening boots.

'Hello Paul,' he said opening the door wider to admit me, 'do come in—how nice of you to visit.'

I stamped my feet on the grid—making him smile—and crossed the threshold into a world of antique furniture, tapestries and fine paintings.

'You must be the only visitor in twenty years to arrive from a car and yet still take care to clean the imaginary mud from your shoes.'

He laughed as he spoke and led me into the drawing room with a hand on my shoulder. The fireplace there hosted a huge blaze, a sublime contrast with Gerald's kitchen fire of yesterday. Richard dropped unceremoniously into one of the fireside armchairs and indicated me to do likewise in the other.

'Now then Paul, tell me what you've been up to.'

'Not a lot really—just thought I might pop along and take advantage of your magnificent library—that is if you don't mind.'

'Not at all—just help yourself, it is so nice that you find a genuine use for the books. Tell me is there anything new in the rarefied atmosphere of the Mount—how's that girlfriend of yours—Kate wasn't it?'

I'd forgotten that the last time we'd shared dinner, the worse for several bottles of fine wine, I'd mentioned something about Kate.

'Fine,' I said, 'no complaints—she is quite a personality and very good company.'

'Lucky dog—oh to be footloose and an author on leave—you should bring her here sometime. I enjoy the company of pretty women.'

I refused his offer of a cigarette and he lit one for himself, watching me studiously through his smoke.

'They are all characters up there. Strikes me that every single cottage has its own peculiar individual tenant—don't you agree?'

'You are right of course—in one way or another they are all a bit strange. I've just met Celia and Jim Smith for the first time—gave them a lift down the hill—it would be difficult to imagine a less likely pair.'

Richard's smile broadened.

'Sammy is certainly an odd lady—they do say she is of uncertain gender—a hermaphrodite.'

'Really?'

'Yes—she usually dresses as a man but sometimes, on occasion as a woman. She shares a surname with Jim but no-one is quite certain what the relationship amounts to . . . . father-brother-husband; mother-son—who knows. I don't suppose it matters in the end. Are you thirsty—how about a coffee?'

As he had made his observation I found myself thinking about my neighbours on the Mount. It suddenly struck me that each of the residents was possessed of their own peculiarity—their own physical oddity. They all had some kind of deformity or another.

'Coffee would be very welcome thank-you . . . . but tell me, how is it that everyone living up there—save perhaps Kate and Duggie—they all appear to suffer,' I wasn't sure how to phrase it without appearing crude, '—they all seem to be crippled in some way?'

Richard smiled and nodded.

'I wondered how long it would take for you to notice. You're quite right—they all have a deformity of one kind or another. I can't speak for Kate but Duggie—her brother—has two toes missing on his left foot—see how he limps next time you meet.'

It was true—when I recollected Duggie he did favour his other foot. I had not noticed before. Richard went on to itemise the list.

'There's fat Bessie in the shop, an elephantine figure, gross in the extreme; her husband Gerald with his hunch-back; Jim the dwarf and Sammy the hermaphrodite; club-footed Malcolm—just skin and bone; Jim Brotherton the farmer missing a couple of fingers and Duggie missing toes—quite a collection eh?'

Put so baldly it was indeed quite a list—a list that only increased the curiosity value of its content. After a moment's silence Richard amplified his observations.

'Of course not all their deformities are simply physical. You may well discover that they each have other kinds of oddities too.'

He paused as if that was enough.

'Now don't go all enigmatic on me Richard. What on earth do you mean?'

He stood up smiling again.

'You're the writer Paul. I should have thought your instinct for research would have been tickled by now. Let's just say there's a lot going on in your little community even if so far you've been oblivious to most of it. Now I'll just get us that coffee. Throw a few more logs on that fire and I'll be as quick as I can.'

I was left sitting staring into the fire, trying to assess the degree of my ignorance. Finding a group of people with such a range of deformities was not in itself such a surprise. There could be hundreds of explanations—genetic or environmental . . . . But other oddities—behavioural—moral—psychological—even spiritual or cultural, that was a different proposition. According to society's inherited value system, morality—for example—is usually the anvil on which one's peers test the temper of one's personal iron: the heated test of acceptability. I searched my memory to see what I had missed.

The spectre of my own activities soon focused my attention—Kate and Duggie—and I—a very different sort of triangular involvement—was that what Richard had meant? Certainly one could assume that incest and a penchant for three in a bed could well be seen as moral deformities, no-one could argue with that. It was a view that only a few weeks ago I would have supported myself.

The guilt came back bringing more questions. Who had corrupted whom? Was I inherently weak in character? Were Duggie and Kate's motives other than what they seemed to be? In this context, how does one assess culpability? My personal devil continued to ask for definitions that I was not able or willing to provide. And what of James—where did he fit into this jig-saw. Could he have known about Kate and our situation? Does he know?

By the time the coffee appeared I was flushed by my confusion. The guilt that had been such an important part of my childhood gnawed again at my conscience. However, despite the quality of my understanding my real dilemma was that I could not bring myself to regret anything. In the more normal atmosphere of Richard's company recent events seemed all the more extraordinary—more like a dream than reality. I knew then that in seeking his company I had sought the voice of logic; a sense of normality. Unfortunately the relief had been short-lived. Richard had raised ghosts that would undoubtedly plague my conscience for some time to come. My apparent lack of perception also raised questions about my gullibility—I was once again the inexperienced schoolboy—the odd one out—the one being laughed at.

I badly needed to discover who was doing the laughing.

To make matters worse Richard refused to be drawn further on his earlier comments and soon after I excused myself with a sudden headache and left him. I drove back stopping briefly at the Post Office to buy cigarettes only to find a letter waiting for me. It was from James and it told me that he was on his way to pay me a visit. A surprise I could well have done without.

*

Reluctant to return to the cottage immediately, I lunched at the local pub, a down at heel place sporting only one bar and a snug. I found it an ill kempt place with none of the attractions one might normally associate with a country tavern. The seats in the snug where I was directed to wait for my meal were a patchwork of homespun repairs. The stuffing and occasionally the springs burst from cushions; the desultory decor stained walls brown proving it to be the haunt of generations of heavy smokers and other than one old man who sat reading a newspaper and nursing a pint the place was deserted.

The Landlord was surprised when I asked for a menu and instead recited a sad litany of local fare. Tripe and onions was beyond my preferred taste as was black pudding with mash so I played safe with sausage and chips. He did not seem concerned and shouted my order through to a back room. I took my cloudy pint of bitter to a corner seat, avoided the torn leatherette and the wire springs and sat to reread James's letter.

The phraseology was redolent of a style long since past for example him calling me, 'My dear Paul' and expressing the hope that my stay had proved propitious. It was nevertheless a nice letter, warm in tone despite its archaic manner. On that occasion I had no reason to question his motives and took his letter at face value. It was only later that I wondered why he made no mention of the celebrations anticipated by the people on the Mount and claimed his visit was a spur of the moment affair. The excuse he claimed was on account of him discovering a manuscript written by my mother that he felt sure I would want to read.

My meal arrived and I laid the letter aside. Two fat glutinous sausages protruded akimbo from a mound of creamy potato mash. My raised eyebrows drew the response from the Landlord who muttered that 'chips r' off'. The shiny brown fingers pointed accusingly from a quagmire still pooled in melted butter. I picked at one sausage sufficient only to allay the critical overview and accepted that my appetite had vanished. I regretted not asking for a sandwich. My performance must have been acceptable as my host took my thanks and my expression of satisfaction with just the trace of a smile and I was left to finish my beer. It was only then that I noticed the date on James's letter. Due to the vagaries of the Postal service it had been delayed and if my calculations were correct, he would be arriving that afternoon.

I rose immediately and went to pay my bill. The Landlord gave me my change and with a stage wink at his only other customer advised me that I could increase my appetite only if I took more exercise.

'Folk from yer big towns ride about in cars too much.'

I agreed but took some satisfaction nevertheless in rattling my car keys as I left.

Although I had half suspected that they may lay in wait for me, on my return journey there was no sign of Jim or Sammy. I decided that as a consequence they would have to walk back. The hill was just as deserted as it had been when i left. However, as I turned the final bend I could see a group of four or five people standing outside the cottage deep in conversation. Unable to access my usual parking spot I slowed to a crawl and stopped in front of them. Malcolm appeared to be the centre of everyone's attention facing Jim Brotherton and Gerald with Bessie in close attendance. As soon as I left the car the whole group turned to me. Someone commented, 'Here he is . . . ' and Malcolm limped in my direction his face was whiter and even more skeletal than usual.

'An' ave you passed a driving test?' he said.

He stopped directly in front of me pushing his face forward aggressively. Before I could answer the others crowded round, their faces tense with concern.

'Sorry?' I asked uncertain of his context.

''Cos if you 'ave—you still needs t' look where yer bloody goin.'

I frowned and shook my head.

'Sorry—but if you'd like to explain what you're talking about I'll make some attempt to answer you.'

The thin man stepped even closer and for a second I had the impression he was about to hit out at me. This time Bessie interrupted.

'Malcolm 'ere believes that you killed his dog . . . . ran over him in yer car. I've been arguing that yer much too careful a driver t' do such a thing.'

'S' th only vehicle that left' ere this mornin . . . . an' Rastus my old dog was layin . . . . just there.'

He turned and pointed to a spot in the road directly outside of the parking bay next to the cottage. At first the mention of my driving caused me to wonder if Jim and Sammy had reported our near accident. This new turn of events therefore took me completely by surprise. I felt my face flush. Secretly I supposed that the bump I felt when I reversed out that morning could have been the dog.

'What the devil was the dog doing lying there in front of a parking spot anyway?'

My question was greeted with derision.

'Sleepin—what the hell d' you think he was doin—he always sleeps there—everybody knows he sleeps there—till you comes along and runs him over.'

With the lack of a firm denial I could feel a sudden animosity even Bessie fell silent. They all stared at me.

'To be entirely honest Malcolm—I cannot say if it was me or not. I didn't know the dog slept there—and if I did run him down he didn't make a sound—well none that I heard.'

Gerald grunted.

'He wouldn't anyway—y' see he had no voice box—hasn't barked or whined fer years.'

Malcolm resumed his attack.

'So what are y' gonna do about it—that's what I'd like t' know?'

'Killin a man's dog is serious business.' Bessie said clearly convinced of my guilt.

The voices involved in this exchange had gradually risen in volume until they were almost shouting. So much so that before I could offer any kind of solution the door next to mine opened and Kate stood on the threshold drying her hands on a short apron.

'What on earth is going on out here—it sounds like a riot?'

Malcolm quickly stepped in.

'I'll tell yer what—yer fancy man 'ere has killed Rastus—ran him over in bloody cold blood an' left him t' die in the street—now what d' ave to say about that?'

Her mouth fell open and she turned to stare at me—they all turned to stare at me. I had to respond quickly.

'At this stage,' I said quietly deliberately lowering my voice, 'I don't think anyone can be certain that I was actually responsible—I'm not saying that I didn't do it but before you accuse someone you need to have evidence—proof that you're correct.'

This time Gerald answered asking that if it wasn't me who else it could have been. I wasn't sure if he was offering me a way out of the predicament or if he was setting a trap. I thought for a moment before replying.

'Well I'm not accusing anyone—please understand that but—I did here Jim Brotherton's tractor pass by before I left.'

'Hold on now—s' no good tryin t' pass th' blame onto me. Yes I passed by 'ere like I do every day—an' I'm sure I see old Rastus in his usual place—like he always is—an' he was fine when I passed.'

There was not doubt that he would be the one to be believed but I wasn't ready to give up then.

'There might be a way to settle this once and for all—let's examine the tyres on both vehicles. If poor old Rastus was run over there might be some evidence on the tyres.'

I could see Malcolm thinking about the proposal. He was deeply suspicious but in the end the idea appealed to him. Finally he said, 'Okay—let's 'ave a look at yer car first.'

I began to wish that I'd stayed on at Miles House.

Chapter Eleven

James brought two cases of red wine with him and if for no other reason this made him a welcome sight. Due to the frequency of my dinner parties my stock of alcohol had been seriously depleted. He also brought two bottles of single malt whisky, four of a reputable Champagne and a bottle of vintage Port. In my view we were therefore secure for some time to come: immured against the ravages of the weather as much as against the possibility of being isolated by the other residents of our little community. And up until James appeared isolation certainly seemed to be likely option that would top the agenda. Fortunately James's arrival coincided with the last act in our canine murder investigation. His appearance could not have been better timed.

Having taken my advice however reluctantly, the group led by Malcolm had just discovered traces of blood and tufts of golden hair in the back tyre treads of my rear wheels. As far as they were concerned that was evidence enough for their suspicions to be confirmed. Their accusations appeared to be proven. In fact Malcolm had already begun to advance on me with blood in his eye and a heavy walking stick in his fist just as James drew up. Given that it had been my suggestion to seek evidence by examining the tyres, it seemed that I had been hoist by my own 'Pirellis'.

To give him his due James realised that there was a situation and with a surprising turn of authority, he took charge immediately. He asked questions and listened carefully to the answers given. He even listened when with suitable venom Malcolm, as the self-appointed foreman of the jury pronounced a verdict of guilty.

'We can't be 'avin the likes of him, comin 'ere and runnin over our animals without so much as an apology—and then trying t' blame one of our own t' get himself off . . . No matter if he's a friend of yours or not'.

The others stood back exhibiting varying degrees of embarrassment in the face of which James was as cool as an ice cube.

'It seems to me,' he said quietly, 'that a verdict has been reached without the case for the defence having been properly heard.'

Malcolm's temper flared again.

'S' nothin more than we might expect—you takin his side . . . you've been gone too long James and we . . . '

Suddenly James was afire; he interrupted Malcolm in a loud voice.

'How dare you Sir!'

Malcolm visibly wilted.

'How dare you presume to make that kind of stupid remark—an entirely unwarranted accusation? Get a grip of yourself man. If you're not careful you could be in danger of losing more than your pet dog.' For a moment or two there was a complete silence. No-one moved and no-one spoke. It was manifestly clear that James had a prestige amongst these people far and above any he might have enjoyed elsewhere. It left me to wonder how this might have come about. James continued quietly.

'Now—if I may be permitted to continue.'

He turned to me.

'Paul—you suggested that Jim Brotherton's tractor may have killed the dog—inadvertently of course?'

I nodded in agreement. 'Inadvertently' was not a word I would have used but I made no comment.

'And has anyone seen fit to examine the wheels of the tractor?'

No one answered and as if to demonstrate his point James marched across to where the vehicle stood some twenty feet away. He looked around one side then the other and after a second or two he called the rest of us to join him. There were blood stains in the grooves of both front and rear tyres.

'What time were you up and about this morning Jim?'

'The farmer muttered something about being out by five o'clock. James nodded.

'Then it was still dark . . . and . . . ' He examined the tractor's controls in the cab. 'And just as I thought—the lights on this contraption don't work. You must have run over Rastus without ever seeing him—perfectly understandable as the stupid animal chose to sleep in the middle of the road . . . . and Paul must have reversed over him some hours later when he went out which is why only his rear tyres were bloodied. But—and this is important—by then the dog was already dead.'

If I had been found innocent of murder by a judge at the Old Bailey I could not have been more relieved. Malcolm was less satisfied. He glowered at me and then at James. Finally unable to control his frustration he spat on the ground in front of me and stormed off down the street. James put a hand on my shoulder as we stared after the thin man as he limped away.

Thankfully the others were remorseful about the mistake and their apologies followed in quick succession. In turn they shook my hand expressing their regrets. When it was Bessie's turn she kissed me on the cheek and whispered that she hadn't believed a word of it from the start. Kate just stood on the doorstep grinning. I felt exhausted.

It was a delight therefore when, after the others had left, James opened the boot of his car and the wine and sundry other bottles appeared—a compensation thoroughly earned. Dinner that evening was made easy by the fact of a pre-cooked chicken with all the trimmings that had accompanied the booze in the car boot. It was not until I was clearing away the dirty pots that I had time to consider the significance of James's performance. These people who lived on the Mount were not easy to persuade still less to control. The speed at which they had closed ranks and concluded their case against me was significant. God knows what the outcome may have been had not James turned up when he did. Certainly Malcolm had demonstrated an uncharacteristic capability for violence and who knows how the others might have reacted. By contrast James had shown amazing fortitude as well as foresight. His inclusion of the word 'inadvertently' when describing Jim Brotherton's role allowed him an escape clause and defused the anger. I wondered how he would have reacted if the tractor tyres had been found to be clean. Would there have been an escape route left open for me—fortunately it was a question I would not need to ask.

During both our previous meetings James had appeared to be a quiet and somewhat reserved person. His surprising assumption of control and his very convincing air of authority had quite shocked me. Small in stature with white hair and glasses James left an impression of a retired academic—more used to books than boxing gloves. I had perceived him wrongly as the ubiquitous face in the crowd—part of a silent majority—never as the face on the rostrum—still further proof of my faulted perceptions.

At James's invitation, Kate and Duggie joined us for our evening meal. After my qualms of conscience concerning our last evening together I was relieved to have James present. Not surprisingly the conversation revolved around the coming celebration the so-called 'party' I nevertheless found the talk something of a strain. Kate and Duggie were relaxed and appeared to be perfectly at ease, unaffected by the nuance and double meanings I saw in almost everything said.

Since infancy I have had a penchant for drawing an association between seminal events in my childhood and specific pieces of furniture. There was the chair on which I banged my head aged four years causing me to have two stitches; the three legged stool bought on the day I started school—the one that collapsed the first time she stood on it to reach a high shelf; the chest of drawers in my bedroom behind which I hid my first 'girlie' magazines. All these and more populate my memory of my early life. Not surprisingly then the dinner party was spoiled for me by my recollections of what had taken place on and about various pieces of furniture the previous night—on the couch; against the table; over the armchair and even in the fireplace. In trying to arrest the progress of theses associations I turned my thoughts again to James's high profile presence. The previously quiet man had become increasingly loud and increasingly overbearing hogging the focus of everyone's attention. It was an intriguing change of character and I was curious as to the origins of this transformation.

Despite James's claim to a long term friendship with my mother, I could remember little of the man. There were only two occasions when I thought he was dimly visible in my home, two vague and indistinct memories that may have been inspired or prompted by him mentioning the visits during our time together in London. My lack of recall was understandable because for most of that period I was seen simply as an insignificant appendage by my mother and her visitors.

Several times I heard Kate congratulate James on the way he had solved the riddle of Rastus's death. She made much of his apparent ability to cut through the prejudice that had biased local opinion. I thought she made too much of it—after all—all he had done was to take my suggestion to its logical conclusion. It was uncharacteristic of her to gush like she did. She seldom gave unwarranted praise and was not easily impressed—as a rule. It was a situation that reminded me of home visits by the parish priest when I was a child. These were usually week-end visits during which I was instructed to be on my best behaviour, not to argue or contradict and whenever possible to agree with what he said.

The most significant change however, was in Duggie's new found abstinence. He took a little wine with the meal—but sparingly and given his one glass of brandy after the pudding clearly set a new personal record for sobriety. As a consequence he played a much more lively part in the after-dinner conversation. I could hear him holding forth dredging up anecdotes from his various employments: mainly office stories. He seemed to glory in the apparent stupidity of those people representing management and inevitably included tit-bits of salacious gossip usually at the expense of a female member of staff. It was clear why he had not lasted too long in any of the jobs he described and I was glad to be washing the pots rather than being obliged to listen to his tawdry tales.

I was at pains to play the host and had cleared the crockery to the kitchen sink where I proceeded to wash up. The others had retired to the living room with their drinks and whilst no-one had offered to help I was glad to have a few minutes to myself if only to apply some better order to my thinking. Questions and queries surfaced like foam from the washing-up liquid. However, whereas the bubbles in the sink popped and disappeared, the intensity of my curiosity remained.

How could I have misread James to such a degree? Why was he held in such high regard—almost in awe in this strange and remote place? And why had he been so keen to loan me his little cottage? I recalled his recent outburst and the threat implicit in his comment to Malcolm—'you could lose more than your dog' It was not the exchange of equals—much more like the thing a master might say to a minion—a servant or an underling—an attitude more typical of a seventeenth century scene. Then there was the business of my mother's manuscript.

What the hell was he doing with a document belonging to her—and why had he not mentioned it previously? The man was fast becoming an enigma. I struggled to find explanations at least sufficient to restore a balance.

I am aware that often I tend towards romantic interpretations of events and that such a bias can sometimes distort what is actually mundane, elevating its importance to a level of unwarranted significance. Throughout my life I have been accused of exercising an over active imagination one my mentors claimed that verged on paranoia.

The sound of laughter drew me back just as I finished in the kitchen. Perhaps I was being silly after all I told myself. Quickly I dried my hands and went in to join my guests. As I entered the sitting room James was just finishing an explanation of some historical circumstance. I caught him mid-sentence.

'Because of the pogroms really—they just upped and left . . . . took their carts, their animals and their families and trekked off across Europe. It was a reaction with a tradition of course, one that can be traced back to Ancient Egypt. There are many who believe that the Romany people were in fact Egyptians . . . '

I pored myself a drink and perched on the arm of the settee next to Kate. I had heard such fantastical stories before.

'I think you'll find that the Egyptian story is just that—a story. There is evidence from a number of different authorities—some specialising in linguistics—that agree the first Gypsies were Indo-Aryan peoples.'

Duggie asked, 'So they came from India?'

'Yes, 'I said, 'and although there is some difference of opinion about precisely where they originated in the sub-continent, there is a substantial consensus for the general location.'

James interrupted to explain that they had been discussing the ancestors of the people who now lived on the Mount.

'Legend would have it that they were actually from Romany stock.... apparently arriving here in the middle of the Sixteenth century. They were looking for somewhere to put down roots, to raise their families and to earn an honest living.'

My interest was aroused.

'And where did they actually come from?'

He smiled as though he knew a secret.

'Well of course that depends on who you talk to and who you believe. I know that at least some came from Armenia ....'

I couldn't resist and stopped him short.

'That would tie in with the research findings exactly. It is reckoned that there are three variations of dialect amongst Romany people: Asiatic, European and Armenian. Apparently it is only the Asiatic that has preserved the treatment of the original voiced aspirates of Sanskrit ...'

Kate laughed.

'Gosh this is getting to be heady stuff. I hope I'm not the only one who has any idea what the hell you are on about.'

'Sorry—I wasn't trying to show off—it's just that the sound and spelling of words can give a clue to the origins of the people using them. It's an area in which I'm especially interested. I wonder ...' I turned again to James. 'Do any of the local residents still have the Romany language?'

He shook his head.

'No it was lost generations ago. Some still have a slight 'twang' but it's mixed with an Irish brogue. By the time the Mount was settled, the blood-line had been well and truly mixed with the Irish. The language has gone but some of the beliefs and practises remain.'

I felt sure that his last statement was meant to be provocative so I deliberately resisted the temptation to ask about it. I was not in the mood to be manipulated, instead I redirected the conversation.

'James you say in your letter that you have a manuscript belonging to my mother—do you have it with you?

He paused before answering, patently unready to discuss the manuscript. After a moment or two he smiled and looked my straight in the eye. This time when he spoke it was with obvious sincerity.

'Ah yes the manuscript. I finished reading it this week. We must have a long discussion about it Paul. Your Mum was a very bright lady. It's in my case at the moment. I'll dig through and get it for you tomorrow—perhaps we can discuss it then?

I had no clear idea where the lie occurred in his statement, only that he had lied. His sincerity was a sham, as disingenuous as a second-hand car salesman. His overly conscious eye contact was a subterfuge and the level and timbre of his voice almost equalled that of a TV advertisement. I was annoyed.

'Fine—anytime will suit me—but tell me how you came to have the thing in the first place?'

Entering into the spirit of the play-acting ethos, I made my question hard-edged with just a hint of sarcasm.

'She must have left it in my flat in Town. She often visited me there—whenever she came up . . . . it was on a bedside table in the spare room. My cleaning lady found it—stuck it on my desk along with a bundle of other papers. You know how it is . . . . '

I continued quickly deliberately not giving him time to mobilise his thoughts.

'You must have only just found it . . . . literally in the last couple of weeks?'

'Actually—now I think about it—I believe that the first time I saw it was a week or so before she died. I shoved it in a brief-case intending to return it but events overtook me.'

I pounced, 'So having forgotten about it—I presume that was the reason it wasn't given to the lawyers—as part of her estate?'

The barb struck home witnessed by his deepening complexion. He was embarrassed and I almost felt sorry. Then he laughed a forced half strangulated laugh.

Neat,' he said, 'you are certainly your mother's son. She could always catch me out. I know it's a hollow excuse but the fact is I simply forgot about it. As soon as we get back to London I will make sure that her solicitors are made aware of it.'

He paused and then added, 'Of course it isn't as if it is going to be a best seller. In fact I doubt her publishers will have any interest in it.'

'Fair enough—but can you tell me what the subject is—what did she write about?'

'I haven't read it too carefully but she'd done some research on immigrants to the UK and made her findings into a book—sort of.'

Duggie commented that it sounded a pretty boring subject and Kate admonished him for his lack of interest. James took the cue and endorsed Duggie's sentiment.

'I must confess it wasn't exactly riveting.'

His confidence returned and he emptied his glass in a way that seemed to indicate that the subject was closed. Kate was on her feet immediately dutifully asking if anyone would like a refill. She went over to the dresser to pour the drinks and as she was so engaged I renewed the assault.

'I would have thought that as the community here are all descendents of immigrants that you might have found the subject quite interesting.... I don't suppose the research was about Romany people—was it?'

Again my adopted tone was innocence itself and again James looked flushed and embarrassed.

'As a matter fact—yes that's exactly what the book is about.'

He stopped short but as I did not respond immediately his pause was limited. My facial expression made it clear that I expected more and eventually he continued.

'Most of it was fairly well established stuff . . . . as you said yourself Paul . . . . they migrated from India some arriving in Persia by 1000AD where they split into two groups. One of them travelling south and west through Africa the other going north through Europe and the Balkans—she claimed that they didn't reach Britain until the 16thCentury.'

'About the time our predecessors arrived?' Kate stated seeking confirmation.

James nodded.

'It must have been hard,' he added, 'They were notoriously unpopular. There was a decree issued stating that anyone who consorted with Gypsies could be considered felons and could suffer death and loss of lands without ever appearing before a jury.'

I added that as late as 1819 anyone who wandered the land could be imprisoned and whipped if they were dressed in the manner of the 'Egyptians'. 'The only place they were given rights was in Scotland. James the Fifth published a decree giving them all manner of privileges. On that account I'm surprised more didn't move to the north.'

'Perhaps our relatives were heading in that direction when they settled here.' Kate offered.

It was obvious that by now both Kate and Duggie were intrigued by the tale contained in the manuscript. They were attentive to everything James said however; he was still a little uncomfortable. A condition that grew worse when Kate said she would also like to read the manuscript herself. Knowing how it would add to his discomfort, I could not resist joking that after publication my mother's book might yet prove to be a best-seller. Despite this I still had no real clue concerning his reticence. If he had possession of such a manuscript and had told me of its existence then clearly he must have known I would want to see it—so why the prevarication? I couldn't help but conclude that the issue of timing had to be a factor. Although when that time might be or why such an advantage might accrue because of it remained a mystery.

After the discussion about my mother's research the evening passed more harmoniously. James settled to tell tales, some of them outrageous exaggerations about the life of Gypsies. He claimed that in folklore it had been a Gypsy who had stolen the fourth nail at Christ's crucifixion. A fact they claimed that had so reduced his suffering that ever since he had applauded and approved of their status as thieves. He also said that although Gypsies were well known to steal, they never stole from anyone poorer than themselves. He described in some detail the workings of the 'Romano Kris' the Gypsy court telling us that the worst punishment they could exercise was banishment from the clan.

It became increasingly obvious that James's association with Gypsy culture had been earned through first-hand experience. His knowledge and insights were supported by far too much detail ever to have been gained simply through reading. I slowly began to accept the fact that James himself had sprung from Romany stock a fact that he admitted a few minutes later. At some point much later when the effect of the quantity of alcohol he had imbibed began to show, he described his maternal grandfather's funeral.

'It was always the custom that real Gypsies should be born in the open air and die in the open air. It was also a tradition that after a leader or headman passed away his possessions—even his animals—should be burned. When Dada died we were camping in Norfolk and families came from as far away Wales and Cornwall for the funeral. He had been sick for months and then one day he had my father and three brothers carry him outside and lay him on the grass. My father said that he must know that he was dying and sure enough an hour later the old man gave in.'

It was clear from his reaction that these were still traumatic memories for James and when he paused his eyes were unashamedly moist. Whilst he drained his glass the rest of us sat in silence and waited and after a small sigh he took up the story again.

'My family were strong on tradition and we built a bonfire—a bonfire as big as a house—everything that belonged to Dada was burned. The funeral celebrations carried on for four days and there must have been in excess of six hundred guests. He was well thought of—the last of an old breed. He used to say he could trace his roots all the way back to Faa.'

Duggie was the one to ask the obvious question making James smile.

'Once upon a time young men like you would be familiar with our history. It would have been taught to you from infancy by word of mouth in the oral tradition of our ancestors. Faa was a famous Romany who was transported to Virginia from Scotland in 1715. Accused of stealing a sheep by a Scottish farmer, he was packed off to America with his family—one of the first Gypsies to land in the new world. The story goes that he was the first Romany Chieftain in that country.'

The conversation and especially James's tales spent the evening quickly. The story of his grandfather ended it on a sombre note and Kate and Duggie rose to leave shortly afterwards. At the door Kate whispered to me that it was probably better if we restrained our love-making during James's visit. It was the first opportunity we'd had to speak about this and I was not surprised at her suggestion. There was only one main bedroom in the cottage and the box-room was filled with packing cases consequently our coupling would have been difficult to achieve anyway. I was reluctant to lose her company but relieved that I did not have to make special sleeping arrangements to avoid James.

By the same token the previous evening had left me uncertain as to my feelings and a break with our recent habit would allow me time to sort out my intentions.

When I returned to the sitting room James had just thrown another log on the fire. A sure sign he was not yet ready for bed.

'So,' he smiled stretching himself out in the chair, 'how is life in the world of publishing—have you finished the book?'

'Almost.' I lied.

'Happy with it?'

'So-so—it's always hard to judge until its finished—and even then sometimes . . . . well you can't always tell'

'Did I detect a certain familiarity between you and the lovely Kate?'

'As a matter of fact you may well have done. We have become rather friendly of late.' I laughed half out of embarrassment, 'She's certainly given me much to think about.'

He sat watching me attentively and then asked, 'Well—don't stop there—go on.'

I just laughed again and shook my head.

'Perhaps when I know you a bit better!'

Suddenly he sat forward leaning his elbows on his knees and becoming more intense.

'About the manuscript Paul—I'm sorry if I was evasive—just didn't want to say too much in company—before we'd had a chance to talk.'

I couldn't help but raise an eyebrow.

'As you've known Kate and Duggie far longer than you've known me I find that a little strange.'

'Not true . . . . I've known you young man far longer than you realise. I knew your dear mother from her earliest days at university and I've known you from the time you were born.'

I was surprised and determined not to let his remark pass without examining it. I poured myself another drink but James shook his head when I offered the same to him. He watched me intently as I sat on the settee opposite.

'I think it is about time you told me the whole truth James. As of today you appear to be a man of many contradictions—certainly not the same man I met at the funeral—or in London. Suddenly you're transformed from the sober academic into . . . . into a Gypsy Chieftain and a man with amazing authority in this community. Apparently you lead a group of characters that could easily spring from a fairy tale by the Brothers Grimm. You turn up a lost manuscript by my mother—coincidentally one about the great Gypsy immigration then you imply that you knew her better than I did myself. I think an explanation is due don't you?'

As I spoke his smile got bigger, his eyes twinkled and by the end of my outburst he was chuckling quietly to himself.

'All true—perfectly true. I can't deny any of it but first I have two confessions to make—and I promise they will begin to throw some light on the things you ask about. I only hope we can remain friends afterwards . . . . perhaps I will have that drink you offered after all.'

I was intrigued. I got up and poured him a generous drink. I found his use of the word 'confessions' a curious choice and my curiosity was aroused. I could hardly wait for him to continue. He sipped his drink first and then resumed his statement.

'First of all—I have to admit that the notion of inviting you to stay at this cottage was decided long before we met at the funeral. I had not seen you for such a long time—twenty years or more—and I wanted to get to know you again—your book was just an excuse.'

'But why on earth . . . '

'Hold on Paul let me tell you in my own way. I promise this time I shan't hold anything back. Your mother and I first met in our late teens.

She was a handsome woman in middle age as you know but in her youth she was a real beauty—heads turned wherever she went. To cut a long story short—we fell in love. It was the real thing but because we came from such different worlds marriage was out of the question—a joint decision. She travelled with me for the whole of one idyllic year—mainly through the summer. In the winter she stayed here at the cottage with me but come the spring she left.'

He paused for a moment or two staring into the middle distance.

'I didn't see her again for seven years, during which time I had become respectable, educated, wealthy and by then she was involved with another man. Her new friend was a work colleague but after a while we fell back into our old relationship—we couldn't help ourselves. The man—the one she told you was your father went off to the USA leaving your mother. She was pregnant. No one could blame him under the circumstances—you see the child was mine. I know this is bound to come as a shock to you Paul but the fact is—I am your father.'

The glass slipped from my grasp and whisky splashed across my shoes.

Chapter Twelve

I hardly felt the first blow. I was suddenly surprised to find myself on my knees. The sound of a wholesome whack on my legs seemed to come afterwards. Instinctively I half turned raising my arm to protect my head—which was just as well. The heavy stick cracked down again firing the nerves in my elbow as it chipped the humerus. It was a blow that would surely have left me senseless had it landed on my skull. I heard myself yell out—more in panic than in pain but the shock shot up into my shoulder and my hand went numb. My voice was as the sound of a frightened animal.

His voice answered in a venomous whisper.

'You bastard—a Kiri like you—before I'm done I'll break yer fuckin head.'

My attacker grunted with the effort and the swish of the stick through the air sounded a sinister warning. I fell forward on my other arm and the blow this time caught me on my back.

I was never much of a fighting man and although I witnessed numerous confrontations during my school days, by comparison these were only amateur. I always managed to evade physical contests. The power of the spoken word had always served me well and despite the shame that occasionally accompanied my efforts at avoidance; the success of my stratagem helped me retain my teeth intact and my bones unbroken. However I had never before been offered violence without some warning. In pain I rolled over onto my back and for the first time I was bale to identify my attacker. It was Malcolm.

Having been unable to sleep I had left the cottage at dawn to take a walk. I had sat up until the early hours talking with James. His confession had been a shock, a trauma that filled me with unaccountable emptiness; a disappointment at my mother's long silence. I needed the sharpness of the cold air to clear my thinking. The contrast afforded by different environments was often a source of comfort to me. Walking along the Thames Embankment or through the deserted streets of Soho worked when I was in London. In the Yorkshire Mountains that same variety was extended due to the extreme difference in temperature. It had snowed again during the night and the white cold cleanliness was attractive. In my preoccupation with my personal problems I had not noticed if anyone else was about. In truth I had not expected to find anyone else at that time of day. I had only managed a dozen or more steps before I was assaulted.

Malcolm raised the walking stick again and I found myself shouting at him.

'Stop—just stop it you bloody fool . . . . '

Surprisingly my effort seemed to have some effect. He paused and stared down at me, the stick still raised above his head, his eyes needle-points of fury. His voice was cool and remote.

'Yer a stinking low-life . . . . a miserable insect . . . an' whatever yer mate James says I know t' was you killed my dog. So I'm gonna beat you . . . leave you broken in the road—see how you likes it.'

I could do little to avoid him. The stick came down again catching me across the shoulder, and again across my torso. It was a calculated methodical rhythm making my senses swim. The pain was intense and I fell back defenceless, convinced he was about to kill me.

In the distance someone called out.

'Stop . . . no more Malcolm . . . . stop.'

The voice was far away. He stopped and looked past me up the street. There was the sound of shuffling footsteps and the voice came again –this time it was closer.

'Malcolm Boswell you're a damned fool . . . how dare you . . . '

It was Bessie. She arrived out of breath, panting with the effort of shifting her considerable bulk at speed. I found myself staring at her ankles and her carpet slippers.

'You madman what d' you think yer doing? Are you alright Paul?'

They both stared down at me and I tried to grin. By then the pain had spread throughout my body like wall to wall toothache. I was light-headed and my smile was more like a grimace.

'Just—just get me home—please.'

At that point I must have fainted because although I remember a muddle of voices, some raised in anger, I only became fully conscious again once I was laid on the settee in my living room. The relief I felt at my rescue almost reduced me to tears. I had never before felt quite so helpless. I had been convinced that Malcolm could—would—cripple me, if not kill me at his leisure.

A cool compress was laid on my forehead and Kate's voice whispered above me.

'I think we'd better get him undressed. It's impossible to gauge the damage whilst he has his clothes on.'

I opened my eyes to find the tiny room full of people. James knelt beside me loosening my collar; Kate stood at my head next to Duggie who was still in his dressing gown and Sammy crowded next to Bessie in the doorway.

'The bloody maniac could have killed him.' James muttered.

'I think he did.' I replied trying to put on a brave face.

Sammy laughed, 'Naw else you'd look better' n you do now.'

The humour relieved the tension and seeing that I was conscious everyone wanted to know how I felt. Given the circumstances, it would have been impossible to describe my feelings accurately. The feeling was slowly returning to my arm, a torment of pins and needles that competed for my attention with the cramps that gripped my legs and my shoulders. My trousers and sleeves were still damp from the snow and my overcoat had twisted round me, a splint for my fractured body. I felt very sorry for myself.

Kate quickly took charge and ushered most of the audience from the room. I could hear her promising that she would let them know the extent of my injuries once an examination had taken place. Duggie brought me a cup of hot sweet tea and as I sipped it, Kate attempted to get me out of my clothing. Without any doubt it was one of the most painful experiences of my life.

Some time later there was a consensus that although I would be badly bruised, miraculously nothing appeared to be broken. By then I was sitting in my underpants with a blanket round my shoulders in front of the fire—this time sipping a large brandy.

'Clearly the overcoat helped,' James said, 'if you'd been in shirt-sleeves I believe the arm would have been shattered, probably the collar-bone as well.'

'He should still be X-rayed.' Kate observed.

Filled with brandy and pain-killers by then I'd had time to digest what had taken place. Malcolm had not been convinced of my innocence and still blamed me for the death of his dog. According to Bessie his animosity had been emphasised by drink.

'Stank like a brewery.' She said.

'I think a visit to the nearest Police Station would aid my recovery rather quicker than a long wait in some emergency ward.' I answered.

At this the others all fell silent and when I looked up they were all staring at me. Eventually Duggie spoke.

'I think you'll find that—up here we don't use the constabulary Paul . . . . I mean . . . well we have a very different recourse . . . sort of a community response.'

I couldn't believe my ears.

'Well that's fine for you—up here—but as far as I'm concerned that man is a homicidal maniac and the sooner he is behind bars the better.'

I was suddenly furious.

'I mean—don't do me no favours—but what happens next time. What if I'd been someone else, someone without a thick overcoat? What if he's attacked Kate; crippled her in the street. I suppose you lot would have held a tribal convention and confined him to his room for a week . . . . well fuck that for a game of conkers. Malcolm is going to prison.'

My vehemence surprised everyone—myself included. I couldn't remember the last time I'd used language like that but at that moment it poured out like bile. The fact that they could imagine me being prepared to let their domestic, homespun group of amateur lawyers deal with such a vicious attack was beyond belief. I was cold with anger.

'Look—I thank you all for your kindness—for all you've done for me but right now I think I'd like to be quiet for a bit—on my own—if you don't mind.'

They said nothing. All three of them went without a word and I was left to my own devices. I finished the brandy and pulled the blanket tighter still around my shoulders. A blue bruise had spread from my shoulder onto my chest and over my neck. My left arm was almost entirely black and blue, so much so that it was impossible to move the fingers on that hand without the most terrible discomfort. As I could not twist round it was impossible to see if the backs of my legs were also showing similar signs of damage. Struggling to my feet I stood with my back to the fire and thought about the last twenty-four hours. Whoever said that life was dull in the country was badly mistaken. Similarly those who imagined that moving to the countryside equated with getting away from tension and distraction were also wrong. Without my conscious help my thoughts turned to James—my father—or so he claimed.

His announcement the previous evening had taken me completely by surprise. Not surprisingly I had questioned him—a cross-examination as if her were the star witness in a murder trial. He was word perfect. The detail he was able to provide about my mother's life left me convinced at least of their close relationship. I was still surprised that none of her other friends were aware of it—or perhaps some of them were. Maybe I was the only one not to know. I recalled my uncle being dismissive of James after the funeral. Thinking about the pros and cons of the situation made me annoyed all over again with my departed mother. How could she not tell me? Her pretence over all those years that my father had absconded to America was shameful. Did she think I would have been ashamed of her? Or was it that she thought I'd be ashamed of him due to his Gypsy blood? How could she think I'd think any the less of her?

Eventually James admitted that my mother's research had focused almost entirely on the community living on the Mount. After her stay during that long cold winter she had spent considerable time tracing the path of their immigration; their conflict with the St. John Smith family and their ultimate settlement. James had been entrusted with the results of her research long before her death. He told me that on the grounds of sensitivity he thought that the manuscript should remain as private as possible. He admitted though that after I'd read it such a decision would be mine alone. The document in question now lay on the table pregnant with the possibility of its consequences. After James had gone to bed I had started to read it but with the alcohol and the trauma I'd experienced with James's announcement, a proper appreciation was impossible.

James had been prepared to say little about his role amongst the residents of the Mount. It was a reservation he claimed that was justifiable until he knew more about my intentions regarding the manuscript. Most of the other information was superficial. He did say that if I were to attend their annual celebration then I would discover for myself more of what their culture signified. He also said that he had a relationship with Richard Smith but other than admitting it was of a business type he would n't amplify or explain further. Privately I determined that the next time I was in Richard's company I would seek an answer from him.

I put another log on the fire and tried to stretch to relieve the constraint in my muscles. It was excruciating. I wandered into the kitchen seeking more pain-killers when there was a knock at the door. James must have left it off the latch because almost immediately the door opened and Bessie came in followed by Gerald.

''Ello love,' she said cheerily, 'and how are y' feelin now?'

'I think I might live.'

She grinned.

'Gerry an me 'ave just comes by t' bring you something fer the pain.'

The little man nodded his agreement. He swung a small knapsack from his shoulder and with his usual lop-sided gait went over to the table and opened the bag.

'Now if you'll just sit y' self down 'ere in the chair we'll 'ave you as right as rain before you know it.'

As she spoke she indicated on of the dining chairs and dutifully I followed her instruction and sat in it. I could not help but wince as she fussed over me, pulling back the blanket and laying a cold hand on my bruised neck. Meanwhile I saw Gerald remove a small tin from his bag; he loosened the top and stood the open container next to where his wife stood. Bessie picked up the tin, peered inside and then gave me one of those smiles. It was a smile that told me what was about to happen would not meet with my wholehearted approval; the kind the dentist might give before he turns on the drill.

'Paul,' she intoned, 'I know you are used to doctors using drugs and technical cures but y' must trust me. My remedies are at least as effective—probably more so—alright?'

I gave a qualified nod.

'Right then—I'll tell you what we are goin t' do. Now that the bruises are appearing we can see where you've been hurt. Bruises are just a collection of bad blood, so the first thing we'll do is get rid of it.'

I started to protest but she 'hushed' me and made me sit still facing the fire. Out of the corner of my eye I saw her take something from the tin and place it gently on my shoulder. It was cold and damp but not uncomfortable. She did this several times but it was not until she was treating my elbow that I saw the nature of the treatment. She was putting leeches on me.

My horror must have been self-apparent because as soon as I became tense, she laid a hand on my neck and whispered to me.

'I know my lovely, I know it's not a nice sight—but believe me Paul it works. Just give it a few minutes and you'll see. These little fellers will take away all the badness and then we can concentrate on treating the deeper injuries.'

Her hand—now warm combined with her soothing tone to calm my nerves and my feeling of revulsion and I tried to relax. 'What the hell' I thought, on occasion I've paid to go to holistic doctors so-called, and some of their remedies were enough to frighten farm animals.

In all Bessie and Gerald stayed with me for just over an hour. As she'd promised the leeches did remove much of the bruising and through the careful application of various balms and ointments afterwards my flexibility improved. She bound warm poultices on my injured parts and the pain diminished considerably—I was already feeling much better.

'You are just magic Bessie.' I told her, 'No small wonder that Gerald is such a happy man. You are a sound businesswoman; brilliant housewife and now I find you are a nurse as well. How will I ever repay you?'

The question was meant to be rhetorical but she took it literally. By then she was putting away her medicines and fastening the buckles on Gerald's knapsack but my question stopped her.

'If you feel you want to repay me . . . . there is something you could do . . . . that is if you're willing?'

'Yes?' I asked tentatively.

You could be a little more patient with us here on the Mount. Perhaps you could find it in yer heart to . . . . to forgive that fool who attacked you.'

The protest was hardly on my lips when she interrupted.

'Yes—I know, I do indeed know. It's hard for you t' understand—despite yer blood yer still much of an outsider—and outsiders always find our ways hard t' understand sometimes. But . . . but if y' leave us to punish the fool—in our own way . . . . then you could consider me well paid fer helping you. I promise you Paul, Malcolm will be dealt with harshly and . . . if you've the stomach for it—you can watch when he is.'

She made me laugh. Her request for this kind of payment was it seemed cultured from a profound understanding of human nature. How could I refuse—we finally sealed the deal with a large measure of Scotch whisky. As Gerald poured the drinks I asked her about a query I'd had since the attack.

'Tell me Bessie what does the word Kiri mean? Malcolm called me a Kiri when he was attacking me.'

She laughed, 'It's a Romany word—meaning insect. I'm afraid Malcolm doesn't have a high regard for you—to use it like that is an insult.'

I raised my glass to her, 'Well here's to insects.'

As we were making a second round of drinks some minutes later, James returned with Kate.

**

It was two days before I was sufficiently recovered to make the walk up to Bessie's shop. During the period of my convalescence Bessie had visited me three times bringing me small gifts of foodstuffs. The things she brought she said would be things I missed through not being in London. It was impossible to estimate her view of the capital but, given the things she brought for me, she obviously imagined my having a Baroque lifestyle in exotic surroundings. I could not remember the last time I feasted on pickled walnuts or chocolate covered honey-bees and I'd not missed the tinned snails in white wine at all. James thought it was a huge joke but cautioned me not to make too much fun of her.

'She's a hard heart to win over Paul—so make the most of your popularity.'

I was certainly amused but equally convinced of her sincerity and I had no intention of letting her see a negative response to her generosity. The last time she called she said as soon as I was able I should visit her shop to receive an extra special present. A promise made with a twinkle in her eye. In return I told that she would be the first person I would call on as soon as I was fit enough to walk. I also said that she shouldn't waste her hard earned money on presents for me. Her reply was typical.

'I've become fond of you young Paul 'an we round 'ere likes the way you've conducted yourself . . . 'an we're glad y' came. So let's hear no more about wastin money. Anyway this present cost very little—but it means quite a lot—and we know yer gonna like it.'

I asked James if he knew what she had in store for me but even if he did he wasn't prepared to spoil the surprise and claimed ignorance.

Despite his recent admission James and I were still somewhat wary of one another. I'd not yet had the inclination to read mother's manuscript so I was unable to declare my intentions in that regard. Even knowing that this was a requirement to gain his full confidence, I still procrastinated. He took this in good part but he was, I felt sure, rather reserved on account of it. For a host of reasons I still found it impossible to accept that he was one of my parents. Consequently we agreed simply to get to know one another better and let nature take its course. We spent a considerable amount of time together during which he continued to ensure my comfort as my injuries healed but our friendship was nevertheless limited. Needless to say Kate had been a regular visitor. Unfortunately partly through James's presence and because of my aches and pains, we had not been able to engage in the love-making we had practised so feverishly before the attack. I had put all the most uncomfortable images relating to the night of our threesome out of my mind. Now when she was with me my imagination was instead full of those reminiscences of our time alone together. If, as they say, absence makes the heart grow fonder, deprivation certainly causes one to focus exclusively on that which one has lost. In one sense Kate's visits made my frustrations worse. She was able to be affectionate but within the limits of polite good manners. She was with me but not able to be with me. I wanted her and convinced myself that I needed her and by the time the week ended, I even began to believe I might be in love with her.

Perhaps frustration caused my recovery to hasten. Perhaps the rate at which the body mends is governed by the strength of its motivation to be mended. I do not know. However, I do know that after two days of pain and irritation, I woke one morning convinced that I was well enough to get dressed and get out of bed: determined to get back to normal.

My writing had lain untouched for days and I'd not been in touch with my agent for weeks. Finally my head felt cleared and my perspective restored. I dressed and shaved; made coffee and toast and even took James a breakfast tray and ignoring his objections and protests I put on my boots and my overcoat and left the cottage. The sun was up glinting on the hardening snow but I was glad to be outside in the fresh morning air. I walked along the street to Bessie's shop.

I was grateful to Bessie and Gerald for all the care and attention they had lavished on me during my stay in bed. Various others had been kind and sympathetic but Bessie always impressed me with the practical concentration of her efforts on my behalf. It was almost as though she felt responsible for me.

As I reached the door it opened and Sammy stood in the threshold.

'Well,' she said to no-on in particular, 'an' who's up and about then . . . ' an I knows who's gonna be pleased t' see him. Come in—come in.'

She stepped back almost stepping on little Jim in the process. He was half hidden in the voluminous folds of her overcoat. When he saw me he grinned showing a line of bad teeth.

'It's our driver.' He called out. 'And lookin like he needs a holiday—let him in Sammy.'

In the process of then moving backwards together the entrance became an area full of confusion, filled with limbs, bags of shopping, scarves and woolly clothes.

Behind them standing at the counter was the other Jim—Jim Brotherton my attacker. He was clearly in the midst of purchasing a bagful of groceries and smiled at something Bessie had said. The commotion at the door caused him to turn and when he saw me his expression changed. At first his was a look of contempt but almost immediately it changed and he smiled sheepishly.

'Glad t' sees you about.'

I squeezed past Sammy and little Jim as their continuous chatter echoed in the confined space. The door closed and when I turned to the counter top Jim Brotherton stuck out a hand.

'Sorry about all that bother with Malcolm . . . . and all the trouble it caused. Hope you're feelin a bit better . . . thank God he didn't kill you.'

Bessie beamed her approval and looked genuinely pleased. I shook his hand and muttered that he should forget all about it.

'S' nice t' see folk gettin on together despite their troubles.' Bessie said, 'you look so much better Paul . . . fer a while you had us quite worried.'

The farmer nodded enthusiastically and Bessie rang the till and handed him his change.

'That's two pounds forty-seven and thank-you fer shopping with us.'

I noticed a bandage on his hand as he held it out. Guessing that working with his hands must be a continuous danger I assumed he'd had a minor accident at work. He grinned at me again, pocketed his change and left the shop.

'Now,' Bessie said breathlessly, 'at last—I'll just get that husband of mine.'

She turned and made one of shouts at the door to the passage.

'Gerald . . . . Gerry my love—Paul's here!'

His distant response caused her to smile.

'He's on his way . . . . made me promise to call him if you came by . . . wants to be 'ere when I give you our little gift.'

Really Bessie—it should be me buying gifts for you. You've been so kind—don't know how I would have managed without your special medicines—and the blessed leeches.'

I shuddered at the memory and she laughed—pleased at the sentiment. A moment later Gerald appeared his face was hardly visible over the counter-top display. He smiled when he saw me.

'Good to see you Paul—glad you must be feelin better.' He then turned to his wife and asked, 'Have you got it?'

Bessie nodded and reached under the counter. She produced a small package, a thin box about the size of a cigar wrapped and tied with a fancy cord. When she handed it to me she made her short speech with exaggerated care, clearly well rehearsed.

'Me and Gerald . . . . and the other residents 'ere on the Mount would like you to accept this token—as an apology fer the torment you suffered and as an apology fer the treatment you had. Take it as a sign that your patience in trusting our sense of justice has been rewarded . . . there.'

I took the box nodding my appreciation.

'Thank you both—as I said before after all the attention and care you both gave me—it's really me who should be rewarding you . . . . and if my outburst after the attack upset you please accept my sincere apologies.'

They stood there expectantly as I unpeeled the wrapping paper from round the little box. The lid was tight and it took me a moment or two to prise it free. When I finally looked inside I was horrified. The bile rose in my throat and it was all I could do to stop myself from vomiting. In the box, mounted on a bed of cotton-wool I found a neatly severed index finger. I was completely lost for words.

'Malcolm's finger—it was the agreed punishment fer what he did t' you. He'll remember it fer the rest of his life.'

Gerald joined in, 'Our way of satisfying the need fer justice. His was the more serious crime so it cost him a whole finger—Jim Brotherton donated one joint of a finger fer killing the dog.'

Chapter Thirteen

The mystery of the missing digits—the missing fingers and toes had been explained at last. It was an in-house solution to crime and punishment. It was certainly original in the modern context. However, it was hardly commensurate with society's view of penal reform let alone the Christian ethic of forgiveness. I found myself with very mixed feelings and wondered if an assault charge and a Police caution might not have been preferable to the victim. On the other hand another side of me relished the notion of whatever pain that was inflicted on Malcolm.

A little while later I left the shop with the box in my pocket. I was still so revolted by the thing that I considered throwing it away at the first opportunity. I was conscious however the Bessie's feelings would certainly be offended should she ever find out what I did. I felt a regard for the big shopkeeper but given her recent actions it was one tinged with new prudence. The demonstration of the treatment of those who transgressed was enough to inspire a new assessment of my new friends. Even given the agreement of the whole community, punitive mutilation was the most extreme example of primitive behaviour so far exhibited. I was to discover later that even Malcolm himself agreed the treatment in preference it was said to a report going to the local law-keepers followed by court appearances. It seemed that Gerald, acting as the local executioner had removed the finger in Bessie's kitchen with one of her steak knives. He told me himself that he was charged with the duty of carrying out all mutilations in the community. He did the chopping and his wife offered first aid afterwards. Gerald did add that the only time Bessie would wield the knife was at very special ceremonies when a new Headman was appointed for example. I did not ask for further clarification on this point.

It took me considerable time to accommodate the significance of their behaviour. Despite my outburst after the attack when I demanded justice, in the calm of my more usual demeanour, I liked to consider myself a liberal humanist. The notion of mutilation as a form of institutionalised punishment was therefore abhorrent to me.

After leaving the shop I went for the walk I'd promised myself originally. I took myself up the hill and across the fields. I ploughed through increasingly thick layers of boot-high snow eventually to a small wood that stood atop a nearby peak. At the summit my breath came in visible gasps but the air was clean and the landscape Spartan under a bright sky. The trees were bare, a skeletal framework against the pale blue cold of the winter sky. A virginal environment devoid of complexity: a relief. It was a million miles away from the claustrophobia of the shop, the cottages and the Old Testament thinking of the primitive inhabitants. Surveying the scene the single row of cottages looked idyllic—a typical country vista: a perverse distortion of the fact.

To the west a Dutch barn housed the machinery belonging to Jim Brotherton and on that same slope I noticed the tips of a small group of headstones breasting the carpet of snow. I guessed it to be a private cemetery perhaps with its back to the prevailing wind. The skies to the north were heavy with the coming snows bringing the promise of even greater isolation. Kate had often warned me that unless I was prepared to spend the season marooned at the cottage, I had better leave before the real snow fell. At that time I was so intrigued by her company that leaving had not been an option. Now I was beginning to have second thoughts. It was all well and good to be amused and interested by this group of odd individuals; to study them from inside their community but, like the changelings of legend when they grew fangs and claws they became an alien race. They could become quite different from the easy-going country-folk of my first acquaintance. As yet I was still welcome. What might happen when that changed was a question I was left to wonder about. Like the threat implicit in the coming clouds, the possibility that my social environment could also change drastically was a reality I had to take seriously.

By the time I started back small flakes were already drifting down to mask my footprints and as if to confirm my fears the clouds had moved that much closer. Back at the cottage I found James still in his dressing-gown sitting before a huge fire. My mother's manuscript was on his knee and he clutched a mug of coffee in his fist.

'Ah the wanderer returns.'

I pulled off my coat glad of the heat from the fire.

'Not the best weather for invalids to spend on the mountain though.'

I smiled and without a word took the dreadful box from my pocket and placed it carefully on the table nearby. He made no comment leaving the impression that he was waiting for me to say something.

'Lots to think about—inspired by Bessie's little gift. Did you know anything about this James?'

He took off his reading glasses and looked me in the eye.

'Of course I did. I chaired the meeting. Bessie was only there to make the case against Malcolm explicit.'

'And did anyone speak in his defence?'

'There was no need for a defence council. The facts were not at issue. We all saw what happened. We witnessed your distress and accepted your request for justice.'

'My request was for legal redress.' I snapped back.

Now my voice was raised. If he imagined that I would be taken in by his argument and share the blame the scandalous outcome, then he'd better think again.

'At no time did I ever ask for the stupid man to be mutilated—it's barbaric.'

He did not answer straight away. He put the document on the table next to the box and got to his feet all the while watching me.

'I can see that you are upset. Let me make you a hot drink and I'll try and explain our thinking.'

As he spoke he went to the kitchen door. For a moment he stopped and over his shoulder added, 'You have a lot to learn about the folk here Paul—don't judge us too harshly until you better understand our history . . . . and remember it's also part of your history too.'

A little while later we sat before the fire. The hot coffee was welcome after my outing but it did nothing to allay my feelings about the subject of our conversation. James went to great lengths to explain the background ignoring my basic objection that civilized behaviour precluded the need for archaic punishments. He talked over my objections until at last I gave him his head and simply listened. What emerged was a tale of hardship and adventure, of persecution and death, of coercion and finally of escape. It was a story that would easily match the efforts of any modern thriller writer however well-versed in the design of suspense they might be.

He told me that in 1545 a group of friends decided to leave their native Estonia and try for a new future in Western Europe. Originally six families comprising seventeen adults and twenty children took their wagons and all their belongings and made the trek through Lithuania and

Poland into Germany. It took them six years to reach Germany only to find that the population there demonstrated the same level of antagonism that they had met with in every other place they had stopped. They were seen as parasites, pariahs without roots or rights; a people who could be abused at the whim of whatever chieftain, warlord or aristocrat whose land they crossed. By that time three deaths had occurred amongst their group. Most notably one of their number was stoned to death in the streets of the port of Gdansk by fishermen. Despite their hopes for a new beginning in Germany the situation grew worse. In the town of Koblenz on the Rhine they were placed in custody en masse and for a while it seemed as if their children may be taken from them and they themselves condemned to indentured labour. This time they escaped by bribing a local dignitary. They used whatever was left of their jewellery and other valuables and were allowed to flee. Despite the bribes however, one of their young women was kidnapped and was never seen again. They reached England's shore in 1553.

At this point James stopped. He reached over and picked up the manuscript again.

'It's all here Paul—you really should read it.'

'I will but only when I'm good and ready. Nevertheless, if your argument is an attempt to excuse your brutalism today because of being ill-treated four hundred years ago—then it is a nonsense—and I believe you know as much yourself?'

He shook his head.

'I was simply trying to establish an historical framework. Without a proper understanding of the background, one cannot hope to comprehend the issues involved in the development—and—and you must know as much yourself.'

I ignored the sarcasm and shrugged my shoulders conceding the point and he continued.

'Like most immigrants the group made its way to London. Now at that time the city if not the whole country was in a state of flux. King Henry VIII had died in 1547 leaving the throne to the boy Edward. Unfortunately Edward succumbed to his illness and died in 1553—the very year our people landed. Despite an attempt by a tiny minority to install Lady Jane Grey as the successor it was Mary, her father's favourite who became Queen. In those days it is well worth remembering that heretics or at least those judged to be so, were burned at the stake. I might add that society—then as now—considered itself to be both civilized and humane.'

'But!'

'No buts if you please—the Tudor Court was regarded as one of the most sophisticated in the modern world—after all it had been Henry who had constituted the English Church no less. Despite the situation for a while the families prospered in a small hamlet west of the city. It was a place called Uxbridge . . . . But a year or so later they were driven out by the local populace.'

'Why on earth would they do that?'

'Does prejudice need logic? Does bigotry justify itself with reasoned argument? When has anyone been able to answer the 'why' of persecution—the 'why' is immaterial—except for the fact that this seems to have been the last straw—as they say. They packed up once more and headed north—and as far as we are concerned that's when the story begins to affect us. They arrived in this locality in 1558 the year Elizabeth was crowned Queen. It was not however, until 1794 that the lands hereabouts were ceded to them and their descendents. By then of course there had been a steady influx of Romany people travelling the highways and byways of the whole country.'

The history lesson was obtuse and I was becoming bored with the lecture. Whatever his argument my concern was with the present.

'But what of their religious practises—the moral standpoint for example? How the hell do we reach a stage when, rather than involve the legitimate authority of the Police, it's found preferable to hold a Kangaroo court and design punishments better suited to the Dark Ages?'

'Paul you can't have been listening—After so many occasions when the so-called legitimate authorities cheated, persecuted and rejected these people; when even after they tried to fulfil useful service they were driven out—is it surprising that there was no trust?'

His argument was understandable despite my disagreement. It was the same rejection as felt by some ethnic minorities after rough handling—but for the reaction to persist—to last over four hundred years—that was incredible. Usually cultures that last over a long period can be seen to evolve—to change according to prevailing circumstances.

James finished his drink before he continued.

'You mentioned religious practises and the scorn in your voice doesn't do you credit. Our beliefs—rely on an appreciation of natural forces the seasons, the power of nature—we know about the needs of the harvest; about self-sufficiency . . . '

'And you know all about employing blood punishments as some kind of instant justice.' I interjected.

My interruption didn't trouble him.

'Yes—true—and one might add that is about the need to maintain order, even if that means minor mutilations. To us a corporate identity is a reality—we value our society. By comparison the ethic of your Christianity is a muddle of contradictions. 'Thou shalt not kill' but bless the army; 'forgive thine enemies' but hang the murderer; prohibit the heretic from his place next to God. The Christian heaven is a senseless meritocracy based on the cult of the individual. Even the slogans are nonsense 'Be born again of water and the Holy Ghost' before you can enter God's kingdom. I find it hypocritical of you to criticise our so-called cruelty when your religion is based on the crucifixion of Christ and is commemorated by symbolic cannibalism.'

I felt uncomfortable but I could not let it rest there.

'Is it not a mark of a civilised society that those who have, will look after those who have not. You certainly looked after Malcolm's interests by cutting off one of his fingers. Revenge cannot replace rehabilitation can it?'

'Paul please don't preach mealy mouthed humanism to me. Remember how you demanded a pound of flesh—wasn't that revenge? And your politicians' example: greed under the guise of public service—immorality is fine as long as you don't get caught. Let the Third World starve unless they can be exploited; screw the environment in the name of profit.'

I couldn't deny any of these accusations but he wasn't finished.

'I also see your disapproval of our predilection for sexual freedom—a disapproval that is a shallow posture given your own behaviour in taking advantage of it.'

'What you describe as the attitude of 'my' politicians also represents the effects of your generation—they are 'ours' not 'mine'. And your business interests have certainly used the system—dare I say with greed in mind; you've taken advantage of free education and no doubt the Welfare State. You cannot pick and choose which bits of our society are convenient for your current philosophy.

James suddenly laughed a short bitter guffaw.

'D you realise that we're actually beginning to sound like father and son.'

However, by then the temperature of my anger has risen to justify the flush in my cheeks.

'Well if the sole responsibility of that relationship is that we share disagreements, I may eventually accept you as my father.'

That hit the target. For a moment or two he sat with his lips pursed, clearly finding it difficult to control his temper. When he next spoke it was with a calculated deliberation.

'Oh no Paul we've shared much more than that . . . . I can assure you that our generosity to one another is just as great as Duggie's has been to both of us.'

'What the hell do you mean by that?' I snapped back.

Now he wore a thin smile.

'However shocking and unacceptable you may find the notion, you should be aware that normally when I stay here—especially over winter—Kate usually shares my bed.'

I was shocked, shocked and furious. My imagination raced making me feel sick to the stomach. He rose, smiling at the distress I could not hide.

'Surely that doesn't bother you. From what I hear you don't always object to sharing her favours . . . Duggie says.'

**

At the far end of the row of cottages stood an old disused bus-shelter—a remnant of the halcyon days when the local service could include such far flung destinations. The logo of the bus company was only just visible through the peeling paint; the bars of the wooden bench seat were cracked and the bus schedule, framed in a plastic cover had faded beyond recognition. A metal pole signifying the arrival point was half rusted through and the pendant sign at its mast-head now declared 'US TOP'.

A claim I did not feel matched the facts.

Kate sat alongside me and we were both glad of the meagre cover the shelter afforded. The gentle drift of light snow had become a blanket reducing the view and disguising nearby landmarks making an unusual uniformity. It was bitterly cold and despite the heavy clothing we both wore we shivered in unison.

I had stormed out of the cottage unable for once to find the words to express my revulsion. I was still pulling on my scarf when I rang Kate's doorbell. When she answered her enquiries after the state of my health went unanswered and I almost dragged her from the house. She had time only to grab her coat and a woolly hat and came protesting the insanity of the action but sensing its urgency nevertheless.

Later when faced with my accusations she refused to answer or to comment.

'I've asked you nothing about your past Paul. There have been no investigations on my part and no recriminations. I took you at face value—as I found you. You have no right to cross-examine me.'

'Right!' by now I was almost shouting, 'If I've no right to ask then who does?'

Kate was sitting on the bench by then her hands bunched between her knees and her shoulders hunched. She had pulled down her woolly hat until it almost covered the whole of her face. Only the hurt in her eyes was visible.

'Don't you think it might be just a little irresponsible going around fucking anything in trousers? Don't you think you might be in danger of spreading some of those nasty diseases . . . '

At last she flared and shouted me down.

'Stop it . . . stop it right there. How dare you Paul and don't try and disguise your jealousy with fake concerns about hygiene and health . . . . For God's sake neither of us made any promises. I didn't try to deceive you . . . . you were only too glad to have your fun . . . and it was just that. It was fun.'

To begin with I had marched up and down in the shelter as we argued but as she spoke this time I sat down, as far away from Kate as the bench permitted.

'Whatever we might hope to have together Paul—don't spoil it please.'

'I don't think it's me that has spoilt it.'

For several minutes neither of us spoke. I sat with my head in my hands and the wind built in the distance. The snow drifted and corners grew wedges of white. Eventually Kate slid herself along the seat and put her head on my shoulder and an arm around me. Her warmth was comforting.

By this time I knew I was being unreasonable—I could hear myself ranting. I knew also that it had been James who had upset me and wondered how much of this upset he had planned. Or was that just more paranoia?

'Can't we be friends again?' Kate whispered.

I studied her through my gloved fingers. Her hat was askew and her nose was red. A whisp of hair trailed across her cheek and her eyes sparkled. On an impulse I turned quickly and kissed her and she responded in kind.

'I've missed you,' she whispered again, 'and believe it or not there's no-one else I miss.'

I held her as tightly as I could and felt near to tears.

'I'm sorry Kate—I'm really sorry. It was just James—the bastard—he knew he could wind me up. I could have killed him—and the thought of him with you . . . '

She pulled back and looked determinedly into my face.

'Let's make an agreement. All this emotion is too much to handle right now. Let's agree that we'll sort all this out and make whatever confessions are appropriate—after the party. That's only a couple of days to go—Friday tomorrow then the celebration on Saturday night.

We'll meet on Sunday. You can take me out for lunch—somewhere nice and we'll decide once and for all what we want from one another. What do you think?'

Her proposal was more than I deserved and I agreed without a second thought. In a strangely perverse way, it was gratifying to have expressed my concerns and made my accusations and yet still have access to the woman I most desired. The Catholic conscience is ever filled with capricious ambiguity. The fact was however that Kate had not capitulated, far from it. There had been no denials and no apologies. She had sought only to maintain the relationship. Why then did I feel that she had given ground and why was I suddenly so satisfied with myself?

We must have sat there in the old bus-shelter for more than forty minutes, in silence our arms about one another and cheek to cheek. It was only when the cold intensified so as to permeate the heat of our closeness that we walked back. I allowed myself to be persuaded to take coffee at Kate's house reasoning that I did not yet feel like facing James again. I could have saved myself the effort. When we entered the living room there was James, sitting in front of the fire with Duggie in close attendance. The smug satisfaction in his smile left me annoyed and suspicious all over again. It was almost as though he had borne silent witness to our conversation—a wild imagining I decided that was further testimony to my ever present insecurity.

Chapter Fourteen

I awoke at five-thirty on Friday morning. It was still dark and the silence suggested that a heavy layer of snow had fallen. It insulated the house. I switched on my tiny side-light and saw that James in the other single bed was still fast asleep. The duvet was pulled tight around his head emphasising the singularity of his face. In repose and without his glasses he had a childlike appearance: the wrinkles smoothed and the expression placid. The disingenuous pretext of sleep, a sophistry of nature like the bright diamonds on the adder's skin, designed to attract the unwary.

As a consequence of my conversation with Kate and our joint resolution, I had determined to observe a polite distance from James. I had no more desire to engage with him on either an intellectual or an emotional level. His motives were his own affair and if he wished to pursue them by whatever devious means then that was fine by me—as long as I was not drawn in to an involvement at any stage.

Downstairs I sat and nursed a cup of very black coffee and studied my last page of writing. The world of Sir Walter Scott about which I had been so intrigued now seemed like a yesterday consideration. His images, his metres and his meanings were of a different generation of thinking: an academic pursuit, suddenly distant and inconsequential. I read a few more pages and then put them away. It was the present that possessed me not the past.

My understanding with Kate implied that I was definitely staying on for the celebration, a decision I did not recall actually making consciously. Curiously, there could be no doubt that almost everyone on the Mount wanted me to stay for the party although why my presence should be sought after by anyone else but Kate remained a mystery. After comments from Gerald and Sammy I began to feel that somehow I was being seen as the main attraction. By contrast my view of the events of the last few days was increasingly distorted; even those occasions to which I might attach importance were unclear. I began to suspect that my paranoia increased in direct proportion to the gradual limitation of my options. I needed the comfort of opinions that were untrammelled, untainted by the immediacy of my own confusions and fears. I decided that I should seek solace in the company of Richard Smith. He was a person who could be relied upon to pour the oil of his logical thinking on the troubled waters of my concerns.

Enervated by my decision, I stole quietly back to the bedroom and collected my clothes. I dressed downstairs and after a shave at the sink, I cooked myself a breakfast of bacon and eggs. I was hungry not having eaten the previous evening and the breakfast went down a treat. However, the food and the act of its preparation helped fortify more than simply my physical appetite. I had spent too long being the passive recipient—the blotting-paper for the emotional ink-spill of those about me. Now I experienced a new determination.

After clearing away the debris of my meal I opened the curtains and rubbed at the window to view the outside conditions. As predicted the night had seen a heavy snowfall: a picture post-card scene greeted me. The landscape undulated in a continuous white surface without definition. Roofs and window ledges were thickly laden; hedgerows mounded under drifts and in the dimness of the early morning the outline of the hill opposite was lost against the white of the sky. I estimated the snow to be about twenty inches or more deep, certainly more than Wellington boot high. For a moment I considered changing my plans. The voice of my guardian angel whispered that it would be unsafe and unwise to venture out alone in such a terrain. The steep hill down to the village would be treacherous and a fall, perhaps even a broken bone might leave me at the mercy of a cruel environment. On the other shoulder my resident devil laughed and asked if I was afraid of a bit of snow. And what would be the result of my staying indoors, isolated with only James for company: a trauma of a different sort. I decided to go anyway.

I borrowed a pair of waterproof pants from the kitchen cupboard and pulled their elasticated tops down over the top of my boots. Two sweaters covered by a Kagool left me secure in a warm cocoon. A woollen cap fitted neatly under my hood and once I had pulled up my collar and tied a scarf round my lower face only my eyes were left exposed. I resisted the temptation to leave a note for James that would smack of too friendly an act. The first inclination was to write down the words of Captain Oates implying that I would not return but I decided to keep my intentions to myself. Further to this same end I left by the back door. There would be no tell-tale footprints from the front of the cottage giving an indication of my direction.

On my way at last I strode out into knee high drifts behind the house. The early light filtered through a fine mist of powdery snow. Agitated by the wind the top dressing swirled in miniature flurries but as I progressed to the road I was protected from the gusts by the huge drifts covering the stone walls. These towered on either side a good four feet higher than my head: a virtual tunnel almost perfect in its symmetry. As expected the going was hard; the softness of the snow deceptive, it offered more resistance than I imagined possible. By the time I reached the downturn of the hill I was therefore breathing heavily and beginning to sweat. To make matters worse, it appeared that the earliest snow fall had frozen over before later falls had covered it making it perilous underfoot. I was fortunate in that although I fell three times before reaching the base of the hill, my padding allied to the depth of soft snow protected me from serious injury. It was only my dignity that was bruised.

The driveway to Richard's house had been cleared already. Ever efficient in matter relating to his property Richard must have been out at the crack of dawn to effect the clearance. Long before my arrival the drive had been salted and the excess snow stacked on either side. He was surprised but nonetheless pleased to see me when he opened the big front door and with his usual good nature invited me to share his cooked breakfast. The kippers and scrambled egg were tempting but I only accepted coffee. Once divested of my waterproofs and outer layers I began to feel human once more. His fire was as ever of the most generous proportions and within a few minutes of arriving before it, my circulation was restored and my spirits were raised.

'Now then,' he said at last pushing his plate to one side, 'what are you doing out on a day like this. I would have thought you'd be crowded round a nice fire with a large scotch in your fist.'

He poured more coffee as he spoke.

'When I saw you coming down the drive you bore more than a passing resemblance to a runaway schoolboy. Are you sure it's Walter Scott you are writing about and not Scott of the Antarctic?'

I laughed and admitted that in my waterproofs I had felt like a Polar explorer.

'I had to call in for a chat Richard—things up there are even more bizarre than before.'

I told him about the manuscript and the dog and about Malcolm's attack; about James's arrival and his apparent change in personality and I ended by describing Bessie's present—the dismembered finger. As I told my tale Richard sat sipping his coffee staring into the fire. I said nothing about the relationship James claimed to have with Kate or of his claim to be my natural parent. I was still too sensitive about both subjects and despite my latest conversation with Kate my pride was still scarred. My friend looked pensive.

'Sometime—if you don't mind, I'd like to have a close look at that manuscript of your mother's. I met her once—just the once—briefly. She and James came out for a walk before the snows came. They stopped here for lunch. My father was still alive at the time and he loved to play host to any newcomers.'

I was surprised at this admission and had to interrupt.

'And you never thought to mention that you knew her?'

'No—and I'm sorry if that seems deceitful but I suspected their relationship was serious—and—and I didn't feel it was my place to make such an observation.'

I could understand his dilemma. However, I could not help but feel left out—like 'piggy-in-the-middle'. He must have read my thoughts.

'I understand—you must be shell-shocked by all that has happened. I wouldn't be surprised if you felt you had been used. I'm sorry about that—sorry especially if you feel I've behaved badly.'

I assured him there was no permanent damage done and that his was a minor part compared to that of James and the others. I did however press him for information about the coming party.

'On another subject tell me what you know about this so-called celebration.'

He grinned.

'Well I've never been invited to attend myself but I must admit that once as a young man I stole up there and watched proceedings from a distance. I came to the conclusion that they certainly knew how to enjoy themselves—lots of booze, dancing and sex. Does that answer your question?'

My imagination raced ahead.

'But did it have any . . . . any undertones of . . . of the supernatural?'

Feeling silly to have voiced my suspicion I added quickly that it seemed the importance they attributed to the occasion and the gaggle of strange ideas associated with it were hardly justified if it was simply reason for a 'swingers' party. As my last sentence ran out of steam I felt myself flush with embarrassment. Richard ignored the fact and paused before he replied.

'I suppose—if you regard the practice of primitive rites as such then the answer is yes. They get themselves worked up over the Solstice but in my opinion their activities are just self-indulgence. It's just an excuse for an orgy. James inspires and organises the event—he even imports a group of 'bimbos'—girls from his magazine connections I suspect.'

I knew nothing of James's business but I was surprised again at Richard's familiarity with his affairs.

'You know James quite well I imagine?'

'Not really—we keep in touch and he occasionally visits me but most of our conversations are fairly superficial. He knows a bit about fine wines and has put me in the way of one or two good buys—a bottle or two of good claret and the like—but that's the extent of our contact.'

'You mentioned a magazine connection?'

This time Richard's laugh was nervous and it was his turn to look embarrassed.

'As I understand it James started to publish a magazine back in the 1970s. You must have seen it. It's called 'Creative View' . . . . CV to its regular readers. It was started apparently on the back of Playboy's success . . . .'

'You mean he publishes a 'girlie' magazine?'

'I suppose it is. He claims that its popularity—by way of nudes and risqué poses allow him to encourage new writers . . . . in his words 'serious writing' that would be otherwise ignored.'

I found myself unable to stop the smile. After that had been said—James the intellectual, the philosopher was after all—simply a pornographer. His outbursts about society; his criticisms and rejections of the prevalent value system—they were all a pose. He had even used his Romany heritage to his own advantage. I wondered what Bessie and the others would think if they knew the truth about their friend. No small wonder that he didn't want attention drawn to his captive community on the Mount. I determined then to read my mother's manuscript at the earliest opportunity. Bearing in mind her religious complexion, how she had ever become involved with such a person as James was almost beyond belief.

At Richard's invitation I stayed for lunch. He showed me the wine cellars situated next to extensive kitchens beneath the drawing room. Clearly the cellars were his pride and joy and although I am not the possessor of anything that could possibly be described as a discerning palate, the wines he insisted I should taste were certainly impressive. He also gave me a conducted tour of the rest of the house and although most of the larger rooms were no longer used, the place was well-kept and the eclectic collection of antique furniture a joy.

He told me that his family was one of the oldest Catholic families in the kingdom. He also said that their support for the Roman faith had cost them dearly over the centuries especially during the Reformation. Traditionally his ancestors had been soldiers, a fact exemplified in his coat of arms: The mailed fist denoting the warrior, the white rose signifying Yorkshire and the crown meaning loyalty and fidelity. It was only when we discussed the coat of arms that I realised the name of the house—Miles House was also consistent: in Latin Miles means warrior.

Sadly Richard was the last of his line. His brother had died unmarried—killed during WW2 on the Normandy beaches and his own wife Mary had died childless only a few years ago. By a cruel twist of fate his last remaining relatives—two cousins had been killed in a road accident and the family hierarchy had thereby been devastated. He said that he had already approached the National Trust and that barring some stroke of good fortune, he intended to bequeath the property to the nation when he died. His family had become used to the depletion of its numbers through war and persecution but this was clearly the last phase of its history.

In answer to my question about his hope for a stroke of good fortune he replied that there was always the possibility that he might meet some willing young woman who would bear him a male heir.

'I know it's unlikely at my time of life—but one never knows.'

I encouraged the idea agreeing with him that the termination of such a long line would be a tragedy. His response was a secretive smile and I took this to mean he accepted my good wishes as a compliment. After lunch we spent some time in Richard's library, my favourite place in the house. Due to my own background as a Roman Catholic he showed me an ancient register from the sixteenth century: a secret record of Catholic families in England. I was startled to find the name Denley there. Apparently according to the inscription one, John Denley was executed for his faith—one of the last in England to be burnt at the stake in 1555. I knew little of my ancestry so could claim no particular kinship with this unfortunate man but I was nevertheless intrigued by the association. Richard went on to tell me that he had shown the document to my mother and claimed it may well have been the thing that prompted her research project.

'I could well have been this register that set her off. She was certainly amused to find a namesake listed and expressed an interest in discovering more about her family tree.'

I experienced a peculiar nostalgia in handling a volume that had so impressed my mother. It concerned a period in her life to which I had no access: a private time to which she had never again referred leaving me to wonder at its possible significance. Not surprisingly I found myself considering her secret life with James. It was a situation I had deliberately avoided thinking about previously. I knew there would be a temptation to be judgemental, to apply fresh criticism and accordingly to feel the hurt of rejection; of being left out. I came to the conclusion finally that, like me, my mother was a self-reliant person and as an adult I had not shared much of my life with her—so why should I feel such a sense of betrayal when she was found to have her own secrets.

As I knew it would, the time spent with Richard proved a balm for my state of mind. Whether it was the quiet luxury of his home; his obsequiousness relative to his family's demise or the calming effect of his acceptance I do not know. I was nevertheless grateful to him. I left him in the middle of the afternoon and began a hard walk back up the hill. I felt better for my excursion and although the journey back was long and hard it all seemed to have been worthwhile. Curiously, on the doorstep Richard made me promise to keep in touch with him whatever happened. He renewed his request that he might one day read the manuscript and finally asked me to be patient with my mother's memory.

'The sins of our parents,' he said seriously, 'are just like other crimes we might read about—without the immediacy of their consequences, they lack distinction and therefore passion. Through learning to forgive sometimes we learn to understand and that has to be a bonus. For what it might be worth Paul, my advice to you is to get back to your writing as soon as possible—but most of all to forget about James.'

The trip back was infinitely more difficult that the outward journey. During my time at Miles House there had been another snowfall and by the time I set out to return the temperature had dropped several degrees. The original problem of walking in knee-deep snow on a frozen under-surface was as child's play. Now the nature of the snow had changed. It was no longer soft, it crystallised, freezing all the more with each step. Each step was a hazard magnified by the incline. Within the first ten minutes the cold gripped me, sinking icy teeth into my torso daring me to stop to rest. By the time I reached the cottage I was in a state of exhaustion. My vision was blurred and my other senses insecure. As I approached my front door Duggie appeared at his and I heard him call to Kate.

I suppose that many of us in our first world comfort are tempted to forget the power of the natural world. We spend our lives protected from the elements with our fitted carpets, double glazing, central-heating and cars. On those rare occasions when we find ourselves exposed to the ravages of climate we find—as I did—any resistance we might once have taken for granted has vanished. We cannot even make an informed assessment of the degree of the danger.

Not surprisingly, I once again found myself in a state of near collapse again surrounded by generous neighbours.

Chapter Fifteen

I slept, not waking until well after dark. Bessie's ministrations had worn me out. She had been called again to apply her skills and again she had wreaked a miracle cure. This time the leeches were left at home and the mainstay of her remedy was a tortuous massage. I had been carried upstairs, stripped to the skin and left to Bessie's tender mercies. She attacked me with some kind of pungent liniment, her big hands pounding the lazy circulation into action once more. The acrid smell of this particular nostrum was nothing compared to the stinging sensation it generated once it touched bare flesh.

'I use it in a poultice often,' she told me, 'draws out boils and abscesses—takes all the bad an' makes the blood surge—do you a power of good—silly fer goin' out in this weather.'

Her descriptions of the use she put the poultice to did nothing to inspire me with confidence. When she stopped speaking she made a violent attack on my body. It was an attack that comprised two distinguishable techniques. At first she snatched handfuls of flesh and muscle apparently in an attempt to tear them loose from their location. In the second she chopped, punched and poked me with fists, with scaffold-pole fingers and with the hammer-side of her hands. I found myself flinching away and wincing each time she renewed her assault. Occasionally she paused to catch her breath; terrible waiting periods when my anticipation of the punishment to come was often worse than what followed. She avoided those parts of my carcass that were still showing bruises but that still left her more than sufficient body surface on which to exercise her remedy. That her treatment was effective I could not deny, within minutes I was warm again and a little while later I was sweating. I was never certain how much of the perspiration was due to increased circulation and how much was due to fear. I decided privately that whilst Bessie had the good intentions of Florence Nightingale she undoubtedly also had the musculature of a mature male gorilla. Once she was finished with me I was wrapped tightly in a coarse blanket.

'Just so the rubs don't stain yer nice white sheets.' she said.

Before I was left to sleep the ritual was completed by her placing a hot-water bottle firmly on my chest.

The most amazing tingling sensation surged throughout my body. It was almost as if the nerve endings were singing the hallelujah chorus in thanksgiving. In truth it was a very pleasing sensation, one of well-being—of healing. My last thoughts before I fell into a deep sleep were of how much I owed to the big lady shopkeeper.

The darkness confused me when I opened my eyes and it was seconds before I realised I had slept away the rest of the day. The fumes from the liniment had all but disappeared and what was left mingled with that of my body's perspiration. My bindings were still secure, they had held me in the same position throughout my period of unconsciousness and I had to struggle to release myself. However, it was only a short while before I was dressed and ready to face James.

At the top of the stairs I could hear laughter coming from below. It sounded as though there may be a dinner party in progress. I crept quietly down the stairs and opened the door into the living room. James wearing a hairy sweater sat spider-like surrounded by his web of followers. Duggie and Kate squeezed together on the settee next to where James sat in the armchair. Sammy sat on the floor next to little Jim and Malcolm was slouched on cushions. When I entered all their heads turned.

Ever the first to speak James quipped, 'Ah the Polar explorer has awoken.'

Kate got to her feet and came to me. She kissed me on the cheek and whispered to ask if I was alright. I performed as cheery a grin as I could and nodded.

'I'm fine thanks to Bessie—where is she by the way?'

This time it was Sammy who answered.

'She's away back at the shop—got work t' do tonight—making sausage rolls and jam tarts.'

With the exception of Kate everyone fell about laughing at this last remark. When they fell silent again Malcolm spoke up, 'An' she's very good with finger pastry.'

This caused another round of screams and giggles. It seemed that Malcolm's presence as much as his black humour was once more acceptable. His left hand was still heavily bandaged and I found myself surreptitiously looking round to see where I might have left the box with his finger in it. Fortunately it wasn't to be seen. There were glasses of all sorts strewn about the room and I therefore assumed that the drink was at least in part responsible for the hilarity. I had never seen any of them in quite such high spirits and as if to confirm my suspicion, little Jim sprang to his feet and offered to pour me a drink.

'There's still some single malt left—I know that's your preferred tipple—and it'll warm you just where you need t' be warmed.'

'I think Bessie got him nice n' warm already—treats 'im like a long lost son she does.' Sammy said.

'And no-on could ask for a better mother substitute,' I answered, 'that's twice she done the business on me so I've a lot to thank her for.'

Heads all around the room nodded their agreement.

Little Jim handed me a large measure of scotch and resumed his place by the fire. Kate pulled a couple of dining chairs across so that we could sit together facing the assembly. For a change James was noticeably quiet but by contrast Duggie was talkative. He told me that he'd read some of my writing and that he's enjoyed it.

'Hope you didn't mind Paul but I was in here alone for a while and I noticed some of your papers—so I started to have a read. That Walter Scott was quite a guy eh? You don't think of a poet being in business and being a qualified lawyer.'

'Did you read anything else?' I asked, curious to discover if he'd looked at my mother's manuscript. He presumed I meant Scott's poems.

'No not really—I glanced at a bit but it was . . . well it was too fancy for me . . . and a bit soft . . . . all those knights in armour . . . '

Before I could comment James chipped in changing the subject completely.

'I suppose your trek to the nether regions was in order to visit Richard Smith?' he asked.

'Yes.' I replied.

My answer immediately bred suspicious looks from most of the others and it seemed that James had deliberately set out to alienate me from them.

'Not that Richard Smith down at Miles House?' Duggie demanded.

'Why not?' I asked.

Sammy took up the cause.

'He's not welcome up here—not one of us he isn't. An' I'm surprised you spend time with the likes of him.'

Kate attempted to quell the tide by offering explanations.

'You see Paul he's . . . . persona non grata. His family have been so for ages past. The community here has nothing to do with him.'

Her sentence tailed off leaving the question of my affiliation hanging—yet to be answered. The others sat in silence as if waiting for me to explain. I performed a cheeky smile for their sake making it to be as nonchalant as possible.

'Okay so you don't like him—or don't approve of him—so what?'

Duggie came back at me quickly.

'So it's a bit odd you going to see him—and in a snow storm as well—as it was some sort of emergency.'

I fixed my smile and said nothing.

Then James asked, 'Perhaps you'd like to tell us why you made such a trip?'

I paused, still smiling, 'No—I don't feel it is any of your business. Believe it or not, I go where I like when I please . . . '

Kate's grip on my arm had tightened implying a warning.

The next silence was broken when little Jim stood and deliberately drained his glass. He placed it with exaggerated care on the mantle and turned to James.

'It's gettin late James. I think it's time I was gettin t' my bed. The atmosphere here isn't as friendly as it was.'

Sammy stood as well nodding her agreement and staring at me as she did so.

'Jim's right—we'll not stay where we're not welcome.'

They began to shuffle towards the door and from his expression of disapproval I could see Duggie was almost ready to join them. Just then the atmosphere was broken by someone banging loudly on the front door. Outside the sound of a distant voice permeated the room.

'Hello—hello in there.'

Little Jim was the nearest so he opened the door. A small crowd stood on the threshold. Two men and three women huddled together next to a mini-bus that was parked outside. One of the men, clearly the one who had shouted spoke first.

'Is this James Collin's place?'

He was a tall man with a dark complexion and the snow had settled on his beard giving him the appearance of a fairytale figure. James was on his feet in a second.

'Ben—Ben is that you. I'd almost given you up for lost.'

They shook hands with one another in the doorway grinning like long lost friends.

'Come in—come on in all of you. We're a bit crowded at the moment but I'm sure we can squeeze you all in somehow.'

The furniture was shuffled about and in no time the five newcomers were pulling off their coats, rubbing their cold hands before the fire and gratefully accepting various alcoholic drinks. James and Duggie served the drinks and James carried on his conversation with Ben all the while. It was some time before things were sufficiently settled so that James could effect introductions. Long before that I had identified the visitors as those forecast to arrive by Richard. The three women were all in their twenties and beneath their overcoats they wore very short skirts and skimpy tops; their jewellery was cheap as it was abundant and their make-up better suited to Soho night-life rather than a night on this bare mountain.

Once more James seemed to change character. Now he was the effervescent host, bubbling with good humour and his archness of only a few minutes ago had disappeared. Now his was the epitome of good humour.

'Let me introduce my colleagues—friends with whom I spend my working days.' He announced grandly, 'Ben is my picture editor and Peter here is his assistant—both indispensible to my operations.'

The bigger man with the beard wore a tartan shirt and nodded to his companion. Peter was shorter but even more bull-like and he grinned back obviously pleased at the compliment. The three women looked on wide-eyed as though they were about to appear on stage.

'And the girls—models all—all beautiful, Emma is the redhead; Jane the blond and Sally the brunette.

It was a curious introduction, not least because of its bias but despite the sexism all three women seemed to revel in the attention. They smiled big Cheshire cat smiles and purred a simultaneous response, taking over one another as formal acceptance speeches were mandatory. Essentially the said the same kind of thing: how glad they were to be invited; what a nice welcome and what a charming village. Fortunately world peace was never mentioned.

The word 'Bimbo' sprang to mind unbidden.

The influx caused space to be even more limited. I gave up my chair for Sally, refusing her offer to sit on my knee with as much good grace as I could muster. Emma a girl of very generous proportions squeezed between Duggie and James on the settee. She made a virtue of the limitation and declared in a high-pitched voice that she needed as much body heat as might be available, 'Just to get warm again.' She said. Jane the last of the trio parked herself on the arm of the easy chair, sitting astride it provocatively and causing Malcolm at floor level opposite to flush with unashamed excitement.

Due to the number of people involved a large variety of conversations sprang up round the room. Kate became involved with Sally trying to answer her questions about country life and trying to persuade her that it was not at all boring. Occasionally she found time to smile in my direction—for which I was grateful. Having been alerted to the motive behind our visitor's appearance, I preferred to stand back from the melee and watch and listen. In any case I suspected that any attempt I might make at conversation would be unwelcome given their irritation with me for visiting Richard. I wondered privately what they might have thought had they known of James's continuous association with the Smith family.

Watching the room and its occupants proved amusing. I saw little Jim vying with Malcolm for Jane's attention. He sat on his heels before her his face animated and his little body in a constant spasm of attention-seeking excitement. His posture and his excitement were as much to do with the shortness of her skirt as with the subject of their conversation. Sammy seemed to focus on Emma who sat opposite her. She attempted to distract the redhead's attention away from Duggie by telling increasingly risqué stories. So much so that all three were soon in fits of laughter.

Not surprisingly the equation between the quantity of alcohol consumed and the noise generated by those who drank it was as great as at any stag party. At some stage someone started to play records on a portable CD player and although the volume achieved was insignificant, added to the general hubbub in the room, it was deafening. People spilled over into the kitchen still talking, laughing and drinking and eventually the smell of fried bacon and onions seeped through.

By this time Kate had extricated herself from Sally's cross-examination and after refreshing our drinks she joined me in the corner near the front door. Not wanting to declare my hand too soon I asked her who these people were and what they were doing here.

'They're James's friends as he said and he has invited them here for the party tomorrow.'

She seemed reluctant to expound further on the matter but I pressed her again asking how he came to know girls like that.

'They work for him . . . . on his magazine.'

'Magazine?' I asked innocently.

Not wanting to be overheard Kate put her face close to mine and whispered.

'James is the proprietor of a magazine—a glossy—the kind you might find on the top shelf in newsagents—lots of pictures of girls. You must know the sort I mean.'

I raised my eyebrows feigning surprise.

'And these young women are—are some of his models?'

'Well obviously they aren't from the tying pool are they?'

Kate was amused by my show of apparent innocence and she teased me about it for a while. Misleading her made me feel less than honest but there was still a question at the back of my mind about her loyalties.

Whilst we whispered to one another we were ignored by the others. By now the noise level had increased in the room and other conversations had become seriously animated. The music was loud and Malcolm had even begun to try and find sufficient space in which to perform a cheek to cheek with Sally. Kate leaned against me, her arm about my waist whilst mine was draped over her shoulders. She looked the worse for drink but pleasantly so. Occasionally she kissed my cheek but turned away each time I tried to reach her lips.

Eventually she asked, 'Should we go next door—this lot will be busy for ages and my house is empty?'

I didn't need more encouragement and a few minutes later we were outside in the cold. As Kate turned the key I looked up the street. The night had settled under chilled high-blown sky. The air was crisp and a frost had hardened the fallen snow. It was never a more solitary place on such a night. In the distance however I thought I could see lights. By then Kate had the door open but I hesitated trying to identify the source of the illuminations. She saw me looking into the distance and leaned towards me.

'What's the matter?' she asked.

'There's something going on up there—near the hill-top. I'm sure I can see lights.'

Oh, that'll be Jim Brotherton and Bessie—they're getting the place ready for tomorrow night.'

'And what does 'getting the place ready' entail.'

She did not answer me straight away but instead she pulled me inside the house.

'Curiosity,' she whispered, 'killed the cat.'

'And,' I whispered back at her, 'it was satisfaction that brought it back.'

We both laughed as the door closed behind us and when I pulled her towards me she was unresisting.

My intention had been for a relaxed encounter: slow to mature and long lasting. But Kate was in a hurry. Her passion came quickly and she forced the issue brooking no delay. Once more I was left to wonder at the fury of her appetite.

Some time later we retired to Kate's bedroom. In the past we had always come together next door where the settee, the armchair and even the carpet had served our purposes every bit as much as my narrow bed. By contrast the bed she brought me to was double sized providing a rare feast of space. We took full advantage of the opportunity. It was a couple of hours later that I heard voices outside. I could identify Malcolm, obviously the worse for drink and Emma who was not a lot better. They were arguing about where Emma should sleep. In the background Sally and little Jim were singing discordantly accompanied by Sammy who made attempts to imitate musical instruments. Kate's room overlooked the front of the house making the voices sound very close indeed. So that when Duggie came to the door with James their conversation was as clear as if they had been standing in the room.

James asked, 'Surely you aren't going all the way up there now—they'll have finished by now.'

'No,' Duggie replied, 'I don't think so. Anyway I promised that I'd give Bessie a hand. They never get round to the wood-pile until the early hours and, let's face it, that's where the hard labour is.'

The pause in their conversation was filled by the various sounds of the others leaving.

'See you tomorrow.' Emma called out and little Jim echoed her sentiment.

'Sleep well.' Sammy said and the voices grew less as they moved away. Malcolm was still arguing albeit in the distance.

'D'you have any idea where Kate took him?' I heard James ask quietly.

I waited to hear Duggie's reply and the time he took to answer indicated that perhaps he was making sign language. Possibly explaining that he thought we might be in the front bedroom directly above them. His answer confirmed my suspicion.

'No idea . . . . they could be anywhere,' then he laughed and added in a louder voice—clearly for my benefit—'Wherever they are, I'd like to bet by now he's rubbed out. She can be so demanding when she's on heat.'

His provocation almost succeeded. For a moment I almost shouted down at him and then I decided it would be better to let him stew in ignorance of the facts. He would never know for sure where we were. Kate must have also heard what was said because she suddenly laid a hand on my arm.

'Ignore them Paul. It is a performance designed for our benefit.'

Of course she was quite correct. Instead I drew her to me and nibbled a convenient ear. Duggie had been right at least in one respect—I was exhausted. However, the proximity of Kate's charms could not be ignored even in so close a state of collapse. She giggled.

'You aren't going to be able to stand up tomorrow.' She whispered.

'And is it so important that I can stand—tomorrow?'

The query in my question was implicit and she saw the meaning immediately.

'It's only a party Paul.'

She struggled to a sitting position her back finally resting against the bed-head.

'I don't know what you imagine our little celebration might represent but the chances are you've let your imagination run away with you . . . . It's related to the religious beliefs of our ancestors only in as much as it celebrates the Solstice—combined with the start of the Celtic winter—Samhain—a kind of Wiccan festivity; a boozy-do if you like. Okay I admit some of the others see more significance in it than I do and sometimes Bessie will dress up in weird costumes . . . . but it's all light-hearted—like I said a party.'

I did not know to what extent she might be telling me the truth. My passion for her was real enough but it did not extend to a blind faith in everything she told me.

'And what about the sex?' I asked, 'I have it on good authority that there's a certain amount of random coupling takes place.'

'Paul you can be such a prude. Sometimes I think you have split personality. In the last few hours we have behaved like wild animals—what price your morality? Besides that you cannot have been under any illusion about James's three female friends. They are probably at it right now with Malcolm and little Jim and even Sammy.'

Her voice rose as she became more irate but after a brief pause she continued in a quieter but more mischievous vein.

'Incidentally did you notice that Jane stayed back with James?'

I laughed, 'You can't resist a bit of gossip can you?'

'There isn't much that I can resist—and anyway who was this so-called authority you were quoting a moment ago?'

'Richard . . . . Richard St. John Smith to give him his proper title.'

I knew that mentioning his name was a gamble and that her reaction might be extreme. I was not proven to be wrong. Her body stiffened and for a moment I thought she might pull away from me.

'After you saw Jimmy's reaction I would have thought you'd appreciate the depth of feeling about your Mister Smith. Really Paul, making friends with him is one thing but discussing our business is something else.'

It was now my turn to take offence.

That is utter garbage Kate. Richard is as friendly a guy as you'd find anywhere; he's cultured and is an excellent conversationalist; he has an intelligent concern about his family's history and their responsibilities. He is interested in the community in general and whether the folk up here approve or not I've found him to be a generous and attentive host.

Now the exchange came fast and furious.

'But he's a St. John Smith . . . . '

'And that's just like saying he's Black or a Jew or if you will—a Gypsy,'

'It's nothing of the sort—his ancestors were murderers.'

'And yours were thieves.'

'Mine were persecuted by the likes of the Smith family—women seduced, men killed. It's in the blood and Richard is just as guilty as if he's been there himself.'

At last it was out in the open.

We both stopped partly to catch our breath and also to lick our wounds. During the course of the argument Kate had slowly risen until she sat completely upright next to me. Now we were poised face to face—a pair of hissing cats.

It took a moment or two before our tempers cooled at which point I reached out to take her hand: an olive branch. She looked up into my face her eyes still furiously alight and pulled her hand away.

'No Paul . . . it's not that easy. You were welcomed here—every hand opened to you. James told us you were ignorant of your heritage and we were all prepared to make allowances . . . . but not—not for the Smith family. You can call it prejudice if you like but it is rooted in a communal consciousness; our folk memory. He represents all the things that we rejected centuries ago. In our mind his is the face of our persecutor; the privileged face of the establishment—the one you sometimes wear yourself.'

The cold of her emotion wafted over me distancing us, confirming the nature of our separate cultures. The subtle distinction between her description of the party as a, 'light-hearted affair' one minute, then as their, 'business' the next had not escaped me. A gap had opened up between us making her inaccessible and I found myself shivering involuntarily. Clearly further discussion would be fruitless; the strength of her conviction was insurmountable, brooking no possible compromise. If, as I suspected, it represented the consensus argument and an accurate representation of the strength of the feeling about the occupant of Miles house, then I had no place here.

Without further comment, I left the bed and dressed in silence. I went back to the cottage next door convinced that I should leave the Mount as soon as I could pack my bags.

Chapter Sixteen

The sitting room next door stank like the aftermath of a rugby-club party. The air was thick with stale tobacco and fumes from spilt beer mixed with the sweet smell of whisky. Dirty glasses and plates of uneaten snacks were stacked in the sink and on the table and in odd corners. It was a mess. However, it was James's mess and in my present mood I decided that it should be left for James to remedy the situation.

I dug through the detritus searching for my notes and despite my determination not to do so, in the process found myself tidying the room. Eventually I discovered my typewriter under the table and my manuscript was beneath it. I found it to be in a jumbled state; someone had begun to read it but not bothered to return it to its proper sequence.

'Bastards!' I said out loud. I remembered then that Duggie had been reading it so it was probably his fault. My brief-case was in the corner and I packed it without bothering to put the documents in order. There would be time enough for that once I got back to London. It was the first time I'd thought about my apartment in days and I felt strangely guilty on that account. It was like forgetting a friend's birthday or the like and this only reinforced my determination to be gone. I am not usually given to impulsive reactions but on this occasion I felt justified. The main objective of my stay had come to rely on Kate's feelings for me. If they had become diluted then there was no point in remaining in the cottage.

Upstairs I opened the bedroom door as quietly as old timber would allow and tip-toed over to my bed. My suitcase stood on a nearby chair and the contents strewn about. I began to pack my things as quickly and as quietly as possible. I had deliberately avoided looking at James's bed. If as I suspected he was sharing it with Jane I had no desire to be a witness. On this occasion my sensibilities were wasted. I was in the act of fastening the straps on the case when James's voice rang out.

'What the hell do you think you're doing Paul?'

He turned towards me propping himself on an elbow.

'It's still the middle of the night for God's sake!'

The mop of hair on the other pillow behind him shuddered and raised itself. In a sleepy voice Jane asked what the matter was.

'My boy Paul here is trying to do a moonlight flit by the look of him.'

His tone was drenched in sarcasm and as he spoke he swung his bare legs from beneath the duvet and sat facing me. Why it should be the case I do not know but when men past middle-age, show their bare legs they always seem to look ridiculous. He caught me smiling and immediately grabbed his trousers and pulled them on.

'Hardly a moonlight flit,' I muttered, not bothering to stop what was doing.

'Originally I came here for a few days only—I've obviously outstayed my welcome so I'm going home. It's as simple as that.'

By now James was buttoning his shirt. I saw him look up from his task.

'But Paul—the party—it's tonight. We all thought that . . . .'

'Well let's hope you all learn something from trying to second guess your visitors.'

'But where will you go?'

His tone was more plaintive now and he sounded disappointed.

'Where do you think I'll go? I'll go back to London to my flat. After all that's where I live.'

Jane stretched and yawned, a bored sound and a clear message that we were disturbing her.

'Come back to bed James.' She whispered.

He chose not to reply but instead followed me down the stairs. I the kitchen I switched on the kettle and glanced at my watch. It was four thirty. Without a word James washed out two cups.

'We still need to talk Paul. There's too much left unsaid.'

He spoke over the sound of running water.

'Our little disagreements are insignificant in the scheme of things... really they are.'

'I'm glad you think so. However, I'm sure you'll understand if I disagree.'

My response was deliberately curt and I busied myself getting milk from the fridge as I spoke. He put a spoonful of coffee in each cup.

'And what about Kate?' he asked.

'You'd best ask her.'

'Ah now I see.'

'I don't think you do—in fact I don't think you could.'

The kettle boiled and I switched it off and poured water into both cups. There was a noise on the stairs and Jane's voice called through from the sitting-room.

'James if you're making a drink, I'd like a cup of tea please.'

He ignored the request completely, instead sipping his drink and studying me.

'I think you're being childish.' He said eventually, 'why not sit down with me now and we can sort out our differences once and for all. It is only a matter of differing cultures, value systems... a different way of thinking about things.' He paused and then added, 'Sex is less important to us . . . morality is . . . . '

Before he could finish his sentence Jane strolled through and interrupted him.

'Sex is less important is it? That's not the impression you gave me last night.'

She laughed a high-pitched squeaky sound, entirely foreign to the atmosphere in the room. I could see James was annoyed. Her comment was made all the more ridiculous by the fact that she was naked. She stood in the doorway unashamed without the slightest trace of embarrassment and content to be the subject of our attention. Without clothes she was a startling sight: her body well-formed and her skin vibrant. In the context of our discussion however there was an element of the surreal in her appearance. Whatever else I may have felt at that moment I had to admit she was a shock to the system. James was as ever quick to take the initiative. He snorted a deep laugh.

'Now—here's a case in point, another cause for some cultural discrepancy perhaps. Not at all acceptable in your average kitchen . . . . however, feast your eyes for a moment Paul. Have you ever seen anything quite so provocative?'

In the spirit of his comment Jane did a slow pirouette. There was no denying the fact that due to her nakedness she was still vulnerable, culpable and careless of her lack of protection. My mouth dried out.

'You like it?' James asked wickedly. 'Of course you do.' He answered his own question. 'Now step two—come over here Jane. My friend Paul has a surfeit of damnable conscience—a Christian complex. The kind we old 'uns used to read about in Boys Own Magazines and Hotspur comics; all stiff upper lip and limp willies.'

Jane approached me playing the part he demanded. Her eyes sparkled and it was an Oscar performance.

'Is he shy then?' she asked coyly.

I suppose it was the total inadequacy of her Munroe impersonation that finally caused me to question the mirage. Until then I had been mesmerised but suddenly I saw her for what she was—merely a pastiche. She had belonged to the inside pages of glossy magazines for so long that she had become two dimensional. Indeed the whole thing lacked credibility. Fortunately, I remembered from painful experience in my own past that it was the employment of ridicule that would guarantee to flatten the affectation of a sexual posture. The memory made me flush for a second but I adopted a knowing grin.

'But James, Jane isn't even a natural blond . . . perhaps I should try the redhead instead.'

Involuntarily Jane's hand dropped to cover her pubic mound. Her advance was arrested and she flushed deeply. For a moment I thought she might cry but instead she whirled about and scampered back to the stairs calling me a bastard in the process. After she disappeared we heard her stamp across the bedroom floor and bounce on the bed.

When I turned James was studying me once more.

'She's quite right Paul—you really are a bastard, Jane is one of my most popular models and she isn't used to rejection.'

I stared back at him. The arrogance of the man was almost beyond belief. I drained my coffee-cup before replying.

'My experience of tarts is obviously more limited than yours—but not to worry—Jane will eventually get used to rejection—they all do in the end. Now I really must go.'

I picked up my cases and my coat and turned to go.

'My thanks for your hospitality James—it was an education. I'm sure I will always remember this place.'

He stood there in silence for a moment and then he leaned forward and pulled back the curtain. He looked out through a steamy window.

'I don't think your visit is over just yet.' He said.

I waited.

'Last night we had a severe frost and since then we've had about four or five inches of snow. You will find it impossible to get the car out of the drive let alone navigate the hill.'

When he turned back to me he was grinning—a mean grimace signifying his delight at his advantage. In my moment of anger I had completely forgotten the capricious Yorkshire climate.

'Why not put your things back upstairs and have some breakfast. Tonight, all being well, I'll extend your experience of 'tarts' as you call them . . . . although, given the implications of your definition of such ladies and your apparently extensive coupling with the lady next door, I would have thought you knew all about tarts anyway.'

It was a mean comment from a mean-spirited man.

My capitulation was an ignominious climb-down—but given the circumstances there was no alternative. I was furious with James's reference to Kate but due to my state of mind found myself without a smart answer for once. Had I been a more heroic person I would have hit him in the mouth, unfortunately that had never been a role I was capable of filling. The self-indulgence of my dramatic exit thereby turned into an extended embarrassment—rather more than just an awkward moment.

To some extent the situation was relieved when Jane appeared once more. This time she wore a diaphanous silk dressing-gown—a coverall that covered nothing. She swanned past me with her nose in the air as if the gown had put her in possession of a new respectability. It did not matter that everything was just as visible as before. As she passed by James he smiled and patted her bottom. Her response was predictable—a wiggle and a coquettish grin. I felt nauseated. Nevertheless the diversion created by her absurd reappearance allowed me a sufficient smoke-screen under which I gratefully retired upstairs, defeated but unbowed.

**

At first light I left the cottage and walked up to the shop. A winter sun lit the snow and although it was still very cold I considered it might be possible to drive the car down the hill. I was still undecided. It had always been my intention to visit Bessie and Gerald to say my good-byes before I left. They had shown me profound kindness on several occasions and whatever my feelings about the rest of my neighbours I felt I owed them a face to face thank-you before I left.

The smell of fresh baked bead greeted me just inside the shop door and when Bessie appeared a moment later her hands were still covered in a residue of flour and yeast.

'An' good-mornin t' you Paul—Up bright n' early eh.'

She wiped her hands of her white apron and dusted the flour from her cheek as she squeezed behind the counter.

'Now what'll it be. The bread won't be ready fer another half hour but I'll save you a nice cob if y' wish.'

Bessie was the one constant star in the little universe that was the Mount. She was always reliable and dependable and her smile was like a beacon. Ensconced in her tightly packed environment she dispensed far more than groceries and it seemed that her crowded shelves were only a medium for her influence.

'To be honest Bessie I really don't need anything. I just came down for a chat—sort of.'

She stared at me wrinkling her nose as though I'd introduced a bad smell.

'Sounds like you might be having troubles t' me. You haven't been upsetting someone have you Paul? S' not likes you t' go round being unkind . . . . '

'Perhaps I have . . . . but to tell you the truth Bessie I really came to say good-bye. I'm leaving.'

Perceptive as ever Bessie immediately saw through me.

'And what does Kate say about that?'

'I don't think Kate wants to see man any more—we—we sort of fell out.'

Despite my close scrutiny it was impossible to tell what Bessie was thinking. She studied me for a moment longer, wiped her hands again on her apron in what could have been a Pontius Pilate gesture.

'We disagreed—completely on some—well some fairly fundamental issues.'

I found myself filling the gap in our conversation. It had always been a problem for me to leave spaces like that even when the things I said didn't help.

'All this emphasis on free sex—sleeping around—making out with anyone that might take your fancy—I find that difficult to accept . . . difficult to take.'

'But not too difficult t'give eh?'

Clearly the lines were being drawn. Identity with the community interest would inevitably supersede new friendships and perhaps I'd been a fool to think otherwise.

'What I gave, I gave in all honesty—I suppose my mistake was expecting the same in return.'

Bessie laughed—a good loud laugh however incongruous.

'Lord above but you're an innocent,' she said, 'and a typical product of the male society you've sprung from. I suppose it's alright fer you t' screw around—You took Kate without so much as a by-your-leave and only when you get hooked d' you start t' ask questions about her. You like your bit of fun Paul—but you find it inconceivable that she should do the same.'

'But she's even been with James.'

My retort was almost a shout. I'd not meant to make this public but in the heat of the moment it was out. Bessie didn't bat an eye-lid.

'And you've just discovered that James is yer Dad?'

Her tone was almost sympathetic.

'Yes I have.'

She was smiling again.

'Lad, y' must understand that in some societies some folk don't place the same importance on that kind of thing. Up here we gets by without serious jealousy. See—it's just another bodily function. On the one hand it's a pleasure taken on the other a generosity perhaps. We don't seek to own one another on the Mount.'

I shook my head. It was so much Hippy nonsense; so much unhealthy, uncivilized self-indulgence—so unfair.

'We all knew you'd have a problem with our ways, that's why we wanted you t' stay fer a while; why we made you welcome an' all. It's always difficult fer those from a split home: yer mother's Christianity versus James more natural ways.' She paused for a moment or two and then added, 'Now listen to Bessie . . . the party we're holding tonight is . . . . '

I interrupted, 'I'm sorry I can't be there. I just couldn't face it.'

It was her turn to shake her head.

'And I suppose you've fallen out with James as well?'

I nodded.

'When you do it you certainly does it properly don't you? Have you had a go at anyone else?'

'I suppose I wasn't too kind to Jane—one of the girls who . . . . '

'Yes I know who Jane is.'

'And little Jim got upset when I argued with him about Richard Smith . . . . Now I think about it, it was Richard's name that set the scene for my argument with Kate also.'

'Okay let's us start at the very beginning,' Bessie said. 'Come round to the kitchen and you can make us both a cup of tea while we talk. Then maybe I can get on with the bread.'

I sat in Bessie's kitchen until lunch-time. Gerald was off doing something else so we are left alone to talk: to discuss and occasionally to argue the pros and cons of our various beliefs. It was not long before she convinced me that the hurt I felt was based on an unfair reaction. Although she did not accuse me of it directly, I had to admit privately that my attitude might be reasonably seen as hypocritical. Our conversation raised my awareness of the difference between the philosophy I claimed as my moral standpoint and the fact of my recent actions. The contrast was clear. By the time I found myself again in the street, the practical dilemma of my behaviour had been solved. At least now I knew what I should do. Nevertheless the confusion I felt regarding the morality of my new resolve was worse than ever.

As my conversation with Bessie had progressed and my appreciation of my personal paradox became clear, I had offered less and less objection to her argument—another case of pragmatism as opposed to honesty. Sensing my capitulation she had produced a bottle of good French brandy from her kitchen cupboard. After several 'tots' as she liked to call them, I felt warmer and more secure. This was a feeling confirmed by my having made some decisions.

When I left the shop for the street outside a piercing wind swept down from points north scything its way across the countryside. It was a thin, mean current of ice cold air seeking out bared flesh with the intensity of a surgeon's scalpel. The warmth afforded me by the brandy was soon dissipated.

As usual the doors along the street were shut tight and the curtains drawn against the cold. I glanced up the hill as I turned. I was surprised to see a group of people up at the copse of trees. Jim Brotherton drove his tractor to and fro and with the bulldozer blades out in front. I presumed he must be clearing the snow—perhaps for the site of the party. Although why anyone would choose an open site for a party at this time of year in this location was beyond my powers of reasoning. Had it been a Pop concert it may have been understandable—teenagers always seem to be impervious to the climate.

If I'd felt braver I could have returned to Bessie's shop and asked her what was going on—the truth was however, that I was embarrassed. There was a presumption that everyone knew all the details about the organisation of the party—everyone that is except me. It was another case of my being excluded; another occasion when I'd been omitted; shunted to the side-lines, as a child there had been a myriad of situations when occasions like this had caused me to feel shunned. These were times when I'd stood apart from my peer group and whilst I envied their freedom of action I'd guarded my opinions and pretended to conform. It had been equally problematic at home. I was fed a diet of the Christian religion and expected to imbibe the ethic. In reality I grew to feel superior to the beliefs orchestrated by the established church. In my view it lacked a basic humanity. Not surprisingly by the time of adulthood I had become a moral snob.

The sudden realisation that my behaviour was after all an affectation was a trauma. It was nothing more than a sham—another embarrassment.

Chapter Seventeen

Standing there wearing only the heavy cloak Bessie had loaned me I stared into the bonfire and tried to decide how the hell I'd arrived here.

The snow had been mounded into a giant amphitheatre with walls fully eight feet high. Three feet from the floor it was stepped to provide a continuous bench seat around its perimeter: a well for containment or a stockade for protection. Beyond the wall stood a ring of trees but only the tops remained visible: Alder, Pine, Oak and Chestnut were half submerged poking their sparse fingers into the cold night air. Access was by way of an opening cut into one side—it was the only access and in the centre of the space a huge fire blazed. It was a bonfire of grand proportions. The heat melted the surface of the surrounding walls leaving them with a damp shiny finish.

The people present wore only a robe, a cloak made of thick woollen material similar to the one I wore. These coveralls were decorated with various patterns and emblems mainly reflecting cabbalistic signs. Shoes had been abandoned outside the circle and bare feet were protected from the cold ground by layers of rushes. Nearest the fire the rush mat had burnt back but otherwise left a carpet sufficient to resist the mud underfoot. Outside the night air was freezing but within the confines of the snow mounds the heat from the fire kept the temperature high.

I was completely disorientated. Time passed in a disjointed sequence comprising only limited periods of consciousness. My vision swam. It was as if I was drunk. I was aware of generalities but not much of the detail. There was laughter and movement; shadows against bright flames; glimpses of bare skin and the heat on my face. Shouts pierced the sound of crackling wood and roar of burning; smells of meat cooking mingled with wood-smoke and the fumes filled my throat. It seemed that only a moment passed but suddenly the fire had burned down. A container of wine was pushed into my hands and I drank from it greedily to relieve the dryness in my mouth.

I saw little Jim and Sammy rake back the red embers and retrieve a pig's carcass from beneath the flames. They prised the hard-baked mud shell from around the beast and immediately a strong pungent and appetising aroma filled the arena. More logs were piled on the fire as Sammy began to carve the carcass. Whatever the reason my appetite was exaggerated by the smell and suddenly I was ravenously hungry. At the first cut the whole assembly gathered round clamouring for a share; dozens of hands reached out for every slice. There was not even pretence of civilized behaviour and not a plate or eating utensil in sight. Chunks of meat were taken and eaten with greasy hands and the noise that accompanied the feats was like that of a wolf pack: sounds foreign to human-kind. Throughout there were howls and cries of those seeking to attract Sammy's attention; the moans of disappointment when quicker hands took the meat; shrieks of success; gasps when fingers and lips were scorched by the heat of the meat and the harmonious sounds of loud chewing. Finally there were the sounds of gratification as digestion began and inevitably the breaking of wind of those momentarily replete.

At some stage I found myself in the thick of the throng and after several missed opportunities I finally succeeded in grabbing a large chunk of pork. I took this over the head of Jane who crouched on all fours before me. My prize scorched my fingers and hot fat ran down my chin and along the length of my arm. Like those around me I fed quickly and turned immediately to seek more. The process was as vultures fighting over carrion. Between the mouthfuls of hot pork I took long draughts of wine, drinking it straight from the neck of the flagon.

The scene was one of confusion and I struggled to recall the sequence of events that had led me to this place. I knew vaguely that I was under the influence of some kind of hallucinogenic drug. This was probably ingested via the punch we had been served before we set out from the shop—perhaps it was also in the wine. The extent to which everyone else was also affected was difficult to decide. By comparison to the quantities imbibed by Jim Brotherton and Malcolm my draught of the spiced wine had been modest. Since then however, I had taken more than my fair share of wine. Unfortunately as my vision was increasingly faulted I had no idea where to look to make a judgement.

I remember sitting back on the rush matting whilst the world about me slipped into a rainbow of colour and each silhouette that passed by brought with it a halo of brilliant white light. Somewhere at the back of my mind I decided that my safety could only be secured by laying flat on the ground. Each time I attempted to make this manoeuvre I found myself floating in the air, hovering above the ground until I put down my feet. It was almost impossible. After numerous attempts someone took hold of my left arm and began to lead me round the bonfire. We joined a ring of people who skipped and danced and leapt around the flames. Now their faces sparkled and one—a woman's face—suddenly burst into a torch of bright flames. Her partner a small man whose cloak hung open exposing a sagging red belly, grabbed at her head putting his hands into the mass of burning and I heard her laugh. They disappeared and I made my staggering progress in pursuit still supported by the guiding hand.

By now I was unable to orientate and the snow walls all looked the same. The gyrations of the other celebrants made the task of locating my position all the more difficult. At some point I slipped and the hand let me go and I ended up with my face pressed into the rushes. Another face appeared close to mine—a fuzzy detail unrecognisable save that it was female. She licked my cheek and cold hands searched beneath my robe. Probing fingers found me soft and unresisting. The face screamed and the hand gripped tight. A pain like no other convulsed me and I contorted like a jack-knife. The severity of the pain momentarily cleared my head and I found myself staring into the girl, Sally's face. Her eyes were glazed and her mouth slack. Her cloak was pushed back over her shoulders and I could see her breasts pressed hard against the tangle of rush-wood. With some difficulty I managed to release her fingers and roll away. However, as soon as I moved the clarity slipped away again and the figures meshed with the reflections of the fire. I found myself adrift and sleepy in a sea of reds and oranges.

It must have been some considerable time later that my consciousness returned. The fire had again burned down and for once the area surrounding it was quiet. My face felt scorched. I had slept facing the fire and now my eyes were tender and the skin on my cheeks tight. The hand I put up to cover my eyes was cold—a welcome relief. I sat up and saw that groups of figures in twos and threes had collected around the bonfire. Having abandoned their cloaks they could be seen plainly in various stages of copulation.

Opposite the entrance on the far side sat a man. He was perched in a niche carved from the ice wall to make a wider than usual seat. His identity was difficult to make out through the flames but he appeared to wear a complex head-dress that obscured most of his face. His cloak was pulled around him disguising his body and only the scale of is proportions gave any indication of who he might be. I struggled to my feet still feeling light-headed still uncertain. Now my head throbbed and a steam-hammer worked itself into a frenzy behind my eyes. A yard or two from where I stood a two figures were locked in a bundle under a cover. The woman's bare legs stuck out they quivered and her toes grasped at the air. As they were so well wrapped it was impossible to see who they were even if the activity in which they were engaged left nothing to the imagination.

As I approached the seated figure his image became clearer. The head-dress was in fact a complex of animal skulls and of horns and teeth. But the eyes that peered out from under the leather cap could not have belonged to anyone else. They turned to me as I drew near.

'Aha—Paul come and sit with me.' Bessie grinned as she spoke.

She flung back her cape to reveal the horror of her nakedness. Her monstrous pot-gutted body was a nightmare. Swollen porcine breasts were perched atop mounds of fat that rolled down to rest on gross thighs. Everywhere the skin was stretched almost to bursting point. It shone, glazed and almost translucent in the fire-light; glistening like a mammoth joint of roast pork. However revolting, the sight of her body was insignificant compared to the other revelation beneath her robe. The nipple of her right breast pointed downwards—a blind snout, wrinkled and sheathed in hair. The other breast was completely hidden by James's pouting mouth. He crouched before her, his eyes tight shut with one hairy arm across her middle hanging on to her pap like an obscene incubus. Her dimpled hand lifted the spare tit and pointed its brown nose to me.

The shock of the image had a similar effect on me as Sally's physical attack. My head cleared and in a flash I had a vivid recollection of the events that had led me to this place.

**

After leaving Bessie's shop and noticing the activity on the hill top I made my way back to the cottage. I was still feeling irritated at having been obliged to stay but after my conversation with Bessie I felt I had accommodated the situation better. Whereas before I had tried to maintain my moral stance theoretically despite the evidence of my actions, now I accepted that my appetites were real. The option of sexual depravity was a reality however horrendous. Nevertheless the boundary of my conscience had been enlarged and whilst this was a step I could still not claim it to be progressive.

Jane was having lunch when I arrived she sat opposite James reading a magazine. When I entered he looked up and smiled, just as if nothing untoward had taken place. Jane ignored me.

'Fancy something to eat?' he asked.

'Thank-you but no—I had a sandwich up at the shop with Bessie.'

'And a drop of the hard stuff I'll bet.'

'A drop of brandy actually.'

Jane looked up from her glossy magazine and gave me a withering look.

'Well I hope it's put you in a better mood,' she said, 'You were a pig this morning—and there was no need for it.'

I put the kettle on and prepared a cup.

'Anyone like a coffee?' I asked.

They both said yes so I took two more cups from the cupboard. When I brought the drinks to the table James was waiting for me.

'Now about tonight Paul—we've arranged to meet at Bessie's at about none-thirty and . . . .'

'Hang on a minute James,' I interrupted, 'isn't it about time someone told me a bit more about this so-called party of yours.'

Filled with my new resolve I was determined to have the detail explained in terms that I could understand.

'I know it's supposed to be Yorkshire's answer to the sex Olympics—but how does that relate to all the rest . . . . the mumbo-jumbo; the quasi-religious crap . . . . you know—all that Romany mother earth stuff twenty generations removed?'

Jane stood up and folded her magazine, picked up her cup and turned.

'I really don't know what the hell is the matter with you Paul,' she muttered, 'I thought you'd come back in a better mood but here you are just as sarcastic and nasty as ever. I'll take my coffee in the kitchen James—call me when he's gone again.'

She marched out.

James sat for a moment grinning quietly to himself.

'I see that you are still the silver tongued Don Juan Paul. You really do know how to get up someone's nose . . . . Anyway—do I take it then that you are going to accept our invitation to our humble little party tonight?'

I mumbled an affirmative.

'In which case let me tell you a little something about the agenda.'

Most of what he told me I knew already some other stuff I'd guessed. He described the Solstice as one of the most important festivals in the old calendar and claimed that since before the Dark Ages believers had celebrated the occasion with a 'no-holds-barred' party. This he said was especially true amongst Romany people.

'Their only responsibility outside the clan—the only one they will accept—is to Mother Earth. You'll find that much of this recent green awareness is only folk latching onto things that people like us have known for centuries. Your 'Johnny-cum-lately' Christianity has about had its day. The morals it purports to claim are hypocritical; the origins of its beginnings are made up from legends and fairy stories and worst of all it doesn't work in practice.'

He paused, partly to sip his coffee and also to see if I'd taken the bait. I refused to be drawn and sat silent waiting for him to continue. When I did not respond he went on.

'The form of our celebration has evolved over the years into an enjoyable social event and—as you said—a quasi-religious occasion. We volunteer control of our conscious senses; we dance; we eat and drink and make merry. Finally we perform an age old ritual renewing our promises to Mother Nature—there's a bit more as you are a new member—some sort of initiation perhaps.'

He delivered the last bit with a secret, sideways grin. The implication being, that he was still holding something back—another provocation.

'So—in a nutshell, one might say you all get pissed and fuck anything that moves—quite a religious gathering.'

He laughed.

'That's a bit like saying that you Catholics gather in church to feast off the dead body of your God's son.'

Our sparring had reached an impasse and for a few minutes we sat in silence drinking our coffee. James eventually asked:

'I suppose you've read Nietzsche?'

'Yes.' I said lying. The man's reputation was enough to preclude him from any reading list I might enjoy. 'Why—is he back in fashion?'

James moved over to stand in front of the fire—a pose implying superiority.

'I suppose I agree with you—at least in some respect—but one or two things he said made good sense. Do you recall his comments on morality?—He said morality was only the herd instinct of the individual. Nice that—I couldn't agree more! He implied that morality as we understand it is only for those who need to be instructed—ruled; the half humans—the sheep.'

The argument was not new.

'Not surprisingly Adolf Hitler agreed.'

'Forget the politics for a minute Paul. Examine the facts dispassionately for once. Most of our moral guidance is a form of population control—you should be able to have what you want, when you want it. That's the law of the jungle—the law of nature. You Catholics—like the Jews—invented guilt as a straight-jacket to stifle objection . . . . pay the price that the holy insurance-man asks or forgo the promise of pleasure in the afterlife . . . . and if sex isn't one of the heavenly pleasures then I wonder what is . . . . and if it is then why not enjoy it now . . . . better the devil you know . . . '

I couldn't resist, 'I suspect you know the devil a good deal better than I do.' I said quietly.

His reply was prompt, 'Certainly—I'll introduce you to her if you wish.' Then he laughed.

Having had such a strenuous night I slept most of the afternoon, not waking until gone eight o'clock. I woke thinking about Kate and decided I should at least try and patch things up with her before the party.

When I got downstairs James had left already and Jane was fussing about getting herself ready. She stood in front of a mirror over the kitchen sink applying a range of cosmetics to her face. It was the sort of undercoat that might have protected motor-car bodywork from rust for at least a decade or so. She wore a long cloak and it was only when she turned to select a different eye-liner that saw she was naked beneath it.

'If you go outside like that Jane you'll freeze to death.' I said.

She pouted into the mirror and a moment later turned to face me opening her cloak with both hands as she did so.

'Now don't tell me you'd prefer me all covered up?' she whispered.

'I'd certainly prefer you without frost-bite.' I answered.

'Any kind of bite might be nice . . . . want to try one?'

This last comment sounded like the marketing slogan of an ice-cream salesman but I resisted the temptation to say so. There was no doubt that she had a good body and it was easy to see why she had become a nude model. Unfortunately there was silliness about her almost verging on innocence, a culpable ignorance of the way the world would certainly exploit her. Until my stay on the Mount I had always fund innocence to be attractively sexy—not quite so much now.

'Later—perhaps!' I said trying to be polite.

My response was taken as encouragement and in a moment she sidled across to me and pressed her body against me. It was firm and tempting but it was just as I was trying to manoeuvre her away that Kate's voice rang out.

'I hope I'm not interrupting anything?'

Like the proverbial hot knife through butter—the mood changed. Kate appeared at the kitchen window and had clearly misinterpreted my involvement. I feigned a welcome and a cheery smile.

'Kate—I was just about to . . . . '

'I can see what you were just about to do Paul.'

Sensing a possible conflict Jane placed her arm around my shoulders and turned her gloating wicked smile on Kate.

'I don't know what you thought we were doing but we'd hardly got started anyway.' She said provocatively.

Kate was dismissive, 'Well whatever it was—if you don't mind I'd like a word with Paul—in private.'

In the mistaken belief that I would support her Jane turned to me. She enjoyed teasing another woman. In return I removed her arm and nodded at the door.

'If you don't mind Jane.'

At that she swished round hardly trying to hide her annoyance and stamped into the living room. By then Kate had entered by the back door. Her eyes followed the other woman's progress and then she turned to me.

'I don't want to contribute to all that moralistic crap Paul but you certainly don't waste any time do you?' She held my gaze adding bitterly, 'Christians seem to be quicker off the mark than us poor heathens.'

I started to protest but she cut me short, 'I just came by to ask where we stood. After you stormed out last night—I didn't know what to think.'

Her appearance had taken me completely by surprise and needless to say my confusion only worsened in the face of her direct assault.

'I don't know.' I said in a small voice. 'I was left with the impression you didn't want to see me again.'

She looked at me for a moment and then without another word she turned and left carefully closing the door quietly behind her. I took this as a gesture designed to demonstrate her willpower; her control but I was left just as ignorant of my standing with her as I was before she came in.

Half an hour later I squeezed into Bessie's kitchen. The room was crowded as everyone in the village including their guests were present and clearly in party mood. I was the last to arrive. The room had been all but cleared; the furniture had been pushed back against the walls leaving only the long table in the centre. On the hearth a huge cast-iron cooking pot simmered stirred occasionally by Gerald who stood close by. Bessie took centre stage.

'Now friends—as y'all know we've gathered here to make the most of our winter Solstice. A time for the old traditions—whatever your beliefs tonight you can find yourselves free from criticism. So—we'll eat and drink an' make the most of one another; at first light we'll perform a short ritual and with the morning we'll welcome the season of cold.'

She beamed one of her most generous smiles and, like everyone else in the room, I found myself smiling back at her. Her good humour was truly infectious.

'If you'd like to pass the punch-pot now—we'll make a start.'

At a sign from her, her nearest companion shuffled across to a tray of goblets that stood near the fireside on a side table. Using a copper ladle he took the first and filled it to the brim from the punch-pot. James was first in line and he took the goblet and drained it. It was refilled before he took it and retired to one side. The next in line moved forward and repeated the procedure and as each one drank Gerald bowed to them in turn and offered his salutations. As I approached Bessie whispered in my ear explaining that the punch was like the Wassail bowl taken on New Year's Eve.

'It's a nicely spiced drink—keeps out the cold and gets rid silly inhibitions. Drink the first draught down but sip the next slowly.'

By then I had decided to conform to their wishes with as much good grace as I could muster. I accepted the goblet and drained it as instructed. It was a rich aromatic brew with an under-taste of lemon and brandy. Not an unpleasant drink but I suspected probably deceptively strong. I was not wrong. Even by the time I'd moved back to where I'd stood before I could feel the effects. Once we'd all been served Gerald left the room.

Clearly I was not the only person to feel the effects of the drink. Emma giggled over something that Ben said to her; little Jim talked in a very loud voice; Kate was next to Duggie who ignored her and instead spoke intimately to Sally on his other side. Sammy made rude comments to Malcolm who in turn poked fun across the room at me.

When Gerald returned he was leading a fat pig on a piece of cord. Immediately James moved over and took the cord from Gerald.

'Ladies and Gentlemen,' he announced, 'let me introduce you to your supper.'

He then led the poor creature around the room in a complete circle until he once again stood before the hearth.

'As Headman, it is my task to prepare the beast and for any newcomers with weak stomachs,' he looked directly at me, 'it is permissible for them to wait in the other room until the ritual is complete.'

No one moved. The comment was obviously aimed at me and I was therefore determined to stay. However, after what took place next, there were moments when I wished I had taken James at his word.

James and Gerald trussed the pig's legs back and front. Sensing their intention the animal then began to squeal—but by then it was helpless. With some help from several others the beast was bundled onto the table, its feet in the air and its head hanging over one end. An old tin bath was dragged under the head and James was given a long thin-bladed knife by Bessie. He brandished the weapon theatrically over his head.

'Let this blood feed us through the season of cold nights and stir our new beginnings when the sun returns.'

The whole room was transfixed. Ever the showman James moved the fat snout to one side and with what had to be practised care he slit the pig's throat in one easy movement. Suddenly there was blood. The animal screamed and kicked and writhed on the table. Its struggles were such that it seemed it would never surrender its life. When eventually the drama stopped the silence in the room was profound. I saw Sally grow pale and clutch a hand to her mouth; Duggie put his arm around her and she hid her face in his shoulder. On his other side Kate just stared as if mesmerised. James sliced off the animal's head with casual expertise. At that point a sigh sounded round the room, the universal response—the pent-up breath of most of those who watched. For those who imagined that the worst was over the next stage was certainly a shock.

James handed the severed head to Gerald who placed it at the far end of the table, and then he cut through the belly of the animal and allowed the steaming insides to spill out; a multicoloured agglomeration that slipped on a sea of mucus across the wooden surface. Fortunately from my point of view to one side, the sight was mostly hidden by the carcass. I was nevertheless immediately aware of a strong smell, a fulsome graveolent odour that permeated the senses making the gut heave and one's digestion insecure. Surprisingly not everyone was affected in the same way. Malcolm, Gerald, Bessie and Sammy were all apparently entranced, their eyes shone as though the occasion was of supreme interest. Indeed they appeared to study the proceedings so as not to miss one tiny detail.

James seemed to be in his element. Without hesitation he plunged his hand into the mess before him and pulled out the still warm heart leaving his hands and forearms blackened with the pig's blood. After disentangling it, tearing it away from the major veins he held it out to Bessie. Without hesitation she took it and threw it on the blazing fire. A smattering of applause greeted her action—clearly a symbolic act.

The remainder of the carcass was hoisted onto Gerald's shoulders for him to transport. Crippled as he was he nevertheless made an adequate porter with the legs of the beast held either side of his face and the headless body itself draped over his hump. The expression 'piggy-back' sprang to mind. My inappropriate humour was only one of the signs of a feeling of well-being that I experienced. My reservations about Kate and my concerns about James were suddenly the source of some amusement. I was light-hearted and increasingly my head floated and my vision blurred. It did not seem to matter when I was invited—as the others were also—to undress and wear one of the robes being distributed by Bessie. I had abrogated control and it felt wonderful.

**

Now the same woman, the friendly generous shop-keeper sat there an obscene parody of the kindly woman I had grown to like and to respect. She was waiting for my response.

Chapter Eighteen

My understanding of Einstein's theories concerning time is limited. In fact I recall only that time like space is apparently able to bend. For me that night, standing on front of Bessie caused time to warp. In the space of just a few seconds I was apparently able to consider a whole variety of alternatives. It was just as if my mind was able to subdivide. In one the problem was considered objectively prompting questions such as: what will they all think if I run away? ; will I be allowed to leave?; do I want to leave? The other screamed a fundamental objection—a total disapproval taking me to the very edge of sanity. I struggled to maintain a view of normality but my efforts were unrewarded.

However disgusting the prospect of Bessie's offer, clearly there was more to the invitation than the simple pornography suggested by her actions: the killing of the pig and what had followed had taught me that much at least. But without the proper terms of reference how was I to make an informed decision? Ignoring the lascivious sight before me, the Bessie I knew had earned much more than my arbitrary dismissal. Unfortunately matters were not helped by my muddled mind and my lack of control. I had an impression that I was missing a simple truth.

'C'mon my dear,' Bessie said again. 'I can be your Earth Mother fer t' night only-Y' need to be prepared fer the ceremony—your ceremony . . . Come on.'

I was not sure afterwards if it was the surfeit of food and drink or the drugs or simply the fear and revulsion that filled me at that moment. Whatever the cause before I could formulate a tangible excuse, my stomach heaved and I was violently sick. It was not the kind of nausea one might associate with a bout of beer drinking or a touch of food poisoning. My body was suddenly wracked, great spasms shook me from groin to chest, spasms that built in their intensity and culminated in a gold medal performance of projectile vomiting. To make it all the more disgusting the stink of the effluent equated in my mind with the smell from the open pig's belly. All at once it seemed that the delicate balance in which my constitution had been held was ruptured. My physical equilibrium slipped, my horizon grew insecure and I fell forward into my own mess. The physical trauma agitated the more by the mixture of emotions that it accompanied, loosened my control still further and I slipped into a faint.

It was Kate's voice that finally brought me round. I raised my head to find her leaning over me. I lay on my back surrounded by the whole assembly

My mouth felt warm and sticky with a sweet sickly taste clogging my throat and when I opened my eyes fully I could se Kate smiling down at me. Her eyes were glassy and her breathing sounded ragged. She was on her knees, one hand placed under my neck and the other flat on my bare belly. Her own robe had fallen back from her shoulders and her bare breasts hung between us.

'It's time to get up Paul,' she whispered, 'time to complete your initiation. We're all here to welcome you.'

'I just want to sleep.'

The hand that appeared on Kate's shoulder belonged to James. He pushed her to one side and bent forward into my field of vision.

'Come on Paul—we'll give you a hand.'

His attitude was businesslike and brusque. A moment later I was gathered up from the rush flooring by invading hands. They wiped me down with a warm cloth and I was left standing in front of James. Bessie sat to his right hand side, her bulk now covered by the robe and a small table had been erected between them. Gerald stood nearby and as I watched he removed a cloth from the table-top to reveal a gauze pad, a small copper bowl and a thin bladed boning knife.

James smiled. When he spoke it was in a voice redolent of a sermon read by a vicar.

'Paul Denley you are the heir apparent to the clan. You are my natural son and thereby the son of the Headman. The spilling of your blood on this Winter Solstice celebration is therefore in keeping with both the needs of Mother Earth and with your initiation . . . '

His words settled gradually, their meaning slow to be identified. However, with the mention of blood—my blood—my thinking became better focused. I suddenly realised what this was all about and panic made my frame go rigid. Before I could react I was grabbed from behind by strong hands and in my weakened state my struggles were easily subdued. When I was helpless James continued:

'You're to make an offering of live flesh Paul and this will be kept in the clan's mound in which all our flesh is kept making you one with us. Your blood will anoint the ground and your spirit will become part of our heritage. When I die you will be responsible for the well-being and the continuation of this community . . . '

Now I was fully conscious—aware and afraid.

'I want nothing to do with any of you James,' I shouted, 'this is primitive madness—a nonsense—now let me go else you will pay for it.'

My outburst was received in complete silence but as soon as I started to struggle the hands holding me tightened their grip. Gerald stepped forward and picked up the knife and the panic choked me. I began to sweat and tremble, everyone's eyes were on me, watching and waiting.

Suddenly Bessie rose from her seat.

'It's time to choose Paul—what part will you forfeit?'

**

The three women walked in line away from the meeting place and I followed at a discrete distance. The sound of their voices complimented the tone of the wind. It was a high-pitched natural sound almost a monotone and only just above the level of conversational speech. They appeared to be singing and yet although they were not in unison, there was a harmony concordant in the noise they made. Beneath them on the lower hill-side the small cemetery was just visible—the tops of the headstones only just clearing the mounds of the snow. At first light the others had made their way back to the cottages no doubt to sleep a recovery after the night's exertions. The fire had eventually died down leaving only a mound of grey ash covering the glow from the embers and I had awoken to find myself alone in the ice packed amphitheatre. As I left the wind swept across the hill-side—it was a chill reminder of my nakedness. I drew my robe tighter as I pulled on my shoes at the entrance a task made a task made all the more difficult because of my injured hand.

In the distance at the foot of the hill I saw the last of several tiny figures arriving at the row of cottages where I stayed. I was all set to follow when I heard the singing. The sound came from behind me from the opposite side of the hill beyond the trees.

I turned to watch and saw Bessie and Kate closely followed by Sam as they waded knee deep in snow to visit each grave. A curious ritual, they paused briefly at each memorial before moving on to the next. At each stop their singing was repeated and their tone consistent. I had no idea what they were doing but whatever it was they must have been half frozen before they concluded their mission. By the time they were sufficiently close on their return, I could see that they were shivering despite their heavy cloaks. It was the last act in a mystery play that had had me confused completely from its inception.

With the advance of the morning at least my head was clearer and my control over my normal functions was restored. I found I was no longer angry; no longer drugged; no longer afraid and even though the assault I'd suffered was still vivid, I no longer felt the same level of animosity towards my aggressors as I had at the time.

At the appropriate moment and before I could suitably voice my objection, with her usual expertise Bessie had removed the last joint from my little finger of my left hand. My scream had accompanied the crunch as the blade slipped between the joint but the sounds of approval from the rest of the assembly were lost to my ears. Bessie had carried out the operation with the same level of care she had demonstrated when she massaged my chest. Naturally when faced with having to choose a digit that would be forfeit, I had resorted to bluster and it was only when I failed to decide that Bessie took over.

By then my cowardice had reached new levels of embarrassment so much so that it had taken four of the men present to hold me still enough to allow the amputation to take place. I remember being surprised afterwards that the pain had not been worse and that there was little blood spilt. Perhaps the wine and the drugs had acted as anaesthetic; perhaps the trauma was in the anticipation rather than in the act itself. In any case my view of the proceedings had been blocked by Malcolm's shoulder (he was one of the men holding my hand) and it was over—or more accurately off before I fully realised what had happened. I suppose if I'd watched it may well have been that much worse.

Before the women reached the place where I stood I turned to make my way back. Now my hand throbbed and the binding that Bessie had applied was blotched with spots of crimson. I badly needed a coffee.

After the fuss had died down and everyone had returned to their various entertainments, I'd spent the latter part of the night with Kate. Sympathising with my pain she had firstly acted like a mother figure; then later as my Florence Nightingale nursing my injury and finally as my lover. Shepherded to a warm corner well away from the rest, Kate had wrapped us tightly together in our robes and taken the lead in a loving night of pleasure. We'd slept intermittently, waking only to repeat our love-making until at last I had fallen into a deep sleep—undisturbed until the next morning.

I do not know the cause only that the strange experience of the previous night's activities may have contributed but I woke feeling changed. I could not define the nature of the change nor its extent, I was only conscious of a difference. A new passivity existed calming all my feelings of opposition. As a consequence I did not object or question Kate when she whispered that she had to go with Bessie and Sammy on an errand. I slept on after she left.

I arrived back at the cottage long before Kate and her friends. The place appeared to be empty and I presumed that James was therefore off elsewhere courting his friends. I dressed in my warmest clothing, lit the fire and brewed a pot of tea. I then sat comfortably before the fire sipping the tea and enjoying the solitude.

Outside a cold early-morning mist laid over the hills precursor of a freezing fog and the promise of yet more snow. The radiant warmth of the hearth-side was a comfort—quite different from the animal fever of the bonfire night. Now with passions grown tepid and fatigue admitted it was possible to assess the state of my conscience objectively and to rate the possible damage. The mutilation at Bessie's hands was only a memory but I calculated that the trauma would stay with me. On the other hand due to the various periods of unconsciousness some of my memories were out of kilter—the sequence was insecure. I could recall the totality of what had taken place but the uncertainty of some after-images left me confused about their progression. The vision of Bessie's body gleaming in the firelight; the obscenity of her invitation and James crouched at her breast like an aged foetus were all icons of my nightmare. By comparison the antics of the others in their lewd performance of sexual perversity were somehow less offensive.

I examined the mental snapshots one by one; each still-frame a portrait of undeniable and shameless pornography. Why then—I asked myself, was I not as horrified by the evidence of the night as I imagined that I should be. Was the virulence of the infection already evident in the bloodstream of my moral sense? I remembered the comfort brought by Kate as we held together beside the fire; the excitement of her body and the satisfaction of our congress. I also remembered seeing her earlier across the other side of the fire with Ben and Malcolm in close attendance. Erotic pictures of flagrant debauchery flicked slowly past mixing my emotions. I was tired—too tired to try and apply order to my thinking. However, before I dozed off I decided that whatever my evaluation of my new state, I needed to confirm the situation between me and Kate. If—as I suspected we might have a future together we needed to qualify the conditions of the match.

**

It was early afternoon when I awoke. Someone had tucked a blanket around me, built up the fire and left me to nestle in the secure warmth of a dreamless cocoon. The cottage was still silent and it took me several minutes to reconstruct the events that had led me to the fireside. Eventually I flung off the blanket and stretched. Contrary to my forecast the fingers of frost on the window had melted indicating that a thaw had set in. Standing at the window I could see that strands of grass were visible in the nearest edge of the garden and spikes of twigs were poking through the mounds of snow from the hedge. At the front of the property patches of cobbles had begun to reappear and the gutter ran in a constant stream of icy water.

I reasoned that if the snow was actually melting then perhaps the hill would be passable. The front door opened and James came in. He saw me by the window and smiled as if he could read my thoughts.

'And how is the writer this afternoon?' he asked stamping the damp from his boots.

'Fine.' I replied.

'Planning a getaway perhaps?'

'When and if I want to leave James—you know I'll just go—so it's hardly going to be an escape.'

He went over to the fire and rubbed his hands in front of the flames.

'Ben left with the girls this morning. You were still fast asleep but they all sent their best wishes. Sally said she thought you were the perfect victim.' He grinned as he made the remark and then looked across at me. 'So Paul—what now—will you stay on here? You still have a book to finish. As I'm going back to Town soon you could have the place to yourself again.'

Seeing my hesitation he pressed the point.

'Kate called round earlier . . . . I suppose she wants to talk to you—you could do a lot worse!'

'I'm not sure what I will do—but I certainly need to talk to her in the near future.'

James turned his back to the fire, clasped his hands behind his back and rocked on the balls of his feet: a military posture, a general perhaps planning his next stratagem.

'How's the hand?' he asked suddenly.

'Missing part of one finger.' I snapped back.

'A good investment as you'll discover. Anyway in a week or so you'll forget you ever had it.'

'Except when I try to type!'

That fact had obviously escaped him and for a moment he looked concerned.

'Sorry about that Paul. We forgot about the typing—should have taken a toe instead—like I did myself all those years ago. Ever mind what's done is done you'll just have to learn to accommodate the new shorter finger.'

I chose not to argue the point and instead I left him to the fire and went into the other room to sort out my manuscript. As the pages were numbered the muddle in which it had been left by Duncan was easy to remedy. In a short while the table was covered in neat stacks representing each chapter with the accompanying notes. It had been some time since I'd faced my task and in no time at all I was soon absorbed in re-reading what I'd written. It stimulated me sufficient at least to establish a new resolve. I badly needed to get back to my writing and to finish this particular project. The events of the last few days were successfully moved to my mental back-burner.

My method of writing always necessitates a closely read review of newly completed pages before moving on to write the next. It is a process that permits me to focus on re-establishing my direction and to renew the friendship of the characters involved—as it were. As a project nears completion I find that the time taken in this period of editing lengthens. It is also a time for digesting the work when the voice of my inner-self determines if the meal has been worth the effort of the eating. As the piece on Sir Walter Scott was in its final stages there was much to absorb.

I was so preoccupied by my task that I did not hear the front door when Kate arrived.

'And I suppose you've been so busy that you haven't had time for food Mr. Denley?'

I turned to find her leaning casually in the open doorway looking just as she had the first time she'd visited me. Unfortunately James stood nearby ruining the illusion.

'Suddenly I'm hungry.' I laughed.

'I thought you might be,' she replied, 'we missed our date—if you remember you promised to take me out to lunch today.' Now she laughed as well, 'So I made a pan of broth—with dumplings and it's on the stove next door. Leave all that and come and eat.'

James watched the performance with a quizzical look.

'And is the old man invited too?' he asked.

'Why not there's plenty to go round—and I'm sure Paul would love to have you there. Wouldn't you Paul?'

Despite the deliberate attempt at humour my disappointment was hard to disguise—so much for an intimate meal together I thought. However, the meal that evening was as reasonable occasion as one might have hoped for and surprisingly moderation was the keynote. No one made any mention of the party or of any of the events surrounding it.; Duggie was on his best behaviour limiting his drinking to just a few glasses of wine and James restricted his brand of sarcasm to amusing anecdotes about historical figures. To some degree therefore there was a concerted effort to restore a sense of normality a fact that was confirmed when the others eventually retired and Kate was left alone with me.

I helped clear the dishes and washed the pots and afterwards we sat together over a late night drink. It was the ideal opportunity for which I'd been waiting. Other than at the party when neither of us was properly *compos mentis* the last time we'd truly been alone together was the night of our disagreement. Not surprisingly as a consequence I was restive—uncomfortable in the knowledge that major decisions need to be taken concerning our future. Conversely Kate was completely relaxed. We pulled the settee round to face the burning logs enhancing the feeling of privacy and sat close together sipping hot-toddy.

'So,' Kate said at last, 'the scene is set but where do we go from here.'

One of the qualities I most admired in Kate was her ability to ridicule romantic situations. I laughed.

'First of all a truce,' I said, 'no progress is possible without a ceasefire.'

'Or,' she interrupted with a cheeky grin, 'no progress is possible without friction. Friction causes movement does it not?'

'I cannot imagine any kind of relationship with you my love that did not include friction of one sort or another.'

She put her head on my shoulder smiling.

'And does the heir apparent intend some kind of a relationship with me?' she asked.

This was my opportunity.

'I think we could be well-suited Kate. I can't ever remember being so . . . . being so close to anyone before. How would you feel about making an honest man of me? We could live in London—you'd like my flat.'

According to her expression this was clearly not what she had been expecting. Suddenly she was serious. The smile fell from her face and although she still held my hand in hers, a distance opened between us.

'Was that a proposal—of marriage Paul?' she asked in a small voice.

I started to mumble my admission but she didn't let me finish.

'I hope it wasn't a proposal of marriage Paul—not at this stage . . . . Because if it was it's the last thing I expected and—regretfully—I'd have to refuse you.'

Chapter Nineteen

My mother's manuscript was a thorough if somewhat complex study. And although my motive for reading it at that particular time and in that particular place was utilitarian the more I read the greater the significance I found relative to the strange community I'd found on the Mount. Amongst other things it proved to be a documentary account of the history of that community. Unfortunately in one respect the manuscript was incomplete, consequently whilst it provided many of the answers I sought; it also prompted almost as many more new questions.

The detail my mother provided indicated a wealth of serious research and justified her regular visits to Eastern Europe in her middle age. She first outlined the history of the region from which the community's ancestors had originated and, even given the context of Russia's new boundaries it was still easy to identify the localities and to update the geography according to recent developments.

The borders of Estonia are now disputed with neighbouring Russia. A situation prompted by the move to self-rule that has caused Mother Russia to claim a dividing line along the Estonian border that precludes the admission of one and a half million ethnic Russians from her protection. Around the small town of Pechory near the east bank of the Narva River, the new border has effectively split a community of 20,000 Setu people. In particular the village of Vommorski has now been annexed therefore.

In terms of their religious beliefs the Setu are orthodox—as opposed to the rest of Estonian society which is Lutheran. The spiritual centre of their culture is the 15th century monastery in Pechory; consequently in order to visit this place of worship the Estonian Setu must now seek a border pass.

Early in the 16th century things were very different. Before the final and irrevocable commitment of Luther in 1521 the majority of people in the land followed the orthodox Christian faith of the Eastern Church. The Allaveer family were some of the few exceptions. Their ancestors were immigrants and although they belonged to the Setu tribe they practised a belief in an older previous religion: one more closely akin to the Pagan beliefs that had been so popular before the arrival of Christianity. It was a belief system reflecting that period when the predominant ethnic group were the Livs—a Finno-Ugrian race known from runic inscriptions as Liflandi. These had been a people who had been colonised and converted by the Christian Teutonic Knights—known as Knights of the Sword from the early 13th century. The subsequent division of the region into Livonia, Latvia and Estonia was therefore dictated by the three predominant religions: the Lutherans, the Orthodox Christians and the Pagans.

Within the existing framework the Allaveer family, their relatives and friends formed a sub-culture which for a while was entirely acceptable despite the pervading influence of the Bishoprics inspired by the Teutonic Order. Nevertheless the advent of Christianity can still be seen as a first step in a slow process of alienation between the old and the new belief systems. In this regard, the unrest and the changes that occurred in the latter half of the 16th century proved undeniable. The pressure exerted by Estonia's neighbours: Muscovy in the north and the unification of Poland and Lithuania in the south prompted major change and when it came, the Reformation made religious tolerance a thing of the past.

The persecution the Allaveers suffered was profound. It affected their efforts in Trade; their purchase of goods and in the end their very freedom. It was a form of suffering that their descendants were to grow used to in the centuries that followed. Prompted by the evolution of prejudice against them eventually the Allaveers departed from Estonia. The Lutheran bias promoted a new degree of severity in terms of the rigour it demanded and in order to safeguard themselves they took to the open road in much the same manner as their forefathers had done.

It appeared that the original trades practised by the families included livestock trading and butchery. However as they proceeded across Europe they were obliged to rely more on their transferable skills as traders rather than as slaughterers or meat vendors. As merchants they could deal in any kind of goods or produce that came to hand.

The traditions of their Setu heritage were maintained particularly with regard to the practice of singing. Setu women sang their gossip to one another at their gatherings. The practice of singing information was endemic and in Estonia previous generations would even sing lullabies made up of the latest news at the graves of their departed loved ones. One might compare such activities with the chorused responses of Neapolitan women saying the rosary at gravesides.

Reading this part caused me to remember the snow laden hill on the morning after the party; the voices of Bessie, Kate and Sammy chanting —it seemed—irrationally around the graves. My perspective became a little clearer. Not clear enough to forgive or forget the amputation of the first finger joint which was now aching again like toothache. The idea of amputation still inspired my horror but the ritual, however remote from the pedestrian reality of my normal experience was perhaps a symbolic reference to the lost butchering trade of Setu ancestors. A peculiar mix of ancient sematology combined with primitive notions of atonement or redemption. It was a convention layered with conflicting meanings. In that same context my convocation as heir apparent could just as easily equate with Jewish circumcision or indeed any of the 'coming of age' rituals evident in old religions

Kate's refusal was hard to accommodate. She argued that she would find any such formalisation of our relationship too restrictive. She said she had other more important responsibilities that would affect the community more directly and that she expected me as the heir to the position of Headman to leave her free to fulfil them. I was unable to get her to itemise these responsibilities or even to indicate how they might affect the community. In the end I was left with only her promise that she would always make herself available to me whenever I felt the need of her.

I had been so set on marrying her: a relationship of exclusivity that would bind us together in the traditional sense of man and wife that I found her refusal incomprehensible. The notion that after refusing a proposal of marriage a woman could offer herself as she had was beyond my understanding. It was unnatural.

The climate in the highlands of Yorkshire is notoriously capricious. Certainly the cold comes early and the snows often last until late spring, however sometimes, unaccountably the weather breaks and a false thaw sets in. A transient warm current of air provokes the development of new buds and spring flowers. A false promise confirmed by the destruction wreaked by the returning frost a few days later. No small wonder the stoicism of the population; no surprise then that such emphasis is placed on responsibilities or that trust is so hard won.

All these were characteristics found in the community and provided some proof of a sparse but continued cultural development. Contrary to the impression that theirs was a society that stood apart, there were traits in personality redolent of the same immutability found in traditional Yorkshire communities. Even the form their rituals took had something in common with the Christian Church and in its single-mindedness the attitude of their congregation was a similar reflection. With hindsight I began to appreciate that many of my cynical observations were unfounded.

According to the manuscript the difference of opinion between the St. John Smith family and that of the Allaveers was more deeply rooted than simply that between land-owners and squatters. Certainly there was evidence of a dispute over title to land, just as there was reference to the entrenched prejudice of an established community to that of travellers. However, the attendant documentation included photocopies of letters written by Sir Gareth St. John Smith to Gustav Allaveer in which the accusation of murder was made more than once. The implication was that the Setu travellers had been responsible for the death of a member of the St. John Smith family. This made me recall the conversation I had with the Postmaster and his gossip about the death of Sir Gareth. In this instance the facts indicated that he had died after a fall from his horse whilst hunting in Durham. On the contrary however, the claims concerning the abduction of a gypsy girl and the death of a gypsy youth were proven to be correct. As a consequence a treaty agreed between the two groups in 1787 ended more than two hundred years of enmity.

Initially the travellers were granted a seven year lease on the land known as the Mount but at its culmination in 1794 this was changed to one comprising a one of one hundred and ninety-nine years duration. There was no mention of blame made regarding the gypsy girl or of the killing of a gypsy youth but the generosity of the land grant was such that there was a presumption of guilt and that was a major factor in determining the nature of the new lease. An excerpt from the Parish register simply stated that a young man from the gypsy camp had been killed accidentally in the woods probably by a falling tree. The entry was inconclusive and stated only that the burial service was carried out according to non-Christian practises and that the location of the grave was not on hallowed ground. There was no mention of the fate of the gypsy girl.

Reading about Richard Smith's ancestors I was reminded again of the violent reaction the mention of his name had caused when I spoke of him to Kate. It had been the first occasion when her views had corresponded exactly with those of the rest of the community. Until then her attitude had implied that her behaviour derived entirely from personal choices. It was also significant that James had not mentioned his own relationship with Richard—no mention of his long association. Even when Little Jim had taken such offence to my claims of friendship with Richard, James had kept silent.

Since James had left to return to London I had transferred my writing table to the front bedroom overlooking the street. I was well aware that my book had fallen behind the schedule set for its publication and, although there was no emergency yet, it needed to be overhauled if it was to meet the next deadline. The usual quiet of the cottage had been spoilt lately by the comings and goings of the many visitors I now received. Whatever I thought about the new status I'd acquired the response of my neighbours had been more than sufficient to overwhelm me. Now I was consulted about all manner of things from the minutiae of their domestic arrangements concerning hire purchase agreements and credit facilities to prices bid at auction for livestock or animal foodstuffs. It seemed that in the eyes of the residents I had been magically imbued with the Wisdom of Solomon and the financial acumen of a merchant banker. It had been in order to alleviate this situation that I'd retired to the upstairs—choosing not to answer the door.

My position from the first floor also provided me with a vantage point from which I was able to view my neighbour's activities without fear of being seen myself. This was an attractive position for any author.

The downside of the new arrangement was to do with my lack of self-discipline. Despite all my good intentions I found myself spending a lot of time—too much time—simply observing the pattern of life amongst the people who lived on the Mount. However it did prove a fascinating exercise. I discovered for example that Malcolm worked for at least part of the week assisting Jim Brotherton on the farm. When he was not weaving rugs he was herding cattle and helping with the milking; Sammy and little Jim occupied themselves full time making pots in the studio behind their cottages; Bessie and Gerald worked in the shop and Duggie played the part of the local accountant. The only person without a specific role it seemed was Kate.

One Saturday morning early in January I sat daydreaming. I'd been struggling with a particular quotation trying to decide how much of it was pertinent to my text when the sound of a car drew my attention to the street below. It was an old black Ford, one I had not seen before. A moment later I was surprised to see Richard Smith get out from the driver's side.

I had seen Richard only once since the night of the party. My Christmas had passed in almost total isolation with hardly a break in my chosen routine. I had collected a few letters and cards from the Post Office down in the village, bought myself a frozen chicken and celebrated with a reasonable bottle of Mouton Cadet left over from my original stockpile. I had deliberately refused all offers of company from Bessie and Malcolm and Duggie. If Kate had asked me herself I may have capitulated but she had not. Richard's invitation had therefore come as a surprise. It had been delivered by a lad from the village and I had accepted on the spot.

It had been on Boxing Day that we'd got together in the evening. After a superb dinner during which we had already drunk far too much Burgundy we sat by his roaring fire and drank too much Brandy. I began to tell him about my starting to read my mother's manuscript and gave him a précis of the opening chapters. Now at that time I appreciate that my thinking was probably befuddled because of the drink, so I accept that my recollection is no doubt faulted. I was nevertheless surprised when he could fill in some of the gaps. So much so that I was left with the impression that Richard knew far more about the Allaveer family than he had previously admitted. Bearing in mind he'd claimed that his interest in seeing the manuscript had been to satisfy his need for historical fact as opposed to gossip, his virtuosity was unexpected. Naturally I asked him how he had come by such information and he informed me quite casually that he had a chest full of documentary evidence, original documents. He told me that many of the contents of the chest were letters and notes about letters.

I could not hide my surprise but he passed off his ambiguity with a wave of his hand calling it insignificant and telling me that he had his own agenda to which I was not privy. It was the first time I'd seen him adopt an attitude of superior aristocratic indifference. Clearly he had been less than honest with me. Equally perhaps had it not been for the quantity of alcohol he'd drunk the truth may not have been exposed. Previously he'd implied that he was ignorant of most factual detail, not surprisingly therefore I was upset.

The question of his integrity in this context caused me to seek further clarification about other possible contradictions. I asked him about his actual relationship with James and to begin with he dismissed the idea of any association other than the most casual.

'Oh I suppose we've known one another on and off for years.' He said, 'I think I mentioned once before that he occasionally gets me a good bottle or two—he knows a bit about fine wines does your James.'

'But there's more than that—isn't there?' I asked, unwilling to let him so easily off the hook.

He smiled by now his eyes bloodshot and his grin a little lopsided.

'Well . . . ' he said after a long pause, 'I suppose now you're part of the clan so to speak, there's no harm in telling you. You see when my ancestors made contact with the gypsies it was agreed that the Headman would provide the St. John Smith family—or at least the current incumbent male head of the family with other forms of entertainment. In those days the gypsy girls weren't averse to earning themselves a few shillings.'

He delivered this statement with the same evidence of pedigree he had just established. I could hardly believe my ears.

'Are you telling me that James pimps for you?'

He flushed.

'No not exactly—in fact the practice wasn't implemented for years. My father never took advantage of it and neither did his. But when I came of age James approached me to see if we couldn't come to some arrangement. Something to assist him financially and to satisfy my other special needs—so to speak.'

'And those special needs are?'

He studied me for several seconds before replying. He remained guarded still superior but have had his plug pulled there was no way he could stop the flow of information.

'Before I answer that Paul—tell me—do you intend to stay on at the Mount—I mean will you have the cottage—use it regularly—at least for the celebrations and the like?'

The question took me by surprise.

'To be honest I don't really know—it depends.'

'On what?'

'Oh—on . . . . '

'On Kate perhaps?'

'Yes she's certainly one of the prime considerations.'

He paused again this time to drain his glass.

'You should appreciate that the lease on the land that houses the Mount is up this year and if I wished I could achieve a good price for it on the open market.'

It was difficult to follow his reasoning.

'I cannot see what the hell that has to do with anything.' I snapped back.

'Well—if you like it describes the parameters of our relationship. As far as you are concerned I am your landlord and the future of your little deviant colony is dependant on my good will. What I'm saying Paul is that in your new role you need to keep me sweet.'

I couldn't help but laugh. The very idea was ludicrous but I could see he was serious.

'I think you've probably had too much to drink my friend. You are rapidly slipping into a power fantasy—and the role of autocrat doesn't suit you.'

He glanced up at me, still red-eyed from beneath the shadow of his darkening brow; a moment of anger. I had not seen him in this mode before. Our previous drinking sessions had been characterised by one or the other of us dropping off to sleep in the chair. This time we had both stayed wide awake, both continued drinking—perhaps providing a catalyst for the atmosphere that had developed. After a moment or two of his shielded scrutiny and as if to confirm my view of his arrogance, he suddenly held out his glass and nodded at the bottle which stood at my elbow. It was an imperious gesture and for a moment I was tempted to ignore the request. In the end I conceded and filled his glass. I considered it would have been too rude to bring matters to a head by refusing to pour his drink. After all who could be certain of the degree of conscious culpability either of us could claim.

A moment later my reasoning was confounded when, once his glass was full Richard allowed a glow of magisterial satisfaction to permeate his expression.

'Thank you . . . . my man.' He said with a sly smile.

Albeit half hidden I concluded that the bastard was laughing at me. I was furious. It took a special effort to restrain my irritation but as I was still inclined to blame the drink I bit my lip and let the moment pass.

'You were going to tell me about your so-called special needs.'

My reminder did nothing to shake his confidence. He sipped his drink and stretched back in the chair before replying.

'Over the short time we've been acquainted Paul we've discussed philosophy, literature, religion and history—and a variety of other intellectual interests. It's strange perhaps that we haven't discussed sex. I say strange because I believe whatever one's age the act of sex is still one of the most pervasive and influential factors in life. Needless to say therefore, my special needs—as I like to call them—all concern my predilection for entertainments of the flesh.'

He continued to watch for my reaction but I kept my face immobile, refusing to be drawn by his pomposity.

'James has proved invaluable in this regard. He seems to have access to an endless supply of young females—he even insists a belief in the old law: Droit de Signeur: The Rite of the Lord and Master.'

He chuckled to himself as though he had a secret and for a moment I thought he was about to share it.

'It is an ancient custom—submitting new brides on their marital bed to the lord of the manner—her first night taken by her husband's master. I wonder how you'd feel giving your bride's first night—quite a thought eh?'

'Fortunately I don't have a Lord—still less a master—and even if I did . . . . '

He interrupted, ignoring my comment.

'I don't want you to go away thinking these interests are obsessive. I restrict my indulgence to one or two sessions per year—just sufficient to keep an old man happy.'

Faced with such objectionable extremes conversation between us became more a competition than the friendly exchange to which I'd become accustomed. Consequently during my return journey up the hill that night, I gave vent to my frustrations, shouting obscene comments and accusations at the black outline of the trees in the best tradition of a drunken lout.

**

From where I stood overlooking the street I could see Richard was wrapped in an expensive overcoat and he wore a soft trilby. Such an outfit was unusually splendid for both the man and the occasion—almost an exhibition. I was not surprised therefore when he slammed the car door as though wanting attention. But the street kept its eyes closed and remained silent. With James being absent I thought for a moment he might want to see me and I half decided not to answer the door should he knock. However his path led not to my door but to Duggie's. Due to the oblique angle I could not see who answered the door but as soon as it was open he went straight in.

Chapter Twenty

I now realise that those qualities I have most admired in Sir Walter Scott's writing, are singularly lacking in my own work. Scott always wrote with clarity of reason and a nobility of purpose and his characters are impelled by a code of honour. His tragedies are those of self-denial and his heroes persevere with the stamina of the righteous. Often from humble beginnings the victory of his characters are nevertheless those of reputable men and women. Rather, my own history especially since my involvement with the unholy community in Yorkshire, hinges on expediency, physical gratification and self-indulgence. Not surprising that my watchword is guilt and that I find myself increasingly filled with self-loathing.

During the last few weeks that I occupied James's cottage I spent a lot of time examining my conscience in this regard. It is true to say that events became so extreme that for the first time since childhood I found myself drawn to prayer. On the other hand that cynicism developed in me through years of hard won logic argued that any recourse to the God figure was due only on account of imagined hardships. I therefore resisted the inclination more conscious of my self-image than for my peace of mind—a typical reaction of the weak.

In truth I had no time for such theological niceties; no wish to debate the issue with myself and certainly no inclination to seek out more doubt. The vagaries of my fluctuating conscience had become capricious leaving me uncertain and even more insecure than usual. My feelings for Kate competed with the contrast between her beliefs, her sensuality and her history of availability. I knew however, that in the very near future I would be obliged to choose either to stay on the Mount with all that might entail or to resume my life in London and the career I had lately put on hold. My quandary was one that could only be solved by me.

Some time later that day I heard Richard's car leave. Naturally I was consumed with curiosity but I would not allow myself the indulgence of enquiring. As it happened I did not have to. Just after mid-day Kate came to see me. She looked pale but when I asked her she said it was only on account of not having slept well. She said she had been asked by Richard to invite me—along with Duggie, James and herself to dinner the next night.

'He said he would put on a special dinner—something memorable.'

'Why on earth would he want to do that?' I asked.

'Does he need a reason?'

I supposed that he didn't but nevertheless felt in some way patronised by the invitation.

'Couldn't he have knocked at my door to deliver such an invite?'

'How am I supposed to know what he thinks or why he thinks it?'

I noticed she was answering all my questions with questions but then, in fairness, how was she to have the answers I was seeking.

'I'm sorry Kate. It's just that Richard and I had words the last time we met and I feel it is therefore a bit odd that (a) he invites me to dinner at all and (b) that he asks you to deliver the invite.' Unaccountably Kate blushed.

'However, as we're on the subject of Richard St. John Smith—how is it that suddenly you and Duggie are such bosom buddies of his all of a sudden. Only a little while ago I was castigated for claiming his friendship.'

'Hardly 'castigated'—you do exaggerate Paul—anyway his visit was to do with community business and I suppose the dinner is also in that regard. Will you come?'

I grinned back at her.

'If my friend Kate is going to be there then nothing would keep me away.'

In response she slid easily onto my knee and kissed me on the lips.

'There—that's for being such a good boy!' she said in her best teacher's voice.

To seal our new accord I made some croutons and opened a tin of soup for lunch. We sat before the fire downstairs and enjoyed the best cream of mushroom that Bessie's shop could provide. It seemed it was the first time in ages that we were alone together in a domestic setting. Afterwards we shared a bottle of wine and chatted like old friends and it was late in the afternoon before she rose to leave.

'I must get off Paul—I've things to do—but thanks for a lovely lunch—and I'll see you tomorrow evening.'

We kissed again at the door and just before she left she suddenly gripped my arm and looked closely into my eyes.

'Whatever might occur Paul,' she said, 'remember our good times together were really some of the best.'

A moment later and she was gone. Her parting comment seemed a little melodramatic and felt strangely like a goodbye. The more I thought about it the more depressing it seemed and it knocked me off balance for the rest of the day.

The next afternoon was bright. A crystal clear sky of pale blue promised a night-time frost and by the time I was ready to leave that evening it was already bitterly cold. I had decided to walk down the hill and therefore dressed accordingly. As Kate had been the one to deliver the invitation I naturally assumed that she would accompany me, however when I knocked at her door Duggie informed me that she had already left. I hid my disappointment and stood on the doorstep for a minute or two gossiping. It cannot have been hidden so well as just as I turned to take my leave Duggie said, 'Don't take it all to heart Paul . . . . Kate is a serious person very conscious of her responsibilities.'

The door closed before I had a chance to ask him what he meant and I was left to ponder it as I walked down to Miles House.

The drive-way was dark but past the curve, the ground floor windows cast fingers of light through gaps in the heavy curtains. As soon as I knocked at the front door the porch was immediately illuminated. I was surprised to find that it was James who opened the door.

'Ah Paul—come in, Richard will be glad you could make it.'

He played the host with an uncomfortable ease, an attitude made all the more convincing by the smartness of his dinner jacket and black bow-tie.

I suddenly felt at a disadvantage.

'I wasn't told it was a formal affair—'fraid I'm just in my suit.'

Not for the first time I was embarrassed.

'It's no matter,' he smiled patting me on the shoulder, 'you're among friends . . . . but if you feel under-dressed I'm sure Richard will have a spare that he'd loan you.'

The shoulder-patting helped make this further pomposity feel particularly irritating and I was thankful that the act of removing my overcoat allowed me to disguise my discomfort. His perceptions were as predatory as ever and with a supercilious smile he laid my coat on a hall chair. I straightened my tie only to have him step back and scrutinise me as if my outfit was modelled for him alone.

'You look fine Paul—don't worry about it!'

I followed him into the big drawing room and he led the way to a side-board where a drinks tray had been laid.

'Whisky—isn't it?' he asked pouring a large measure from a crystal decanter before I could reply. I took the drink and allowed its fiery taste to brace me.

'They shouldn't be long.' He said catching me looking about the room, 'Richard is just showing Kate over the house. She's not been here before. Let's make ourselves comfortable by the fire.'

He brought the decanter with him and placed it on a small table between our chairs. His careless familiarity with the place and its contents exaggerated the ambiguity in his assumption of the role of host. To the casual observer he might have been Richard's closest friend or even a relative rather than the representative of one side of an antagonism dating back four hundred years. His performance made me feel uncomfortable.

'I'm glad we have these few minutes alone together Paul. I want to brief you—about this business of the lease.'

I waited whilst he lit a cigar.

'Old Richard has a bee in his bonnet about the lease—you see it will be up soon—this year actually—one hundred and ninety-nine years later. In theory he could sell the place out from under us leaving Bessie and the rest homeless—and he'd get a bonnie price, it's a fair piece of land.'

'So how much does he want for its renewal?'

My question made him smile but he drew on his cigar before answering.

'Your perceptions are sharp enough—what he wants depends on you—to some extent.' He watched me through clouds of grey smoke. 'We all need to know how seriously you take your responsibilities as the next Headman.'

I laughed quietly, 'So James—after all this—as the Americans might say—*you want to put the bite on me eh*—Well despite appearances I am not a rich man. I am quite well provided for but I don't have access to large amounts of cash. How much are you looking for?'

He sat forward and shook his head.

'No—no you've misunderstood. I'm not asking for hard cash—and Richard certainly isn't interested in your money—he's more concerned with a sense of history . . . . ' He paused obviously at odds with himself then he leaned forward his face tense.

'Do you know are you aware that Richard can trace his ancestors way back to the Norman Conquest—an unbroken line that includes Crusaders and Knights of St. John. His is one of the oldest and proudest families in Britain. They were soldier Knights originally allied to the Roman Catholic Church—representatives from his family have fought in every conflict—every confrontation since William 1st. Richard was himself a full colonel in the tank regiment in World War Two and in Korea he was an intelligence officer. He only missed the Falklands because of his age and . . . '

I couldn't swallow anymore of this litany and interrupted.

'I cannot see what the hell this might have to do with your lease.'

James stopped and stared into my eyes.

'Okay—let's get one thing at a time sorted out. I've a straight question deserving a straight answer. Will you accept the role of Headman when the time comes?'

Now all his pretence had gone. He was deadly serious—but I was not prepared to be blackmailed.'

'The short answer is—no—but before we get into that there are a few things we need to sort out—for example—how is it that you are so friendly with Richard? Back at the Mount you didn't have a good word for him and yet I find you here swanning about like you have shares in the place.'

James's face paled and he stood up and stretched in front of the fire before he answered.

'At least some of what you see is due to politics. I suppose we are perceived as friends and the fact is I do little favours for him. You see we belonged to the same lodge for a while. I found he is an odd man—full of contradictions and I've used that to get close to him,' he paused but eventually continued, 'If you want the actual truth—I hate the sight of him but I can't help but admire his family. I agreed to satisfy his demands simply to ensure that the lease would be renewed—unfortunately what he wants now will affect you so I need to know that you will not . . . . '

His reference to a Lodge indicated that membership of the Masons was a factor. It should not have surprised me. Before I could comment, at that moment the double doors swung open and Richard stood there with Kate on his arm. His dinner jacket sported a cluster of miniature military ribbons and his face wore a huge smile. There was an air of triumphalism about him: a sense of successful one-up-man-ship and I found it particularly irritating. Kate looked stunning in a lace and silk evening dress: a picture from a fashion magazine.

'Ah Paul . . . at last—I hope James has been looking after you.'

They came forward together, Kate looking intently into my face as she approached. The tiny diamond pendant at her throat sparked a reflection in her eyes. Richard wore his white hair combed back and with his sharp white shirt and his impeccable suit he looked every bit the aristocrat. No one could deny that they made a fine pair but Kate could easily have been his daughter. I rose at their entrance and they stopped directly in front of me.

'It's been a long time Paul—too long—I've missed our little philosophical discussions.'

'He's been locking himself away from all his friends Richard,' Kate added, 'been working on his book; isolating himself—being antisocial.'

She smiled as she spoke as though she was teasing me, but there was a serious edge to her statement that I quickly identified.

'Man is born to labour . . . ' I quoted.

Richard responded immediately, ' . . . and the birds to fly.'

I laughed, surprised that the breadth of his reading included the Bible. He then turned to Kate.

'You see Kate,' he said, 'like you our friend Paul shares a love of archaic, if not obtuse romanticism. It is a quaint but altogether endearing quality—even if it helps negate any aspiration he may have to be taken seriously in debate.'

I felt my colour rise.

'Sadly the indolence of the so-called Upper Classes has left them without any understanding of the world of work,' I directed my response to Kate ignoring my host's presence, 'and as we all know, when faced with a challenge, lazy people with lazy minds will always seek to discredit informed opinion—often through joining secret organisations . . . '

James interrupted with a hollow laugh. He stepped forward.

'Gentlemen—before we come to blows I think we should adjourn to the dining room. Bloodstains are extraordinarily difficult to remove from carpets.

Kate had watched the exchange with a straight face but when James spoke she grinned and added, 'Blessed are the peacemakers for they shall be called the children of God.'

Richard raised an eyebrow and muttered, 'Told you so!'

I applauded, 'In company such as this any knowledge of Christian Scripture should be acknowledged—and in the face of an ancient family rooted in Freemasonry, one that has regarded its members as warrior princes for hundreds of years, a plea for peace must come as a trauma to equal Judgement Day.'

Richard smiled and chose to ignore the gibe. Instead he led the way into dinner with Kate on his arm. As I expected it would be the meal was superb. It was served by two girls from the village, dressed for the occasion in black skirts and blouses and short white aprons. With their able assistance the course followed one another with mechanical precision tempered with the best level of appreciation for the diners: a fitting tribute to the excellence of the food. Richard served the wine himself and clearly took some pleasure in describing the heritage of each bottle as it was poured. It was a feast.

During the course of the meal the conversation relied heavily on anecdotes, largely from James. He took a delight in talking about his magazine and the girls he employed as models. Once or twice Kate joined in but only to speak as a witness or in support of something claimed by James. I could not help but notice that whenever the subject of the Mount cropped up Richard and James seemed to compete to be the one to change the subject and the direction of the discussion. Eventually cognac was served with strong coffee in the drawing room.

In our absence chairs had been arranged around a table located in the big bow window and we were invited to seat ourselves there by Richard. Had it not been for the brandy, the coffee and the casual air, it was almost like the setting for a company board meeting.

As soon as the coffee was served and the bubble glasses charged, Richard handed round a substantial humidor. Nodding in my direction when James paused to ponder its contents he said, 'I'm sure Paul will find the Jamaican leaf to his taste.'

He had not spoken to me directly since before the meal and this oblique reference confirmed my suspicion that he had taken offence to my earlier comments. I was not disappointed. Once the cigars were lighted he opened a black leather folder placed before him on the table and turned to me.

'Paul—this is the lease agreement. Should you wish your lawyers to examine it later I can make it available at their convenience. For the sake of brevity however, I can summarise its contents by telling you that the agreement was to cover a period of one hundred and ninety-nine years. It was signed and witnessed in 1794—the term will therefore be up in four weeks time.'

He paused to allow me to comment but I had nothing to add at that time.

'I've asked you all to attend tonight in order that we might agree the terms of the next agreement.'

He grinned fox-like and added, ' I'm sure you will all understand that should I see fit, I could simply sell the property by private treaty . . . . in which case who knows who the next owner might be. It is clearly in your interest to accommodate my requests therefore and in so doing acquire the freehold.'

Whilst he spoke both Kate and James sat staring silently into their coffee cups as though they had heard it all before. It seemed that Richard's speech had been made entirely for my benefit.

'Do I understand you to say that you are prepared to hand over the freehold if your conditions are met?' I asked.

Richard nodded.

'Okay then what price are you asking?'

James filled the gap, answering in Richard's place.

'Paul you should be aware that once this negotiation is complete I intend to resign my position with the Mount—and—if you are willing, you will become the Headman immediately.'

Having exposed his little trap he paused to await my reaction.

'I need to know what Richard has in mind before I make a commitment.' I replied.

Clearly it was not the answer he wanted but he accepted it nevertheless.

'All right—the deal is this . . . . Richard is conscious of the fact that he is the last of his line—naturally this is regrettable. He has however, proposed a way to solve his problem as well as satisfying our problem over the lease. In brief—he is prepared to sign over the land known as the Mount on condition that—Kate bears him an heir.'

It took several seconds for the proposal to sink in—in fact it may have been even longer. Several things occurred to me attended by memory images: Richard's visit to the Mount; Duggie's parting comment; the insistence that I should attend this meeting and finally Kate's change of attitude at the cottage. The implication of the latter point was that she had in some way agreed to his condition and was only waiting for my acquiescence.

The static finally cleared. The scheme was a carbon copy of the same distorted reasoning that had been the hall-mark of Richard's ancestors. It played on the insecurity of an ethnic minority; the terrible advantage of the powerful over the weak and the willingness of one of those disadvantaged people to sacrifice herself for the good of the others. There was no doubt in my mind that under the conditions given, Kate would play the martyr. Her eyes had remained downcast throughout this last statement—an emphasis to the ensuing quiet and a guarantee that my analysis of the situation was correct.

I struggled to identify my own part in the proceedings—or at least the part others perceived should be mine. My feelings for Kate were obvious enough and—that they sought my agreement must mean that these feelings were reciprocated—that was something worth knowing at least. Unfortunately, as far as the community on the Mount were concerned, if I were to reject the role of Headman then any influence I might have on Kate's future would be forfeit. If I accepted it then in order to safeguard the community's future I would need to accept Richard's proposition. It was an iniquitous plan charged with all the familiar undertones of the corrupt meritocracy to which Richard and his ancestors had always belonged.

The depth of my outrage was difficult to control and it was the effort needed to disguise my sense of abhorrence that made me realise that my feelings for Kate were far greater than the sum of our sexual liaison had led me to believe. My future happiness depended on Kate but the feeling of inevitable failure was overwhelming.

Eventually I asked, 'Has this notion been in your mind for very long Richard?'

He shrugged his shoulders and avoided my eyes.

'I think the answer to that question is largely immaterial.'

'Then tell me—why has Kate been chosen for this dubious honour?'

This time he did catch my eye and again I was aware of the malevolence of his assumed superiority. Before he could reply James interrupted.

'The plan is that they would marry—and once the ceremony was complete then the deeds would be transferred. Naturally on Richard's death Kate would inherit his estate.'

This was seen as bait for me hoping I would wait in the wings expecting an inheritance in some future association with Kate. What James failed to appreciate was that if the deeds were not transferred before the wedding there was at least some likelihood that Richard would renege on the deal. My agreement was an obvious prerequisite and James's tone acquired an untypical quality of pleading.

'And what does Kate think about all this?' I asked quietly.

She looked up at me for the first time in what seemed like an age.

'You know how I feel about you Paul—but I have to do whatever might be in the best interests of my community.' She replied, 'But I'd like your approval.'

Her voice was small and uncharacteristically meek and as she spoke Richard smirked and covered her hand with his. The bile rose in my throat and I felt my control begin to slip.

**

Although I spent the rest of the night stalking the respite of sleep my quest went unresolved. I plagued myself with questions. At best I acquired a half-dreamlike state in which the loop of an action replay of my evening at Miles House was constantly reviewed. I examined the argument in all its detail; I followed the path of my eventual temper tantrum; the sound of the raised voices; the fury and the inevitable violence accompanied by the sound of breaking glass. I seldom lose my temper and have never lost control to such an extent. In truth I had no previous experience of initiating a physical assault and thereby no criteria with which to assess the result. There was nevertheless a perverse satisfaction in seeing Richard go down with blood on his face, with blood on his nice white shirt and as a reward for my frustration—skinned knuckles. Once I'd started I had been unable to stop the progress of my rage. The words of abuse; the crash of furniture overturned; the gasps of surprise; the fear and wide-eyed horror of the others and the noise of feet on the floorboards as I stomped out.

The sound of the footfalls became another reality when I realised in the early hours that someone was banging on my door. Much the worse for my long nightmare and dressed only in my shirt, I answered the knocking to find Bessie and Malcolm on my step.

'There's a fire—a fire.' She gasped.

I was so slow to assimilate her meaning that to begin with I just stood and stared.

'Down in the village,' she said, 'a fire in the village.'

Malcolm pushed his face forward into mine.

'The whole village has turned out—it's Miles House—it's ablaze.'

He was wild-eyed, his long hair windswept and his clothing crumpled. There was a look of madness in his eye. Behind him I saw Sammy and Gerald hurrying past half dressed. Jim Brotherton pulled up in his tractor with little Jim alongside shouting for us to hurry. I stepped forward and saw the glow in the distant sky and panic set in.

'You were down there tonight . . . . weren't you? With James an' Kate . . . . they're not back.'

Bessie sounded stricken.

The door next to me slammed and I saw Duggie pass without a word wild-eyed pulling on his overcoat as he ran past trying to catch up with the tractor. I struggled to break the slow-motion cycle in which I was trapped.

'I'll get dressed—be with you in a minute. Get into the car and I'll drive you down,' I shouted.

A minute or two later we were speeding down the hill heading towards the reddening sky.

Chapter Twenty-One

It was the dull sound of bottles chinking on a stone step that wakened me: a five-thirty delivery of milk. It was one of those mornings when, despite the depth of the sleep enjoyed, a single sound leaves one wide awake in an instant. I lay there in the dark fully conscious, a time for my next day paranoia: increasingly an every day occurrence. It was an hour before the central heating would kick-in; two hours before sunrise at this time of year and four and a half hours before the book-launch. Time enough I promised myself for a shower and breakfast; sufficient leeway to allow nerves to settle and statements to be rehearsed again. I was due to face the Press at ten—my public and my critics—not a task I anticipated with great confidence.

The book had been a long time in coming. The gestation period had been brief but the act of writing it had dragged on for fourteen months, fully two months past the agreed deadline. It was not a record of which to be proud, nor one that had endeared me to the publishing house. There had been moments when the tone of the exchange between Charlie my long suffering agent and Mr. Sullivan representing Meridew and Sons had been distinctly cool. Finally it had been the threatened possibility of having to return the down payment that had energised me. Clearly I had to put in the man-hours or face the likelihood of losing the contract.

Charlie had been surprised and disappointed at my poor showing. My previous performances had made me one of his most reliable writers.

'What the hell is wrong with you Paul?' he'd asked. 'Sullivan is suddenly reluctant to discuss their option on your next two books and it wouldn't surprise me to find them dropping you like a stone.'

I'd said that he shouldn't worry and that I would make up for lost time. Unfortunately at that time all my promises had sounded hollow—I hardly believed them myself. Neither Charlie nor Sullivan's were privy to the cause of the delay and even if they had been, it is doubtful that they would have found it credible.

Two factors had affected the progress of my writing, the first being the untimely death of my lover, Kate and the second my mother's manuscript. When I finally returned to London I spent three weeks studying the manuscript and, as far as I was able in checking the detail of her research. Thankfully I was able to fill the gaps and in it final form it made good sense. Not a sense that I could have ever guessed but one that left me to wonder at the complexity of the coincidences.

I had stayed on at James's cottage until the spring: a time in which I attempted to accommodate all that had happened. The recurring horror associated with the night of the fire had become the cause of nightmares and sleeplessness. My conscience made a meal of it, a repast far too rich for my constitution in turn producing a trauma not easily digested. Consequently all other considerations had been put to one side—including the book. Scenes embedded in my memory had me sitting bolt upright in the midnight darkness and I was tormented by waves of guilt. My immersion in my mother's research had therefore provided the distraction necessary to help blot out the images that plagued my subconscious thinking.

The flames that night had leapt over sixty feet into the black night air above Miles House. It made a column of smoke into a county landmark.

Fearfully I'd parked the car well away from the stone gateway. There was little possibility of getting close due to the crowds filling the entrance. By the time I had forced my way through the whole house was engulfed. The doorway and the long windows on the ground floor had been invaded by a searing furnace of flames. As I watched, the openings on the upper floors imploded, sucked in on themselves by the temperature: the glass disappeared, some showering the lawn but the noise was absorbed by the general racket of the fire. A fireworks display stung my face.

The paintwork blistered; lead flashing melted and slate roof-tiles popped into the air like so many mortar bombs. In places the stonework itself glowed. It was impossible to get any view of the interior such was the ebullience of the burning. I ran to the rear of the property only to find it was equally impenetrable. A sudden change of wind sent a waft of torrid heat to scorch my face, stealing my air in a suffocating envelope of fire. Gasping with my face hidden beneath my jacket I staggered back to the front of the house only to find that the Fire Brigade had arrived at last with two engines. Fragments of frightened faces were pushed back as helmeted men took charge. Arches of water quickly rose from scurrying, bulging pipes outlining the inferno in an organised resistance to the destruction.

Few of those who had come to witness the blaze stayed on until the end. Presumably they drifted back to warm beds as soon as it was under control. The firemen however, worked until long past dawn and by then only Bessie, Duggie and myself remained. We saw the roof collapse under its own weight; the west-end gables crumble and we saw the grey of a cold morning light behind the fading curtain of smoke. There was a weak sunlight marred by capricious clouds of ash but we waited well into the morning to see the bodies removed from the mountains of smoking detritus.

I was called as a witness when the inquest was held some five weeks later but could provide little by way of an explanation that investigators did not already know. It was estimated that the fire started n the kitchens next to the wine cellars. Combustion they said presumably caused by the ignition of leaking gas: the intensity and the rapid spread of the blaze being blamed on the presence of nearby alcohol which acted as a catalyst. The fire investigators informed the Coroner that two bodies had been discovered in what had been the drawing room. Obviously they belonged to Richard and James however; their individual identities could not as yet be identified. Significantly the similarities they shared in life were at last confirmed in death. The female remains were found in the kitchen area, recognisable only by the pendant she wore. There were no other casualties; the gardener was away for the week-end and other part-time help having left immediately after the meal. It was concluded that the gas explosion in the kitchen had spread the fire so quickly that the drawing room above would have been engulfed in seconds. The cause of the gas leak was not identified although no foul play was suspected. The cause of death was stated to be by misadventure.

The remains were released three days later and Kate and James were interned on the hill-side beyond the Mount in a simple ceremony. They were buried at night in a candle-lit gathering according to their custom. The wavering lights guttering in the wind reflected the tears of all who were present. Afterwards I stayed to hear Bessie and Sammy sing the account of the fire over the graves. Later we all collected in Bessie's kitchen where Gerald read James's last will and testament. I was surprised to find that I was the sole beneficiary. Unwilling to accept his bequest I promised that after the sale of his assets, the bulk of his estate would revert to the community on the Mount. To the silent assembly I also regretfully refused the position as Headman arguing that as he was a full-time resident Gerald was better fitted for the job and after much discussion this was finally agreed.

Some days later Richard was placed in a family tomb sited in the local church-yard, a ceremony organised by his solicitors. Although his funeral represented much more pomp and ceremony than that for James and Kate, the altar-boys; the Requiem Mass and the organ music did not make up for the fact that I was the only member of the congregation present. During the service I found myself wondering if the St. John Smiths might not after all have had a gypsy buried in their crypt. No one had sought evidence of DNA so it was possible that James and not Richard had been interred in the family grave. In any event Richard's estate was left in the hands of his lawyers. He had no other living relatives which may be why at that time before his proposal concerning Kate; he had bequeathed the land known as the Mount to James.

I spent the next six weeks trying to make sense of my Mother's manuscript, deciding in the end that I needed access to a good reference library if I was ever to steer it to a conclusion. In order to preclude what could have been difficult goodbyes I therefore slipped away early one morning and set out to drive back to my flat and the sanity of the Capital. On the way I stopped briefly to visit Uncle Desmond and Aunt Polly (in truth more him than her). In their world it seemed that little had changed, he still fulfilled the role of slave and her as the miniature dictator. I was nevertheless made welcome and agreed to stay overnight. I therefore managed to organise a visit to the local hostelry with Desmond and was surprised to discover he was a regular visitor.

'I manage to get away now and then.' he said with a grin.

It had been my intention to tell him of the alleged relationship between James and my mother and the claim of paternity but in the event I chose not to. Given that Desmond still imagined he had had a close friendship with my mother, the news may well have upset him—better to leave him in ignorance even if the claims were without foundation. I left early next morning leaving a note expressing thanks to Aunt Polly for her hospitality.

Back home I had opportunity to study the research more closely. Now I find that the real story of the people comprising the community who lived on the Mount is characterised in my mind by its symmetry. And although believers in synchronicity may well attribute greater significance to the pattern of events, I tend to be somewhat more sceptical. I am inclined to think that the constructions we see are applied afterwards and that such is our search for significance that we consciously seek out coincidence and pursue ambiguity for no good purpose. Consequently I believe only that we provide a necessary post-script.

My research shows that after Gustav Allaveer and his sons and relatives arrived in Britain the only work they could secure was as executioners. Their trade had been as slaughtermen and butchers and in those days the local butcher was often called on to act as a public executioner. In a time of extremes when religious persecution was common, the skills of the Allaveers were welcomed by the authorities and they were kept busy. However in some respect times were changing. In 1555 in a London suburb called Uxbridge three men were put to death by being burnt at the stake. These were some of the last killings of this sort before the Crown, in the person of a new Queen stopped such practices. The Uxbridge burnings proved to be particularly unpopular and a short time later those responsible for fulfilling the death warrant were driven from the town. The Allaveers were forced to make their way north to avoid the hue and cry.

One sunny afternoon I took a tube train out to the end of the Metropolitan Line which stops at Uxbridge. In the centre of the town I found a small cemetery situated on a roundabout that still commemorates the spot where the three men were put to death. A stone there is inscribed with the names of the victims. It states: John Denley, Robert Smith and

Patrick Packingham were put to death at Lynch Green in the year of our Lord 1555AD. Interestingly the Robert Smith referred to was the youngest son of Henry St. John Smith and one of Richard's distant forefathers. Odd that John Denley—my own ancestor should have been burnt alongside one representing the St. John Smith family. Odder still perhaps that four hundred years later, a blood relative of the executioners would seek to marry into the Denley family and later after Richard's death inherit land from the last St. John Smith estate.

Of course there are questions that will remain unanswered. History often thumbs its nose and defies the curiosity of those who pry too deeply.

I wonder for example did my mother know that her lover was related to those responsible for murdering her ancestors. And could that have been the reason she refused James's offer of marriage? Did she perhaps discover the fact after she'd fallen pregnant by him? How much did Richard actually know? The chest of letters he boasted of—was it real and if so what did they tell him?

James's role is even more obtuse. Knowing the man I cannot be persuaded that he was ignorant of the facts about either the Denleys or the St. John Smiths—so what was his purpose? The romantic in me prefers to believe that my mother broke with James Collins despite being pregnant, only when his ancestry was revealed: an ultimate gesture of self-denial; true love subjugated by principle . . . . At last a fact that possibly equates with her son's obsession with the work of Sir Walter Scott.

It is curious also that the community of the Mount, even after four hundred years continue to lock themselves in their time-warped condition: their traditions and practices hardly changing in that time except for their occasional exploitation by James. It is only when their beliefs are cast against the impositions of their feudal overlord; Richard that culpability for their ignorance can be fully appreciated. The history of the Allaveers seemed to be bound uncomfortably alongside the St. John Smith family. They appeared to swim together albeit in a sea of discontent, united by the periodic deaths of their members at the hands of the others. I have to conclude that it is these tidal waves of confrontation that disrupt any possibility of a safe landfall for any of them.

The St. John Smiths were crusaders, members of the Teutonic Knights of the Sword; Knights of St. John and thereby freemasons. As Teutonic Knights they played an important part in the conversion of Estonia to Christianity and as a consequence a part in the forced movement of the Allaveers. Conversely in England, acting as executioners for the Crown the Allaveers put to death Sir Robert St. John Smith, the ancestor of Richard.

The accidental meeting—if indeed it was by chance—between James and Richard at a Lodge meeting was to prove historic. It set events in motion in a last modern context that would prove irresistible. In their own way they were both corrupt and self-centred; exploiters of those weaker than themselves and interested only in some private fantasy fulfilment. And whether that fantasy concerned the continuation of a family line already moribund or the need to maintain the adulation and subservience of a small ignorant community the effect was the same. Richard's private agenda was no worse than James's distortion of his culture. The fact that the said culture had long since lost any real significance is immaterial. In some sense I believe progress depends as much on asking the right questions as it does on seeking answers—therefore as much on honesty as on invention.

My lack of confidence, inspired perhaps by an outdated moral code, made me a willing participant in the excesses prompted by James. I was so bound up in my romantic idyll that I mistook my association with Bessie and the others, imagining them to represent some new or some long forgotten truth. Such ignorance makes me as culpable as the rest.

The book launch eventually proved successful. The critics accepted my interpretation of Scott's endeavours; the publishers were hopeful of their sales initiative and Charlie was able to negotiate the contract on my behalf that he had hoped for. I was the only person left with any sense of disappointment—a disappointment founded again on a feeling of guilt.

Both historically and psychologically guilt is the great leveller often making bedfellows of complete opposites. Jews and Catholic for example have long since shared a reputation for rigour implicit in the practise of their religions. Given the historical enmity between them anything that they share might be seen as a paradox. However, in terms of the effect on their practitioners an aspect of that rigour is the generation of guilt and this might be seen as the most significant characteristic they share. Catholic children undergo a conscience reconstruction and the image of their guardian angel on one shoulder and their devil on the other is still real years later. The struggle between self-indulgence and self-denial is epitomised by this image. No small wonder that a feeling of guilt soon becomes a vital part of every child's lunch-box. He carries it with him from morning till night; he wakes with it and goes to bed with it. In the end he is forced to accept schizophrenia as normal.

Having come to terms with my own personality split, unhappily I now find new cracks turning into fissures—to chasms even and after my outburst at Miles House, I now find I must deal with another form of guilt.

When Richard's proposals became known to me that night, I flew into an unusually ugly rage. All the recriminations I felt were screamed across the table. I was suddenly disgusted by the veneer of sophistication used by Richard and James to disguise their intentions. The expensive furniture; the antiques; the fine silver and the crystal were so much stage dressing. In the face of my outburst James paled into a long silence but

Richard fought back. He said I had been only too glad to use Kate for my own sexual gratification; that my moral outrage was a sham and that I shared the same stupidity that my mother had exhibited. It was this reference to my mother that finally tipped the balance. Before I knew fully what I was doing I had tipped over the table, slapped Richard across the face and grabbed him by the throat. James tried to intervene and the three of us ended up rolling about the floor: a maelstrom of bodies crashing into furniture and scattering fine ornaments. Fortunately none of us were sufficiently fit to be able to continue the struggle for very long and after a few minutes Kate screamed and pulled us apart. We separated panting and red faced and stood our ground in a silent staring match. At that moment I hated them both and wished them dead. I kicked a nearby chair in frustration and in a final act of senseless destruction I snatched the beautiful decanter from the sideboard and threw it into the open fire. The effect was instantaneous. A sheet of flame burst across the room firing the carpet and the soft furnishings on the settee. His possessions threatened Richard shouted for Kate to get water from the kitchen and she ran out.

James tried to beat out the flames with a cushion but only succeeded in spreading the damage—by then the carpet and wooden flooring had caught. I stomped to the door experiencing a perverse satisfaction at the damage I'd caused.

'Tell Kate,' I shouted, 'she is to meet me at the cottage—and God help both of you if you try to stop her.'

James was by now fully occupied fighting the fire. He made the piteous noises of a frightened animal. Richard shouted back threatening me with jail. I responded as I left saying I would see him in hell.

Given the findings of the fire investigation, I cannot understand how a gas explosion could have occurred. When I left the premises the fire appeared to be under control and at that time it was confined only to the drawing room. Curiously by the same token, I had time to walk up the hill; go to bed and sleep for some time before the blaze was reported. The only explanation I can imagine is that they succeeded in dousing the flames and at some time later Kate went down to the kitchen to make a hot drink. The gas from the stove perhaps reacting with the still burning embers in the floor above her head could have resulted in the final explosion.

My possible responsibility for three deaths (one possibly being my father) is yet another albatross to hang around my neck alongside my neglect of my mother. In my heart of hearts there is no doubt in my mind that ultimately the blaze was caused by the brandy being thrown into the open fire; an act for which I will never be able to forgive myself. Whether James and Richard deserved such a fate may be arguable but there can be no doubt whatsoever that Kate deserved better. In this game she was just a pawn. Her only function was to satisfy James's interpretation of an outdated agreement: a sacrifice for what he saw as the general good of the community on the Mount. The tired fabric of the Allaveer weft meshed with the warp of the St. John Smith family is now echoed by my own condition: a terrible textile weaving together a concoction of freedom and blame.

At a time when I was at last beginning to confirm my liberation from religious cant; from the restriction of polite complacency—even from an over active conscience I find myself weighted down by another different guilt. For the first time in my life I was unashamed in being able to express the depth of my emotions both in a physical love and a violent act. Unfortunately the inevitable inheritance is yet another stricture alongside the almost unbelievable loss of Kate.

Those souls who experience a conversion to a new belief inevitably prove to be the most devout of practitioners. Traditionally one finds that the greater the contrast between the new creed and what went before, the more zealous the new graduate. Maybe the converse is equally true—perhaps for the first time that cynicism I have always affected now has a credible sense of reality; an advent of maturity promising the loss of gullibility. With this in mind therefore perhaps the only true cynics are those like me who are converted from romanticism.